EMMA'S FAMILY

Recent Titles by Elizabeth Daish from Severn House

EMMA'S PEACE
EMMA'S HAVEN
EMMA'S FAMILY

RYAN'S QUADRANGLE

EMMA'S FAMILY

Elizabeth Daish

SEVERN SH HOUSE

This first world edition published in Great Britain 1996 by
SEVERN HOUSE PUBLISHERS LTD of
9–15 High Street, Sutton, Surrey SM1 1DF.
First published in the USA 1996 by
SEVERN HOUSE PUBLISHERS INC. of
595 Madison Avenue, New York, NY 10022.

British Library Cataloguing in Publication Data

Daish, Elizabeth
    Emma's family
    1. English fiction – 20th century
    I. Title
    823.9′14 [F]

    ISBN 0-7278-4904-2

Typeset by Palimpsest Book Production Limited,
Polmont, Stirlingshire, Scotland.
Printed and bound in Great Britain by
Hartnolls Ltd, Bodmin, Cornwall.

For Duthey and Jack

Chapter One

Emma turned away from the wide window and the trees in the park. Paul held her close. She closed her eyes for a moment, then smiled. "It's wonderful," she said.

"But a bit frightening?" She nodded.

"I felt scared the first time I came here," her husband confessed.

"You scared? I don't believe that for one moment. You are never scared by anything."

"Listen my love." Gently he shook her to give force to his words. "I am often scared. I was scared when I first saw you in Bristol and had to be the perfect neutral doctor-friend when I fell in love with you. Your father was ill and I had no hope of making you love me because of Guy. I was scared when Guy seemed to fill your mind even after his visit to Belsen ended in his death and you shut your mind to other men. I was convinced that you could never love me as I wanted." He kissed her cheek and gently smoothed her hair. "I can hardly believe my luck now that we are married. It's all too wonderful but this new venture is a gamble and yes, I'm scared too."

She began to protest but he kissed her again firmly as if to instil confidence in both of them, then tried to look serious. "Listen to me! We've been married for what is it? only a couple of months and it's time you knew some of my dark secrets before we take on this house and try to make a successful clinic here."

Emma began to giggle. "Don't tell me you have a

few wives tucked away somewhere? Six illegitimate children?"

"Nothing like that, but you have to know that I am not always as strong as I appear, and without you, this job would never get off the ground."

"And if it fails?" She spoke lightly but he sensed the real unease under her calm.

He grinned. "Then you can go out to work as an agency nurse and earn enough to keep both of us! Why did you think I married you? I had to look ahead."

"Beast!" she said tenderly. "I do love you, Paul." She saw the light in his eyes and the soft full curve of his mouth and felt safe. Marriage had been a revelation, with a love that was deeper and yet more carefree than the love she'd had for Guy. Even the times when they were apart were full of poignant moments of a kind of closeness that she had never experienced with any other person, except perhaps with Bea, her friend over the years in Bristol, and in The Princess Beatrice Hospital in south east London where they trained to become nurses. Apart from anything like natural friendship, the traumas of World War Two and the loss of friends amid the hard work at Beatties, were enough to bind the two girls closely together for all time.

Emma leaned away from him and tried to regard him as objectively as she would have done if she was not married and in love. He made her feel important, including her in everything he contemplated. They were partners in every sense of the word and she knew that she wanted to be with him for ever.

"So what do you think?"

Emma laughed. "You are doing it again! I'm beginning to know what you are like as a psychiatrist. You brought me here today, wondering if you had lost your marbles even to think about taking on this huge house and setting up a clinic, and now I feel that it is right and we have to go forward together in what is, I admit, a terrifying adventure." She shrugged. "You make me feel strong."

"Good," he said mildly. "I shall have to study chapter six now."

"What's that one?"

"The one that deals with inflated optimism. You are very bad for me. I might think it's easy to set up here from scratch."

"It could be perfect," she said cautiously. "These rooms would be quiet for your consultation rooms and the three small rooms at the back could be used for bed cases if that was necessary. I haven't seen the rest of the house but it smells dry and solid and it has lovely proportions."

"No patients to be treated here for a while as we'd need staff for night time," he stated firmly. "The clinic first, with a few long term cases under analysis until we are sure that this is viable and we can afford to continue."

"No patients?" she asked.

"No. I don't really care for the idea of disturbed people living here." He grinned. "Apart from us, and I'm beginning to believe we must be mad. If we can't manage to make it pay, then it's general practice for me and you must decide what you want to do, so long as it's never far away from me."

"You could go to St Thomas's."

"It's possible but I want to work away from a hospital, although I'll keep in touch and never forget my medicine. It's still important to know what physical complaints may have triggered off the quirks of the mind, so I shall keep one session going in the medical clinics, and they want me to take a few psychiatric consultations as a second opinion with some hypnosis. Wonderful experience and will help me more than it will help them!" He regarded her with affection. "What are you worrying about now?"

Emma took a deep breath. "Not just one thing. Possibly the whole of humanity as usual," she said with wry smile. "I can't change overnight, Paul. They asked me to work

3

part-time at Beatties as they have wards full of returned prisoners of war, with nasty half-healed wounds and badly set fractures that need re-doing in surgery." She sighed. "I feel guilty because I said I'd think about it and now I don't want to do it. I'll have to let them know if I'll go for a few morning sessions, but only if they are really very short-handed in surgery."

"I've treated some of the returning men for mental disorders," Paul said. "It's a bad picture and some will never recover. Do you want to go back to help part-time, or will the first few sessions grow into full-time work and take over again? It could leave you no time for leisure and for this place . . . and me."

"What do you think?"

"No, what do *you* want to do? It's a free country, or so we are told. You make up your own mind," he said firmly.

A brief vision of Guy Franklin, the rising surgeon who had been her lover, was almost real, looking hurt and completely without any idea that she could mean it when she said she might not want to give up nursing before her graduation, just to do as he wished. He'd wanted her to be there in the cottage when he was available, though they were not married, but only lovers, to be there even when he was working away from Surrey for long periods.

"Unless we are short of money, I want to make this place into a smart and well run clinic and leave you free to get on with patients, and I know I shall find your work fascinating. It's new to me and I shall let them know at Beatties that I am not available again," she said with sudden resolution.

Paul kissed her gently. "Never ever feel trapped, if that isn't what you want to do. It's what I want, and I do think that you've had enough of the hospital environment for a while, so let's go through the accounts and see what we can afford here."

Emma looked out of the grimy window. "We need an

army of cleaners before we bring in any furniture." She saw the ruins of the houses along the road, bombed one night early in the war and leaving heaps of rubble as yet not cleared away, and the sparse earth of the gardens sprouting weeds and straggling bushes. "It must have been a beautiful part of London," she said wistfully.

"A lot of these houses are Georgian and very well constructed but it's a miracle that this one escaped. It was detatched from the row. There was a gap in between this house and the block that had a direct hit. A high wall took the blast and left this one standing. As far as we can judge, it's intact and has a good roof, and gas, electricity and water are laid on. Bea's father certainly had vision, buying up deserted houses of quality when people fled from the Blitz."

"Bea's father is a more refined version of a man my Aunt Emily knew when she was a child. He bought and sold properties abandoned in the first war and never bought a dud one. His wife and son run his business now, but still listen to what he says although he's ancient. Bea's Pa does his business through an agency as if it has nothing to do with him as a politician, but he makes a lot of money." She laughed. "Bea says he was probably a barrow boy in a past life, or a horse thief."

Paul pictured the urbane, cultured and wealthy man and smiled. "I think Bea had something to do with his generosity over this sale. He has other houses, but told me that this is the plum property and I just couldn't believe how cheaply he'll sell it to us. He's keeping several back, as soon many people will come back to London and want somewhere to live, and to buy houses, so the prices will go up. The government hasn't even started to build brick dwellings for the returning forces, and big houses will turn into apartments or single bed-sitting rooms."

"I can't imagine it happening here," Emma said. "The elegance of some houses by the park is almost intimidating and the houses are not close to factories or markets, so if they converted some buildings into apartments, the tenants would have to be a bit more affluent."

"That's right. I think the area will keep its value as Kensington has always been a good address. It will be rebuilt tastefully by men like Bea's father, who will spend a lot of money on them, making them luxurious and expensive. Aren't we lucky to get this place in such an exclusive area? The park and the shops will see to its future success and some of the remaining houses may become prestigious business premises keeping in tune with the rest of the residential ones."

"Sometimes I can't believe that the war is over," Emma said. "Its difficult to get out of the habit of thinking that it's still with us. I forget and cover the windows at night with blackout curtains, and yesterday I even heard a shopkeeper say, 'Don't you know there's a war on?' The customer gave him a dirty look and said she expected better service now it was over."

Paul led the way through the empty rooms and they made notes as they went. "Fuel may be a problem unless we can have good supplies of wood for fires," Emma said, eyeing an Adam fireplace with admiration. "The peace has been signed but we are still rationed and they say that bread might go on ration for the first time if we don't get more aid from America soon. Lease Lend was a life saver but it's over now."

"Bea's husband says that there is a new idea to send supplies here under The Marshal Plan, but we'll have to pay for them in part as the United States have their own money problems now, and Europe must be helped too."

"Poor Dwight," Emma said. "He's so typical of a high ranking American Air Force officer from God's Own Country, with all his roots and loyalties in America, but after marrying an English girl, he's had to keep a still tongue over some things. He adores Bea and they never quarrel, just argue over trivial things. She's wise

6

to avoid certain subjects and now that they are going to have a baby, he can't do enough for her or his English friends."

"They are lucky to be together now," Paul said.

Emma sighed. "I miss her now that she's staying at the American Base and I suppose she'll be flying to America soon, for ever, unless Dwight is stationed here for another six months or so." She bit the end of her pencil. "There was talk of him going to Germany to Dortmund or Hanover, in charge of a training and operations base but Bea was horrified, mostly by the fact that she might be looked after by German doctors and nurses, and because Dwight would be away for long periods, shuttling between Germany and the States. We tried to convince her that she would be in an American Forces hospital if she had to have the baby over there, but she hates the Germans and wants to stay in this country to have her baby, among her friends. The alternative would be to fly to America to Dwight's family, but she doesn't know them well enough yet to feel relaxed there."

"You didn't do midwifery?"

"No, and it's just as well I didn't as I couldn't treat Bea objectively if she wanted me to deliver her," Emma said firmly. "I hated the idea of being a midwife. I wanted to do a six month course to gain a qualification that would be all I'd ever need, then back to surgery. That was it! It would have been all right just to have the experience, but a law was passed that midwives must practice for a year after the full year's course, whether they wanted to do so or not, so many of us said we couldn't give up two years doing something that we found uninteresting or repugnant or that we wanted as a subject we might never use, except in theatre for Caesarians."

"Surely that robbed the country of a lot of capable midwives?" Paul suggested.

"Yes, there were some who might have wanted to stay on to do second part but who now will never know if they would have been happy in the work," she agreed.

He regarded her with serious eyes. "But not you? Don't you care for babies?"

Emma blushed and looked away. "I haven't been in close contact with many that weren't sick," she said, then added as if the thought had only then occurred to her, "What about you?" It was something she should have considered before she married Paul. Her heart beat painfully. What if she had a baby and resented it as her mother had resented her?

"I like some children," he said. "Some children are lovable and some aren't, and some people are too. To me, children are just small people who I like, or avoid as I do . . . older people."

She laughed. "That's a relief. I'd hate to think that you'd love every squawling infant you set eyes on, and wanted me to have lots of babies to fulfil a subconscious urge to have a large family."

"Bea is having a baby and she isn't really the type, but she's excited about it now," he said gently.

Emma smiled indulgently. "Bea is happy that Dwight is back to normal, and the baby will be good for them."

"So miracles do happen," he said cryptically, and picked up the list of work to be done in the house before it could be furnished. "Why not telephone her today, as she must miss you, too."

"I'll do that as soon as we finish here and go back to the hotel." She looked pensive. "It would be fun to camp out here instead of staying at the Melrose for much longer."

"No electricity connected as yet but we can ask for it and then wait patiently for them to do it. I'll apply for a telephone too. I shall have priority if this is registered as a medical clinic. We'll have to bring in fuel as the nights are getting cold, and central heating will have to wait. Some radiators are workable but I looked at the boiler in the basement and it's very old and lethal, but there's a good stove there where it is of no use to us!" He looked pensive. "I suppose we could move in here if you don't mind roughing it."

"Oil lamps and candles," Emma said decisively. "I have an oil stove at the cottage on the Island and lots of candles that I took with my rations in case Aunt Emily needed them, but she uses oil when there are power cuts, so I have a bundle of them." Her eyes shone. "I can clean two rooms and the kitchen on the upper floor and we'd be quite comfortable and conveniently here on the spot to get the house ready quickly."

"I suppose you can light a fire with two matches, like the good Girl Guide that you were," he said, teasing her.

"Let's try it," she said.

"If we tidied up a second bedroom we could have friends to stay . . . Do them all and we can take in lodgers!" he said, amused at her enthusiasm.

"Idiot," she replied. "But seriously, it's a good idea."

"Lodgers?"

"No, a spare room for Bea and Dwight if they can't stay at the apartment in St James's with her father. She grumbles that he has far too many theatrical people there, now that he's married again, and there's plenty of room here."

He tore off a sheet of paper from the note book. "I have some furniture in store from my family home," he said. "Now that my parents are dead, I have no other relatives who mean anything to me, so I must use that stuff or get rid of it." He hugged her. "It's just furniture, and with you, I can bear to see it again."

Emma ran a finger along the window ledge and it came away covered with grime. "We need an Amazon angel with hefty arms who loves cleaning," she said glumly.

Paul gave a whoop of triumph that beat any hog call that Dwight indulged in when excited. "Mrs Coster!" he said with reverence. "The woman I would have married but

9

for her drunken husband and seven children." He wagged an accusing finger. "You didn't think that you had a rival did you? *Some* women really appreciate a man,' he said complacently.

"Can she scrub?" asked Emma. "And I mean brushes and water and soap," she added hastily.

"She offered to scrub for me," he said with pride. "In fact when she heard I was getting married, she offered to clean my house or flat when I settled, as her wedding present."

"A ward maid from St Thomas's?"

"An angel with a broom," he corrected her. "Also a patient who thought quite erroneously that I saved her life when I diagnosed a nasty cluster of gallstones and had her rushed, dramatically jaundiced, to theatre. 'Yellow as a duck's beak,' as she told everyone!"

"Do you think she'll come?"

"We can try," he said and wrote a note. "I have to see someone at Tommie's so I'll see if she's still there."

"I'll ring Aunt Emily and ask her to have the odds and ends in the shed sent over by ferry and carrier."

"And ring Bea," Paul reminded her. "It's too easy to be caught up in new ideas and to forget people we really care about."

"I could never do that with Bea," Emma said, but felt vaguely uncomfortable. She had put off telephoning and couldn't imagine why. The fact that Bea was pregnant was a source of amused wonder at such an unforeseen accident, not a barrier to their friendship, but soon Bea might become a voice on long distance telephone, the calls lacking spontaneity as they would have to be booked in advance, unless they came from Bea through Dwight's offical sources. News would be confined to a series of letters that might dwindle as their interests took divergent paths.

"Cheer her up," Paul suggested.

"She's on cloud nine over the baby," Emma said. "She doesn't need any cheering up."

"Watch her, Emma. Under it all there is a slight panic and a sense that she might be losing a lot if she goes to the States."

"Like me?" She bit her lip. "She's my best friend and the girl I wanted as the sister I never had."

"So enjoy what you have," he said, and quoted, " 'They look before and after and sigh for what is not . . .' "

"I'll get on the phone as soon as we get back to the hotel and you must demand a phone for here as you are *very* important and your work is vital to the peace effort."

"And if I get some moron who asks me, 'Don't you know there's a war on?' I shall bring him up to date as politely as I can."

"Offer to hypnotise him," Emma said and giggled.

Chapter Two

"Could you ask Mrs Miller to ring me at this number when she's free?"

"Who shall I say is calling?" The flat American female voice asked.

"Emma Dewar . . . no, sorry, Mrs Sykes," she corrected herself. It would take a long time before she was used to being called Mrs Sykes, and of course, Bea Shuter was now Mrs Dwight Miller. Are we two different people? Emma wondered. So much had happened in the past six or seven years, when they had worked together and often suffered together, played together, flirted with doctors and nursed hundreds of patients with tender loving care. During that time we have had to be several different people as the need arose, she thought.

Emma shook away a niggling sadness. I'm too young to fall back on memories, she told herself. I have the future, with or without Bea, with a husband who is wonderful and gentle and so penetratingly aware of what I feel that I find it somewhat unnerving.

It had been Paul who rang the American Air Force base from the hotel room, and handed the phone to Emma as soon as he was connected.

She looked up at him. "Mrs Miller is busy right now," she said, imitating the telephone operator. "She's at the ante-natal clinic."

"Don't look so relieved," Paul said.

"Why not? She was driving Dwight crazy because she wouldn't have regular checks, so this is good."

"Doctors and nurses make bad patients," Paul said. "Much too bossy and sure that we know all the answers better than an objective person making an honest diagnosis."

"Bea has too much sense to risk anything now," Emma said. "But after three months, the baby should be safe, shouldn't it?"

"Stay by the phone in case she rings, and I'll get some coffee from the restaurant. It would be nice to be free to make our own coffee that doesn't taste of dandelion roots," he added wistfully. "What did Aunt Emily say?"

"She must be psychic again," Emma said and laughed. "Why do I bother to use a telephone when her mind is there out in front and she can tell me what I am going to do next?"

Paul draped himself over the end of the bed in the hotel room and chuckled. "So what are you going to do? Anything that includes me, or didn't she say?"

"We have to furnish the new place for a start, with a lot of pieces that Bert Cooper's son found at an auction out in the West Wight. An old manor house and farmhouse was being cleared, but on the day of the sale, it rained heavily and the wind blew a gale, and the crossing from Lymington to Yarmouth was not fit for man nor beast nor dealer, or so Aunt Emily said. They even cancelled a few crossings, which is almost unheard of there and the Island was cut off for people travelling by way of Lymington and Yarmouth. Everything at the sale went for next to nothing and Aunt Emily asked him to bid for her. She was a bit scathing, but if dealers come from the mainland, she *knows* they must be delicate flowers who couldn't take a bit of a wetting or a rocking boat."

"Do you think she conjured up the storm?" asked Paul with a grin of pure affection. "Great lady, Aunt Emily, but a bit of a witch, too. I don't suppose you had ancestors who waited by the cliffs for wrecks to be washed up on to the rocks? Maybe they were the ones who tied lanterns between the horns of cattle and drove them over the rocks to guide the ships to wreck and to their deaths?"

"There were no wreckers in my family and no smugglers as far as I know," Emma said. "I've never seen Aunt Emily's broomstick, either. Talking of broomsticks, is Mrs Coster going to help us with the cleaning?"

"She can come for three whole days and would like to be left alone to get on with it," he said.

"Not have you here? I thought you were her heart throb."

"Partly my idea," he confessed. "She did go on a bit when she cleaned my consulting room and leaned on her mop while she told me about her family and their troubles when she should have been working. Although she wanted to help us for free, I insisted that she be paid the rate for the job, so we can afford to expect her to keep busy." He laughed. "She is like the Mrs Mop in ITMA and really does say, 'Can I do you now, sir?' when she starts on a room. She hinted that she'd like more private work and could do for us one day a week as the trams are convenient for her to come to Kensington."

"Do you want me to be elsewhere while she's here?" Emma smiled. "I could visit the Island and see what we need from the goods that Emily bought."

"What a good idea," he said. "As it happens, I have to give a few sessions at Tommie's, so I shall not be at the house, either. We can leave her a key."

Emma gave him a sharp look, wondering if it had been her idea or what he had intended all along! "You and Emily both," she said quietly as he went from the room to fetch the coffee.

She picked up the receiver, wishing the bell wasn't so shrill.

"Emma?" Bea sounded relieved to hear her voice. "Thank God for an English accent! I get a bit miffed when all I hear is that whining personal aide of Dwight's, drawling on and on and being so boring."

"That's not all the time," Emma said placatingly. "Some American voices are wonderful. Dwight has a lovely deep brown voice, and if the aide wants to talk to you, it's your own fault. He's fallen for your aloof English Rose face, and thinks you are Jus' Darlin.'

"My face is fine still," Bea admitted with less annoyance. "It's my figure that will be ruined."

"Is that what's worrying you? You will bloom and look even better when you are a bit further on. It's a known fact that pregnancy works wonders for a woman's skin."

"If you go on sounding so *smug*, Dewar, I'll hang up!

"Who is this Dewar, Mrs Miller?"

Bea giggled. "Neither of us got a better name on marriage did we? But it's easy for you to be condescending. You aren't pregnant and you haven't been sick for three months. I bet your skirts fit round the waist."

"Skirts can be let out," Emma admonished her. "But you are better now and over the morning sickness. What did the medics say today?"

"I'm fine," she said impatiently. "It's Dwight."

"He's not ill?"

"No, don't sound so anxious. Nothing wrong with his mind, and he's bursting with health. He's so *slim* and sexy, I could hit him! At least we can make love again now that I am over the sickness and everything is in place, but what happens when I am so *gross* that we can't get anywhere near each other? He might fall for some slick little tart with no bum and no tum."

"Come on Bea, that's not likely and you know it. What's really bothering you?"

"He has to go to Germany for a week or so and to Amsterdam for off weekends, and I refuse to go there. After the wards full of prisoners-of-war we had to nurse, I can't even hear the German language without wanting to puke. You must feel the same after the way Guy died of typhus in Belsen."

Emma took a deep breath and forced her voice to sound

15

normal, but her hand clutched the telephone as her tension found a release there. It was only when she was taken by surprise with a mention of Guy that she remembered him now with any clarity, but the sharpness was there.

"Come to the Island with me," Emma said. "I've definitely decided that I am not going back to Beatties as there will be plenty to keep me occupied at the house in Kensington and as I can't do much until it's been cleaned, I am better away having a break."

"Are you and Paul really, really buying it?" Bea's voice went up an octave. "That's wonderful. May we come there to stay?"

"It isn't very comfortable at present," Emma replied cautiously. "I don't think bare boards, even if they are rather nice parquet, would be good for your back just now."

"We can bring in furniture," Bea said. "Please Emma, you have no idea how bored I am at the Base."

"Come to the Island first. I shall make you work there, helping me choose from the furniture that Aunt Emily bought at an auction and when we come back here, I'll need your help arranging it all."

"You sound very, very happy," Bea said.

"We are both happy women," Emma said firmly.

"Won't we be too much for Paul? Me with my winges and Dewar with another efficiency drive about to burst out on us?"

"Paul isn't going to be there," Emma explained, and told her that he would have to be working at St Thomas's hospital for a week or so. "We'll be two women alone and have plenty to do without our men," she added. "We may not even miss them."

"Speak for yourself, Duckie," Bea said, with feeling. "I've had the all clear over sex and it's better than ever!"

"At least you can't get pregnant twice."

"No." Bea chuckled. "It's all very free and easy, not

16

having to bother with birth control, and we make love in some very peculiar places if we are in the mood, which is a lot of the time."

"I don't need to know the details," Emma said primly, but smiled as Bea rabbited on. Bea was back to normal, the baby was safe and Dwight was virile and as much in love with her as ever, so there was no need to worry about anything.

"Can we go now?"

"Tomorrow will be soon enough. I have to pack and arrange a car to take us to the station."

"We'll go to Portsmouth by road. Dwight will arrange a staff car," Bea said casually. "I'll tell him I need it at nine in the morning and we'll pick you up in London and then be driven down and catch the afternoon ferry to Ryde. At least Dwight still has plenty of gasolene."

"I'll ring Aunt Emily and ask if the boy who does odd jobs for Dr Sutton can leave my car at the pier head, then I can drive us to the cottage."

"If I know Emily, she will have put hot bottles in the beds and baked us cakes before she hears we need it all."

"Well she did ask me to go down there."

"What can we take for her? No Swiss biscuits from Pa just now, but she did say that maple syrup was good in cakes and on pancakes, so a jar of that and some chocolate will have to do."

"She doesn't expect something each time you see her," Emma protested.

"Why not? And I can't wait to see her wicked brown eyes glint with a little justifiable greed!"

"I must go. Paul went to get some coffee and I think I hear him now. It will be lovely to have my own kitchen and space to put things. Hotel rooms are fine for a while, but I'm longing to move into the Kensington house. This place has everything. There's even a kitchen on the upper floor and one in the basement as well as the main one. I suppose the families had servants who used that part, or a nurse living in to care for the children."

"I'm bored here too," Bea said firmly. "You needn't think you can get out of inviting us, and even if you get uppity, we shall arrive and expect to be made welcome! I don't mind being a Victorian above stairs servant."

Paul returned from the restaurant just as Emma had finished her conversation with Bea.

"No cake that looked edible," Paul said and examined the nearly empty biscuit tin with sadness. "I do like something sweet with my coffee."

"Tomorrow you can move into staff quarters and beg cake from the ward sisters who are dying to get you into their clutches again," Emma said, heartlessly teasing him.

"While you go to the land of milk and honey, with Aunt Emily to feed you, and I eat slab cake, and baked beans and suspect sausages?"

Emma kissed him. "Will you miss me?"

"Yes," he said simply and held her close. "Isn't that good? We'll do what needs to be done and then you'll come home to me and we'll see if Mrs Mop has done her job. Did I ever tell you, Mrs Sykes, that I adore you?"

"A nice few times," she said with an Isle of Wight accent.

"I brought up the mail," Paul said while she poured coffee.

"All those for you?" she asked. "Not your birthday? Or have I got it wrong?"

He frowned. "It hasn't taken the drug firms long to get in touch after the war. I'm inundated with literature and samples to try out on patients. If one works, then there is a danger that I might become loyal to one particular firm and stay there, regardless of the efficiency of their other products, out of sheer inertia." He laughed. "This could be a job for you, reading the blurbs and making a note of anything that strikes you as good, bad or dangerous.

I have yet to meet the nursing sister who didn't know as much or more about the effects of medicines than the average doctor, especially wet-behind-the-ears newly qualified medics."

"I once thought that I might write articles about some common sense methods of treatments, those that are usually ignored by house surgeons who go by the book and prescribe the official remedies without looking further. If you knew how we had to make do and adapt at times when supplies were bad after D-Day, it would make your hair curl," she said.

"You and Aunt Emily should get together on that, so long as you keep off bat's blood and eye of newt!" he told her.

"I'm not daft!" she said loftily. "I admit that I'm not all that sure of my Culpeper herbs, but I'm going to study them as soon as I have more time."

"So you really have finished with Beatties?" he asked gently. "Just because you married me, doesn't mean that you are in a trap, darling. If ever you need a change, say so and take it, even if it isn't something that I want to do. We all need our own space at times."

She nestled into his arms, her head on his shoulder as they sat in the one deep armchair. "I can't think of anything I want to do that doesn't include you, Paul."

"And yet the woman is leaving me tomorrow!"

"Who is leaving whom? You will swan about the hospital with an adoring staff following you."

"Who is leaving." He spoke with quiet vehemence. "We are just doing what we need to do for us in the future."

"You'll telephone?"

"I'll want to speak to your aunt to make sure you are behaving," he said. "We don't need ornate chandeliers and Georgian whatnots or vast pottery urns, so I hope she keeps you under control."

"I like chandeliers," she said, "but you'll have to trust

me to keep to practical items. We shall sleep in our cottage as Emily has her sister Janey with her for a week or so and it will be better for Bea if she can put her feet up without feeling that she has to be polite."

He laughed. "When did that ever trouble Bea or the people she honours with her presence? Emily will make a fuss of her in a wryly humorous sort of way, wherever Bea decides to stay."

"When will you phone?" she asked.

Paul shrugged. "I really can't say." He saw her tense her mouth, and he turned her face to his so that she saw his expression.

"We are both going to be busy. If I phone and you are not there, I'll try again later. Simple isn't it?"

She still looked worried. "If I am to go to the manor farm to check the furniture that they left there ready for collection, I may not be at the cottage for hours, but I can stay there if I know when you might ring."

"*No*! You concentrate on your job and me on mine. I hate hanging about waiting for calls and so do you. It wouldn't be fair to expect you to waste time sitting by a phone, waiting for a call that might not come for hours if I am with a case. You and I have very important work to do if we are to get this clinic started."

Emma let out her breath slowly, and her eyes were bright. "I've done a lot of waiting by phones for unpredictable calls," she said.

"I know, and it's time you realised that I am not like that."

His mouth was soft and loving on hers and she smiled. "No, you aren't like that." The times when she had refused invitations or left parties early, just in case Guy called and expected her to be there, faded. Paul was so different. "I love you, Dr Sykes," she said.

"Say that at least once a day," he said, softly. "Do that and we may lay all your ghosts."

She levered herself out of the chair. "You weren't

the only one to have mail," she said and picked up her three letters. She slit open the first envelope. "One from an insurance company." She make a wry face. "One from Aunt Janey." She read it with growing amusement. "Remember my long lost cousin George?"

"The naval type who was out in the Pacific as an observer when they dropped the Hiroshima bomb?" She nodded and read on. "Odd isn't it?" Paul went on. "Dwight was there in an aircraft and had an acute psychological crisis after witnessing the drop but as far as we heard, George had no such trauma."

"He's coming home," Emma said.

"Where can I hide you? That man nearly stole you and only the bomb saved the situation when he had to go away."

"He's a very attractive man who was good for my sagging morale for a few days at most, but he's a first cousin and I never felt anything more than an amused attraction for him," Emma said firmly.

"I hope that he isn't still in love with my wife," Paul said with an effort to appear fierce.

"I wasn't married to you at the time." A tantalising dimple appeared close to her mouth and he kissed it. "Aunt Janey hoped for us to get together, but now, he's married!"

"You must be losing your grip! That's two men who professed undying love, that you've allowed to escape." He grinned as if hiding an amusing piece of news. "You don't read the newspapers thoroughly. Your Sir Arthur is married, too."

"I know that! He was a patient and good nurses never get involved with their patients," she said stiffly then smiled. "Can you really imagine me living in a manor house and having to talk horses and hunting?"

"And having a lot of babies?"

"What do you mean?"

"There was a picture of him and his wife at Buck House

when he collected his MC. She looked very pregnant, so he might have an heir very soon."

"He'll call his wife 'Old Girl' and they'll have the county to dinner . . . and his mother." She shuddered. "Not for me, Paul."

"Who has George married?"

Emma giggled. "Bea thinks she will escape all things American and the inevitable talk of baby showers if she goes down to the Island, but George has married an American and is bringing her over to meet Aunt Janey."

"Janey lives in Hampshire so you might not meet."

"You forget that she is with Aunt Emily now while Alex is in the Midlands buying spare parts for his marine engineering factory."

"At least you'll be staying in our own cottage while they are with Aunt Emily."

"You aren't worried in case I have second thoughts about George?" Her eyes widened at the idea of Paul being jealous, but to her secret chagrin, he laughed.

"I'm sorry for the poor devil who will introduce you as his cousin and have to cope with the knowledge that he might still be in love with you!"

"George isn't the type to need your psychiatrist's couch, Paul. Aunt Emily said he has a cabbage heart, a leaf for everyone, so by now he'll have forgotten that I ever existed. Besides, nothing happened between us," she said.

Paul raised an eyebrow and gathered the coffee pots on to the tray. "I'll take these back and pick up a newspaper and *The Lancet* if it's arrived, and then we'd better get our packing done. Remember, we need to pack everything, as I shall give up this room if we are to camp out in Kensington when we come back."

Emma couldn't recognise the handwriting on the third letter. She turned it over, with a marked lack of enthusiasm, almost as if she suspected that it hid a scorpion, and yet curiosity made her open the envelope addressed to

'Sister Emma Dewar at the Princess Beatrice Hospital' and forwarded, first to Aunt Emily and then to the hotel.

She stared, unable at first to put a face to the name at the end of the letter, then she gasped.

"Laura!" she said aloud. Guy Franklin's sister Laura, the girl who had collected his case of personal belongings from the hospital for his mother to keep, and then, as if she suddenly realised, on meeting Emma for the first time, that the family had made a big mistake when they refused to admit that Emma meant anything to their beloved Guy. They had decided that she was just a nobody who they could dismiss from his life as a trivial incident and maybe a sowing of wild oats, before they could find someone of whom they approved.

Laura had hinted when they met for the one and only time that she wished that she had got to know her. This was Laura, writing to her as if she knew her; Laura, who with her parents, had not had the decency to tell Emma that her fiancé was dead, and whose family had excluded her from the funeral service as if she didn't exist.

They had made no contact with her until a friend alerted Guy's commanding officer, who was disgusted with them and told them sharply that if they wanted any of Guy's things from Miss Dewar, they must contact her personally, as she had been engaged to him.

It all flooded back and she fought her tears. Guy's family had been all important to him before he fell in love with Emma, a girl not of their choosing, and they made no effort to meet her. She thought back and knew that Guy had never shaken off the grip of the indulgent and selfish family and now, they begrudged her even her private memories and 'Wanted to talk about Guy'. They wanted to squeeze out the last dregs of her time with him and make them somehow their own, she thought. They were jealous that she might have memories that he had not shared with them.

Slowly, she tore the letter into strips after making a note of the address, then she took another envelope and placed the shreds into it with no note, and addressed the envelope with a clear bold hand. The sticking down was easy but the gum left a bitter taste. She found a postage stamp. Laura was married, so Paul wouldn't recognise the name when he posted it, and Emma smiled coldly.

They would hate her for ever and she was amazed that the thought made her glad. At least the letter had brought a resolution to nagging memories. This letter was cathartic and she knew that Guy, whom she had loved and tried to please, was gone for ever, with the horrible family he had never really left.

"You look nice," Paul said when he returned with the newspapers.

"I feel wonderful," she said. "Let me fold your shirts before you crease them. We've a lot of work to do today."

Chapter Three

The burly GI loaded Emma's bag into the trunk of the car and handed a rug to her as she sat in the back with Bea.

"We'll stop for coffee or something half-way," Bea said.

"Yes ma'am."

"A hotel would be best as I'll need a comfort station," Bea said, and he looked embarrassed at the idea that the wife of his commanding officer should admit to needing a lavatory. He probably thinks the President's wife never needs to go, Emma thought, and giggled. Comfort stations? Would Bea gradually use all the American phrases?

"Yes ma'am," he said each time Bea said anything.

Bea slid the glass partition closed between the driver and passengers in the luxurious motorcar. "Now we can talk. I don't think he would contribute a lot to our conversation unless we needed him to say, 'Yes ma'am', all the time," she said when Emma wondered if he might feel slighted. "Drivers are used to being shut out," Bea said, glancing at the solid back and thick neck and jug handle ears. "Efficient as a driver he may be, and in civilian life would be a good bouncer, but hardly a witty companion!"

"He'll hear you," Emma said in a low voice.

"No he won't. That glass is thick. Often they drive VIPs who have private matters to discuss and don't want to be overheard by the hired help for security reasons."

"This is a wonderful car," Emma said, smoothing the

leopard skin upholstery. "I've never been in one like it but I suppose they still make such things in countries that haven't been in the war. We'll find Paul's old car a bit of a come-down after this."

"A real passion waggon," Bea said cheerfully. "Look at the curtains. They are not there for blackout reasons, they are for sex." She chuckled. "Did you ever hear of Eleanor Glyn who said sex was good on a tiger skin? Or something similar," she added as Emma looked as if she was about to tell her the exact reference.

"I didn't know that such cars were issued to senior officers at the Base!"

"Actually they are not!" Bea said in a suddenly flat voice. "I tried to convince myself that I was amused when Dwight told me I'd be travelling in this crate, as it's the most comfortable one they have . . . remember the awful Jeeps? . . . but I can't wait to get to Portsmouth and be rid of it."

"It's a wonderful motorcar," Emma said again, fingering the tassels on a velvet cushion.

"Loot!" Bea replied. "A part of me says good, let us take as much as we can from our enemies. It's only the spoils of war, stealing as they would do if they came here, and as all invading armies have done throughout history, but under it, I feel uneasy to be driven in a car that rumour says belonged to Goering."

"You're joking!"

"Pa said that lots of art treasures and valuable cars and antique furniture were 'liberated' as we began to advance and the war was nearly over. I noticed he has two very nice pictures that he bought from an army colonel." Bea shrugged. "Most of it was stolen by the Germans from the countries occupied all over Europe, or confiscated from the Jews when they were sent to the death camps. Often, they left no heirs, as most of them were killed as whole families. If any survived, they'd find it hard to prove anything, so who is to say what belongs to which country

26

any more? Possession as they say, being nine tenths of the law."

"That is on a big scale, but you must have seen some of the things that the soldiers we nursed brought back from France and Germany as souvenirs. Trifles maybe, but the principle was the same, I suppose."

"If I'm honest, I don't really care about who owns what now," Bea said. "What I hate about this car is that it belonged to a pervert and murderer! Can't you imagine what went on in here?"

Emma hastily stopped smoothing a velvet cushion cover. "I'd rather not!" she said. "Your delicate state is giving you the hab-dabs!"

Bea relaxed and pulled the rug over her knees. "I feel fine and the car is very comfortable," she said. "I'm just envious of every girl with a flat stomach! Don't tell me yet again that it doesn't show! I shall make Pa bring me a hat from Paris."

"Why?" Emma asked helplessly. "Are hats suddenly slimming?"

"No, Miranda, Pa's new wife, went there with a show and said that all the women wore the most outrageous hats even if they had shabby clothes."

"Hats do brighten an outfit," Emma agreed.

"It was more than that," Bea said. "It was an act of defiance during the occupation. When the Germans entered Paris, they brought female soldiers and nurses and clerks all dressed in dismal grey. The French called them the Grey Mice and the Parisians made colourful hats to make a statement that they were not grey in dress or spirits. I want a hat like that."

"Your morale is high and you have pretty clothes," protested Emma.

Bea chuckled. "A couturier who dressed my mother, made a dark green velvet gown for a pregnant friend and said that if a large ornate hat was worn with it or a bright posy of flowers was pinned high on the shoulder of the dress, it took the attention up and away from the lump! I shall use every trick to stay glamorous."

"Idiot," Emma said, but was pleased to see Bea in such a good mood.

They found a hotel that was open and serving coffee, but the luncheon menu was boring and they were glad that they were too early for it. "I wonder why they call messed up mince and potato shaped as rissoles, Vienna Steaks? Any Austrian chef worth his salt would commit suicide before he served them," Bea said scathingly. "I have a passion for fresh vegetables, so I can't wait to see if there is any spinach left in your garden."

The driver vanished for half an hour and came back smelling of cider. The rest of the journey was uneventful and Emma enjoyed the colours of starkly ploughed fields, and bare trees filtering a wintery silvery sun. It was good to feel free of work and responsibilty after years of tension in her hospital nursing and private life, and it was good to be with her best friend again.

Bea dozed and woke refreshed as they turned into the shore road by Portsmouth harbour. "Home soon," she said when she saw the masts above the houses as the car swung into the docks. The air smelled of salt and freshness and gulls screamed above a fishing boat returning with its catch as they had done for hundreds of years, wars or no wars.

The driver went to find out when the next ferry would be due to leave, and they waited for fifteen minutes in the car, where it was warm and smelled of Bea's perfume, rather than the staleness of old cigarette stubs in the waiting room near the jetty. Emma looked out to sea, avoiding the scene behind her of half derelict bombed houses, and rusting machinery in the yards of empty sheds, and was glad to see that most of the sea defences of corrugated iron and spikes of metal, set in the water to repel invasion, had been removed to allow the safe passage of small boats again.

The ferry arrived and Bea smiled sweetly at the driver and thanked him for his careful driving. He loaded their bags on to the boat, saluted smartly and said, "My pleasure ma'am," and drove away, back to the Base.

Bea turned up the pale nutria collar of her coffee-coloured swing-back coat and shivered in the cold air. "Is it cold or is it me?" she asked.

"It's coolish," Emma admitted. "Let's go inside the saloon. Paul suggested that I bring a flask of coffee and it should still be hot." Bea sat with the warm mug between her hands and sipped the coffee gratefully. "We'll have a hot meal when we get home," Emma promised. "Even if it is only soup and bread."

"You'll have to come to America to stay with us," Bea said suddenly. "I can't bear it if you don't."

"We'll come over later, I promise, but first we have to get the clinic started and you have a baby to think about, which will take all of your time for a while." Her remark was something that Bea repeated often now, as if saying it would make it happen and Emma was worried to hear the muted panic under the words.

"I can't cope alone," Bea went on. "I think I shall hate America and I don't really know Dwight's family. I want to have the baby at Beatties, where they know me and where I know I shall be safe. For the first time in my life I shall be dependent on others and my body will be ruled by the forces of nature. Do you know, Emma? Believe it or not, I hate the thought of being naked in front of strangers, even if they are dedicated to helping me. Being examined by the very nice gynae man was an affront. I sometimes think that I could never have been like my mother, sleeping with anyone with a good body and handsome face. It's a relief to know I am not like her although she could never believe that I was a virgin when I married Dwight."

"But you did fancy a few," Emma said.

"Fancying is different isn't it? A lovely feeling of

29

excitement and power but with something holding me back from going the whole hog." Bea giggled. "I shall flirt as usual, even when I am two tons and ugly," she vowed.

The exquisite face above the soft fur collar looked the same as the face of the aloof and aristocratic girl that Emma had first met in Bristol years ago and who had made her feel like a country bumpkin. But Emma knew that now, their friendship was deep and for ever and they had few secrets they did not share.

"You'll be safe," Emma said. "The baby is fine and Dwight would never let you be delivered by a doctor or midwife who didn't care and was inefficient."

"I like men, but now I feel that I need women round me and I know why men are excluded in some tribes at the time of birth, as they would be quite superfluous. Here, we do have male obstetricians I suppose, but I'd rather have a woman delivering me. I need you to hold my hand as they don't allow laymen into the labour wards at Beatties, thank God." She giggled. "When I suggested that Dwight might like to stay with me, he went pale and wobbly and said he'd rather fly a bomber on one engine than see a baby born."

"If you have the baby in Beatties, I promise I'll be there," Emma said. "It might happen here in England as Dwight still has a few months of duty based over here, and even the times he has to spend in Germany are only a short flight away."

"Maybe I can have it early," Bea said hopefully. "Maybe I can scream that it isn't safe to fly over the Atlantic in my state of health."

"That opportunity has gone," Emma said. "Paul thinks that it would not have been safe to fly during the first three months or so, but after that, unless you have some complication, it would take the kick of a donkey to shift a foetus once it's fixed to the uterus."

Bea's eyes glinted with wry humour. "I'll have that

husband of yours know that this is a baby, in my motherly womb, not a blob of jelly in a uterus, so he can stop calling it a foetus! I've already given it at least three names for either sex."

One of the sailors carried the luggage from the ferry and Bea followed, clutching her coat round her, tightly. Emma made a mental note that Bea's waist was thickening and she looked more than four months pregnant. The car was waiting and Emma had the spare keys in her bag. She unlocked and Bea settled on the back seat, with a sigh of relief.

"Tired?"

"Cold mostly. I shall ask Aunt Janey if she had sore breasts that felt the cold, when she had babies."

"I'd forgotten that she is here," Emma said. "I hope that Aunt Emily isn't too busy, with Dr Sutton's receptionist duties as well as Aunt Janey."

"Janey will do the cooking and make her eat well, and Emily loves to have people around her," Bea said. She smiled. "I'd love to hug her but she shies away from kissing women. She lets Dwight kiss her but then he wouldn't take any hint that it wasn't welcome!" she said. "At least he gives every woman friend a bear hug and a smacker that isn't exactly sexy, so I don't object."

"Nobody could take offence at anything Dwight did," Emma said. "I love him."

"Watch it!" Bea said. She took a long deep breath. "I can smell wet leaves and apples," Bea said, closing her eyes when she stepped out of the car.

"The Cox's Orange Pippins must be ready to pick. They are a late crop and my favourite apple," Emma said. A steam train puffed along the line from Shide Station, just far enough away from the cottage to make a homely background noise and far enough away to avoid covering the house with smuts although the white smoke hung on the air.

Emma unlocked the door and felt a wave of warmth

31

coming from the open grate. Bea pulled aside the mesh fireguard and held her gloved hands out towards the wood fire then sank into a chair. She peeled off her fur-lined gloves at last and shook free from her coat and hat, letting her blonde hair cascade round her shoulders. "Want any help?" she called languidly.

"No. Get warm and we'll have some food." Emma appeared with a note from Emily. "Wilf, her odd job lad, lit the fires and he's chopped enough wood for a week. We have chunky logs for later. She's left us soup and pie and there's a dish of stewed plums and apples and a jug of cream in the larder for lunch, and we eat with her and Janey tonight after you've had a nap."

"Bliss," Bea said. "I'm really hungry and I love wood fires. I hope we have them in America and not just the awful steam radiators that they have at the Base, with no open fire places to keep the air fresh. The air is always dead and dry, and the pipes make strange noises in the night."

"Forget all that. We are here and must make the most of this time," Emma said, seriously. "We are starting a new phase in our lives, Bea, and we may not see as much of each other as we have done, but I know that distance will not make a lot of difference to us keeping in touch." Her lips trembled. "We need each other and we've shared so much," she said.

"'When we are old and grey and full of sleep and nodding by the fire,'" Bea quoted. "It was written for a lover, but it means the same for any close relationship and we can look back on such a lot."

"Not now," Emma said firmly. "We have the future, Bea. Paul reminded me of that yesterday. You will have a family, and I have a lot of work to do, and I have Paul."

"Even if you never have children and that thought is impossible, you will gather people around you as a family. You can't help holding out a hand to those in need of care."

"I can help people now that I've really grown up," Emma said. "I had nothing to give except nursing care at first, but I learned to give comfort during the war."

"Learn to love my baby, Emma." There as note of desperation. "Even if it is as ugly as sin you have to be its aunt."

Emma was shocked, but hid her feelings. "Is this just a fluttering of hormones, or a slight seasickness?" she asked, smiling. "Or is something wrong?"

"When they weighed me at the clinic, they measured my waist and hips and told me to send them measurements each week if I couldn't attend antenatal classes or be seen at the clinic."

"That does seem to mean they are being careful," said Emma to reassure her. "I suppose they do that to every patient in case they want to eat too much and put on a lot of unnecessary weight," she said brightly.

Bea shook her head. "They kept asking me if my dates were right as I seemed further on than four months." She smiled wanly. "I should know! I couldn't say my husband was impotent after the shock of Hiroshima and it was a memorable night when he managed to make love and I had taken no precautions!"

Emma laughed. "It did put that date firmly on the map," she agreed. "Maybe the baby will be a huge Texan."

"Thanks very much," Bea said with feeling. "And I have to be delivered of a giant?"

"Have a nap down here," Emma said, removing the loose cover from a folding bedchair and fetching a rug. "The bedrooms are chilly, so use this during the day if you feel tired and we can light a fire in your bedroom at night."

"I won't even pretend to help," Bea said. "I'll use the bathroom and put on a loose dressing gown and sleep for an hour. Later, when we go to Aunt Emily, I'll phone Dwight and you can phone Paul, but I'm glad you haven't had the telephone put in here."

"We can't have it yet as this is a private house with no war work connections, but Paul will manage to have it installed soon at the house in Kensington if it's to be used as a clinic, so we can keep in touch easily," Emma said.

She cleared away the dishes and washed up, then returned to the fire and Bea, who looked pale but relaxed in deep sleep. After an hour, reading, Emma crept away and took a wooden garden trug out to the vegetable patch to cut spinach and parsley. Apples lay at the base of the trees and she reached up to pick some ripe fruit, before they fell and were wasted, revelling in the scent and coldness of the misted skins. Garden fruit was not rationed and she made up her mind to make preserves while she was at the cottage, using the rationed sugar she had accumulated ready to bring to the Island, as she never used it in tea or coffee.

Maybe I'm being stupid, she thought. Rationing must end soon now that the war is over, but the unbelievable rumours of impending bread rationing had spread. Bread rationing? when it was the one staple food that had never been rationed during the whole of the war, even if it was often in short supply and was the grey chalky bread of the National Loaf? She frowned. The shops were more empty than they had been in the middle of the war and fuel was difficult to obtain, even if people were willing to collect their coal from railway sidings and coalyards, filling their own sacks and taking them away in wheelbarrows and trucks and even in cast-off baby carriages.

She left Bea to sleep until it was time to get ready to go to Emily Darwen's house for supper. "We'll walk," Emma said firmly. "You know it isn't far and the exercise is good for you."

"So they said, but I prefer being lazy," Bea said. "However, I suppose they sent you with me to spy on my condition and I'll have to do as I'm told." She helped herself to a long thick scarf that Emma had hung on a hook by the door in case the weather turned really cold. Bea draped it across her front and crossed it again at the back, tying the ends in a knot and looking like a child sent out to play in the snow.

"It isn't that cold!" Emma said.

"You'll keep warm carrying all that stuff," Bea said. "In my condition, I can't carry heavy burdens," she added complacently. "Isn't it good? I can get out of doing anything I want to avoid now."

"Not everything. You have tiny garments to make," Emma said heartlessly, knowing that Bea hated anything like knitting or sewing.

"They gave me a list at the antenatal clinic. The vests are easy as they are on extra clothing coupons and obtainable for the newly born, the gowns of Clydella will be made by a lovely woman at the Base who loves sewing and will embroider them in pastel colours, and the first size matinee coats will be made by another angel who lives not far from here."

"Aunt Emily?"

"If I play my cards right," Bea said. "Dwight's family are sending shawls and cot things and all I have to do is to have this lump delivered and get back to normal."

The lane near the house was damp under foot and smelled of wet mushrooms as if autumn had lingered and was unwilling to give way to winter. Bea pushed open the green garden gate and almost ran into the house with her offerings of maple syrup and chocolate, while Emma followed more slowly, carrying baskets of apples and vegetables and sugar for Emily.

"Wilf said there was a light in the cottage, so we knew you'd arrived," Emily said and avoided Bea's hug. "You look well, but big for your time, I'd say." Emily Darwen eyed Bea, taking in every detail. "Carrying a lot of water, or is it twins?"

"I've been eating too much," Bea said, hastily.

"You have to eat for two now," Janey said. "Or so my mother used to say."

35

"And what if I want to stay slim?"

The two women laughed. "That would be a miracle," Janey said. "If you starve, your baby will take what it wants from your body. The old saying is that you lose a tooth for each baby."

"You make it sound as if I am carrying a parasite." Bea tapped her waistline. "Behave in there! I value my nice teeth!"

"So you'd better learn to like milk," Emma said.

"Please don't tell Dwight. He has this passion for ice-cream sodas and milk shakes that they make at the Air Base. I'll settle for ice-cream and lovely, lovely cream on my fruit," she said.

"You'll have rice pudding tonight and like it," Emily said. She took the basket of vegetables and saw the spinach that Emma had washed carefully. Emily handed the dish to Bea. "Give this another rinse. I hate grit in my spinach, and we can have that now with the casserole as it takes only minutes to cook."

"I thought you'd spoil me," Bea said in an aggrieved voice.

"We are," Emily said. "We're letting you do healthy activities like washing spinach."

Bea went into the kitchen and they heard the tap running. "Don't give in to every mood she has, Emma. She's strong but could be selfish if she can get away with it. It's in her nature, but she's grown out of most of it, unless she feels sorry for herself." She smiled. "I'm not being hard. I'm really quite fond of her."

"Do you really think it could be twins?

"Time will tell," Emily said enigmatically. "Lay the table and help me dish up."

Chapter Four

"I'd forgotten that Christmas was so near," Emma said. "I went into Newport to do some shopping and Mrs Maple at the cake shop had a cake in the window that looked like a real Christmas cake, but I think it was a plaster of Paris cover over a sponge cake, like some wedding cakes are now, looking traditional for the wedding pictures but hiding a very small cake inside, often with no fruit and very little jam."

"You didn't buy anything in there? She dusts it off each Christmas and puts it in the window. I've seen that model robin at least three times. Never eat her cakes: she has a dirty kitchen," Emily Darwen said with an expression that boded no good for any one of hers eating Mrs Maple's doughnuts.

"Of course not," lied Emma, and hoped that none of Emily's spies had seen her and Bea eating hot doughnuts oozing with red jam of unknown origin, when they sat on a seat in Church Litten cemetery. Well it was my duty to provide Bea with food when she felt suddenly low on sugar, she told herself.

She had needed comfort eating, too. The house and garden that Emma recalled from childhood, that had sat peacefully next to the cemetery, had been flattened by a bomb and was now an empty space where a doctor's house and surgery had once been, and only a few trees in the old chestnut avenue remained.

Surprisingly, the ancient burial place where plague victims were interred, escaped, and the impressive tombstone to the memory of Valentine Grey, the last boy chimney sweep sent up a chimney and who died there, now stood unscathed.

She recalled hearing about the old doctor and his family, spoken of with admiration and affection, and she felt depressed that such a valuable man should have been killed when he wasn't even in the services. She remembered the huge golden gooseberries that had been grown there and were sold when the church held church fêtes in the grounds.

"Will you be here for Christmas?" Emily asked, trying not to sound as if that's what she wanted.

"If Dwight can be here, we can stay with Emma," Bea said. "The Americans make far more of Thanksgiving Day than Christmas unless they are very religious, which Dwight isn't, so he may be able to get away for a day or so." She laughed. "He can bring us food and that will bring seasonal tidings of comfort and joy," she added.

"When I ring Paul, I'll ask him if he can come here, instead of me going back to London," Emma said. "No workmen will be available on Christmas Day to work on the house, and patients don't like seeing doctors over the holiday unless it's an emergency, so he should be free." She chuckled. "Someone asked him to carve the turkey in hospital in Bristol last year but he opted out, saying he was not a good surgeon, and no good at carving anything."

"Turkey? Of course. That's something that Dwight *can* organise, so depend on him, Aunt Emily," Bea said.

"They'll have a bit of chicken at the British Restaurant," Emily said. "A farmer friend said he'll let them have a few birds and the place will be full that day. I finished there last month, but I look in now and again to see that they are all right," she said, but sounded doubtful.

"And are they all right?" Bea smiled, knowing that Emily had jealously guarded her kitchens and staff and took care over the supplies and menus when she had been in charge of the British Restaurant. She'd served good

38

wholesome hot food each day to hundreds of people short of rations at home. Even members of the Council ate there if their work took them close to the two Nissen huts that had been made into the restaurant, and nobody felt too proud to eat there after they'd forgotten the idea that it might look like a soup kitchen for down and outs.

Emily sniffed. "Well enough I suppose, but the woman who took my place tries to serve ox liver once a week as it's off ration, and half of it gets left. Unless it's minced with plenty of onions, a bit of fat bacon and parsley, and put in a terrine, it's horrible the way she has it done. She never soaks it in milk to get rid of the bitter taste and soften it, and it's always over-cooked by the time the customers have it on their plates, all curled up and dry."

"You wasted precious milk on liver?" Bea asked.

"It makes all the difference and it isn't wasteful, as I used it in soups when it was drained from the liver."

"You should write your recipes down," Emma said. "I think you are as good as Mrs Beeton."

"I could write about the rubbish they made us make during the war, and that we have to use even now, but it's interesting that the same ingredients can produce such different results, according to who is the cook. Even Woolton pie, that has nothing but diced vegetables in it and was the butt of music hall jokes, is good if the pastry is light and the vegetables are cooked in good stock, but Mavis at the restaurant, who now makes all the pies, can make any pastry as heavy as lead and it tastes of nothing."

"When will the shops have more than basic rations? I never want to have another fish cake made mostly with potatoes, or a baked bean again," Emma said.

"If it wasn't for Dr Sutton and his grateful patients, we would never have a joint of pork or a fat duck or a boiling fowl," Emily said. "I suppose all through the war I have been quite lucky."

"Do I smell rabbit pie?" asked Bea.

"No, it's rabbit stew and herby dumplings," Janey said. "We're a bit short of fat for pastry."

"Paul sent his ration book as he will eat in the hospital canteen for the time he is there," Emma said. "And I have mine with me too."

"I'll send Dwight a list of what we need for Christmas," Bea said eagerly. "I'll ring now and ask him to write it down and make sure he knows he is to be here on Christmas Eve. He can bring Paul with him," she said as an afterthought. "What fun to be here all together with the people I love most."

Emma looked at her aunt. "If Bea and Dwight stay with us, will you be alone here or could you stay with us too? The spare room is cosy and I keep it for visitors when Bea and Dwight use the bigger room."

"You won't get me sleeping in a strange bed when my own is up the road!" said Emily but her refusal lacked rudeness and her eyes were bright with pleasure.

"Will Aunt Janey be here?"

Emily glanced towards the kitchen door, beyond which Janey was thickening the stew with cornflour. "I hope so, but you never know when George will come back, and Alex might want to be in their own home as he has been away so much lately."

"You'll have room for them all if they come," Emma said cheerfully, "But if you are alone, come down to me."

"In a way, I dread George coming here."

"Why? I'll be fascinated to see his American bride."

"I'm fond of Dwight and I've liked some Americans, but others I've found brash and boastful and that raises my hackles. I say too much," Emily said.

"George wouldn't choose someone like that," Emma said, smiling.

"Don't forget that Janey has never met her and that will be a bad moment for her," Emily said. "She and

40

Alex hoped that you and George might get together. I know it was Janey's dearest wish." Emily paused and regarded her niece with a hint of exasperation. "It was what he wanted, too, and you know it!"

"George and I are first cousins and I never marry first cousins," Emma said firmly.

"I know that, and I think you've done well with Paul. At least you knew Paul for long enough to know your own mind."

"And George didn't know Sadie for more than a month!" Emma bit her lip. "I know that after Hiroshima, people did get entangled in love affairs just as they did when friends were parted in the war and suddenly believed that they needed to belong to each other. Sometimes they were wrong, but a sense of panic made them feel that they might be killed and never have a future or survive to live a normal life. There were times when I thought about my own mortality and nearly made a few mistakes," Emma confessed. "At the time, I knew I was right to live with Guy, but now all sorts of bitter memories come back to me to remind me that I wasn't intended to marry him. I know how lucky I was to marry Paul."

"And what about Bea? She's a lovely person and very attractive and they say that gentlemen prefer blondes! There must have been men in her life."

"Dwight came along at the right time to prevent Bea from being promiscuous like her mother, or so she thinks, but I know her too well to imagine that happening. She was wonderful with Service patients who stepped out of line, and as she nursed a lot of healthy men with broken limbs but with nothing wrong with their hormones, she had to be strong, as we did meet a lot of very fascinating men."

"You and Paul give me no worries," Emily said.

"What about Bea?"

"It's all right, she can't hear us. She's far too busy

41

tasting everything that Janey made. She's in the hungry stage."

"So, what do you think?" Emma asked anxiously, knowing that Emily was feeling a bit fey, and in that mood, was sensitive to the future.

"She's carrying two and Dwight ought to know that she must not travel far now."

"How can you be sure?"

"How do I ever know these things?" Emily sounded impatient as if she wished that she could not see into the future.

"And you are usually right," Emma said flatly. "Will she be all right?"

Emily took a deep breath. "She'll be fine and so will the babies but I feel that there is a tragedy about to happen to someone. I can't tell what, as the person is coming from far away."

"George?" Emma caught some of Emily's foreboding. "He isn't in submarines. At least Aunt Janey hasn't the fear that he will die as his father did, under the waves."

Emily gave a thin smile. "Take no notice of me, but I think we may have another pregnant girl here for Christmas."

"Don't look at me!"

"Not you, Emma. Not yet," she said.

"Be sure to tell me when I am," Emma said dryly. "I'm sure you will know long before I do!" She laughed. "Tell me, is Paul there waiting for a call from me, or should I wait?"

"Cheeky young thing," Emily said. "Get along with you and call him and ask what he wants for Christmas . . . apart from you."

But Bea was already talking to Dwight and telling him what to bring to the Island. "Yes, I'm really fine," she said for the third time. "Don't worry. Just be here when I want you, and that's all the time," she added softly. Emma closed the door quietly and waited for her to emerge.

Paul was unavailable and Emma left a message for him to ring later as she would be at Emily's house until ten.

She put the phone down and it rang again immediately. Eagerly, she picked up the receiver and said the number.

"It's Emma! I'd know your voice anywhere."

"Speaking," Emma said, as if she didn't know who was calling, but she did and her heart gave a curiously heavy extra beat.

"It's George!" he said, as if surprised that she didn't recognise his voice.

"Where are you?" was all she could think of to say.

"What, no, wonderful to hear from you? No welcoming warmth?" His bantering tone hid embarrassment.

"Hello cousin," she said. "Janey did say that you might be back in England and I am very pleased to hear from you. Wait a moment while I fetch your mother."

She ignored the bleating at the other end of the line, telling her to hold on and leave his mother until later.

"Aunt Janey, there's a man calling himself George on the phone and he wants to talk to you." She almost pushed her aunt into the hall and closed the door after her.

"Where is he?" Emily asked.

"I didn't give him time to tell me," Emma said. "Aunt Janey is the one who needs to know that and all his news, not hear it second-hand through me."

"Just as well," Emily agreed. They both turned towards the array of photographs on the polished surface of the grand piano and looked at the one of George's father, Clive, Janey's first husband, the dead submariner. His naval officer's cap was at an unconventional angle and his eyes sparkled with mischief and humour. Beside the sepia picture, taken in the First World War, a later black and white one stood, taken in the war just ended. It could easily have been Clive but was of his son George, with the same quirky smile and handsome eyes, the same confident and almost arrogant bearing and even the cap looked the same.

"Is George really like him?" Emma asked." In ways other than looks I mean."

"What do you mean?" Emily asked sharply.

Emma shrugged. "You know . . . sailors with a girl in every port, and all that," she said and her voice tailed away.

"Clive loved only one woman: Janey, and was devoted and faithful," Emily said. "Luckily for her, she's got another devoted husband in Alex."

Emma raised her gaze from the pictures and was suddenly scared. "George is happily married," she said. "So am I, and we can enjoy being related as cousins, can't we? I felt an immediate family bond when I first met him and so did he."

"You did," Emily said dryly. "George fell for you," she added quietly.

"He is a very attractive man and must have had lots of girl friends," Emma protested.

"He asked you to marry him, didn't he?"

"Yes, but that was nothing. We knew each other for only a week or so and he was a bit lonely, home on leave and having to go away to the Pacific, where he knew something momentous was about to happen, and he observed the dropping of the Bomb. I've met a lot of men who felt they had to have some emotional relationship before going away to unknown danger." She glared at her aunt. "Don't look at me like that! I didn't encourage him and he went to America, knowing that I would never marry him. It was just a passing fancy for him and he fell madly in love with Sadie! You said yourself that George had a cabbage heart, a leaf for everyone," she said triumphantly as if that excused her from whatever her aunt's knowing brown eyes accused her.

"A leaf here and there until he found what he wanted, but his heart is sound and solid like his father's, and

44

you'd best be careful, Mrs Sykes," Emily said deliberately.

"You needn't say that to me," Emma said proudly. "I am very happy in my marriage and it gets better all the time. George would never admit he'd made a mistake, would he?" She bit her lip. "Now you've got me wondering if he might still feel something for me, and I know it can't be true."

"Well, finish laying the table and we can eat," Emily said. "Janey will know if he's coming here, so be warned." She made an impatient gesture. "Unfortunately for George, marriage suits you. You'll look more appetising every time he looks at you!"

"You really are uneasy about him, aren't you?"

"Yes, but it's nothing to worry about now. When you meet him, enjoy his company, but always with Paul and the others, of course." Emily seemed confused and suddenly pale. "Don't ask me any more. I can't see it clearly, and it isn't soon, and I may be wrong."

Bea opened the kitchen door and brought in a dish of steaming potatoes and Emma went to help her with the other dishes as Janey was still talking on the phone. They heard the click of the finished call and Janey joined them, her face flushed and beaming. "How is George?" asked Emily.

"Fine." Janey sat down and for once let the others dish out the food, her eyes rapt and her hands folded on her lap. "They'll pick up Alex and bring him here on Christmas Eve." Her joy was almost painful. "It will be like it was when we were children, Emily. One big family, and George will be posted to the Ministry of Defence in Bath in the New Year, so no more sea-going ships for him for a while."

"And what does Sadie think of being tossed into our family all at once?" Emily asked. Emma saw that she was tense under her smile.

"She's excited, as she has no real family in the States.

She was adopted by rich elderly relatives, now both dead, who could give her everything she needed but company, and left her a lot of money, but she never had brothers or sisters or even cousins, and often felt lonely." Janey frowned. "It sounds as if she needs a rest. George thinks she was upset on the long sea voyage across from America. It was, as he says, a bit rough, so it must have been terrible if he admits it was anything but flat water all the way!"

"Is she over it, or is she being sick?" Emily asked with an innocent expression, and Emma watched her.

"George said it's taking a long time to settle." Janey looked at her sister. "You think she may be carrying?"

"How should I know? I've never met the girl," Emily said and helped herself to sprouts.

Paul rang later and made Emma laugh at the things that his treasure, Mrs Coster, had said when she was cleaning. "You remember the awful old Ideal Boiler in the basement that we want to get rid of?"

"I do," Emma said with feeling. "I think that tramps camped out in the cellar during the bombing and cooked on it. It's full of rust and the top is broken."

"Well, Mrs Coster fell in love with it and her husband and son are coming to dismantle it and take it away! She said, looking at it when she first saw it, and completely impervious to puns, 'I call that ideal.'

"'That's what it says,'" I said. "'It's an Ideal Boiler.'

"She was very patient with me. 'I know,' she said. 'It's ideal.' So I felt put in my place and gave her a lot of old packing cases and some rolls of wallpaper that match nothing in the house and are really ghastly, but they brought a smile as she told me where she would hang them if she was given one of the new prefabs the government are promising will be given to returning service men."

"What are they?"

"A very good idea. Small prefabricated units that can

be taken by lorry and erected on a site, bolted together and plumbed in quickly, ready for immediate occupation. They are like small bungalows and I saw one at an exibition of what the housing people plan to use to fill a gap until real homes can be made. They are very practical, made of aluminium in the aircraft factories, and making work for the men and women who built planes and are no longer needed for that. But although they are basically aluminium, they are very well insulated, and Mrs Coster lusts after one as it will have a built-in refrigerator in the built-in kitchen! All modern conveniences and better equipped than many expensive flats."

"They'll need thousands," Emma said. "Too many people are living with in-laws or in bed-sitting rooms."

"Time I checked a patient with an obsessive desire to be clean! I'll try to convince him that he has no need to wash his hands six times during the night and I'll give him a sedative."

"Not another Lady Macbeth? 'Not all the perfumes of Arabia will cleanse this little hand'? I wonder what triggered it off?"

"I'll find out tomorrow when I put him under hypnosis. I think he was found muddy and wounded after a battle and refused to say what had happened, but obviously has a heavy burden of fear and guilt." Paul laughed. "What a way to say good-night to the woman I love. Sleep well, my darling, and I can't wait to join you for Christmas."

"You look pensive," Bea said to Emma when she had finished talking to Paul. "What did Paul say when you told him that George would be with us for Christmas?"

"With his bride," Emma said quickly.

"Of course. You *did* tell him?"

"I forgot," Emma said. "Come on, you look tired, I'll walk you home and light a few fires."

Bea eyed her with malicious speculation. "Scared you will light a few fires from the old embers? George will never forget you, Dewar."

"Don't be ridiculous," Emma said crossly. "You are as bad as Aunt Emily."

"So, she thinks so too? That's very interesting. We shall watch carefully and be good chaperones," she said seriously. "If Emily thinks he still cares about you, then he does, poor devil. Happy Christmas, George!"

"He's married and so am I, so don't be silly." Emma walked out to the gate and waited, forcing herself to be calm and wait for Bea. She saw again George's face when he said goodbye to her before he left for America, when she told him that she could never marry him and he must find a pretty American girl. She'd said it lightly, but he'd done just that and she hoped with all her heart that he'd forgotten Emma Dewar.

Chapter Five

"Quite a convoy!" Emily Darwen said dryly as she watched the two cars being driven along the lane and into the garden. "I hope the kettle's boiling."

"Tea and coffee at the ready," Bea said in a delighted voice, and ran out to meet Dwight, hugging him almost before he emerged from the car.

"The Boston Strangler," he said when he managed to free his leg from the car door and stand up to continue the embrace. "Hi Honey. Hi, Emma!"

Paul kissed his wife and regarded Bea with amusement. "You seem full of life," he said wickedly, and she tried to hide her thickening waist.

"I look slimmer if I stand this way," she told him and gave him a welcoming kiss.

Janey hurried to the other car and George was enveloped in a motherly embrace before she stood back, suddenly shy, as Sadie stepped from the car with Alex. "Say hello to Sadie, Mother," George said and Janey went forward and kissed the girl's cold cheek.

"Sadie is chilled," Alex said and exchanged a non-committal glance with his wife.

"We've a lovely warm room waiting," Janey said and took the girl by the arm to lead her into the house. "What can I get you to make you warm? Coffee, tea or hot Horlicks?"

Sadie shuddered. "Not tea or coffee," she said. "I'm sorry to be a nuisance but I haven't enjoyed either since we left the States. Maybe it's the water over here."

Emily said a brief greeting that included everybody but no one in particular. "Did you bring any lemons?" she asked Dwight.

"Bea said you wanted them, so I went to great trouble to get some for my favourite aunt," he said and she couldn't escape his hug and kiss.

"Give over," she said but smiled. "You're a good boy, Dwight even if I am not your aunt, and I'm glad you're here. Bea needs to be a bit broody and likes to have people round her, and she misses you."

"I promise we'll be no hassle," he began, his expression concerned. "We do look on you as family and it means a lot, even if you do bully me," he said more laconically than his expression showed.

"You are never a bother," she said. "You and Bea will stay with Emma and Paul and the others here."

"You won't make those wunnerful pancakes with my lemons without asking me to eat with you?" he asked accusingly.

"Don't worry, we'll all eat together in the evenings and for Christmas midday dinner, and I need some of the lemons for Sadie."

"I thought it was me you love!"

Emily laughed. "You could charm the birds off the trees and you know it. Keep it for that wife of yours and for your . . . children."

He gave a boyish grin. "I can hardly believe that I am to be a father, and you said children! Yes, I do hope we have more than one, in time of course, and if Bea wants them."

"Nature will decide that," Emily said briskly. "Now find the lemons and I shall make hot lemonade for Sadie as she's gone off tea and coffee and needs something sour, like my mother did."

"Sometimes, my dear Aunt Emily, you talk in riddles," he said with exaggerated politeness. "What has your mother got to do with this?"

"She went off tea," she said. He looked puzzled. "You

50

may fly those terrible planes but you don't know much. Common sense is much more valuable on a day to day basis but it takes a woman to know that," she added sweetly. "When my mother was expecting, she craved for sour things and my father bought her the finest lemons he could get. She ate them whole, sometimes dipped in sugar, but mostly so bitter that they made my teeth ache to watch her."

"And Sadie is . . . ? How can you know? You never saw the girl until today!"

"Put me down at once!" Emily protested when he danced her round the room. "She doesn't know and neither does George, yet."

He laughed and held her close. "I love you, Emily Darwen! You're a wicked doll!" He held her away from him. "You'd better believe that or I'll have you burned as a witch. We had a place for such as you down in Salem, US of A, so I hope your spells are only good white ones."

Sadie looked better in the warm room and when Emily brought in the hot strong lemon drink, laced with sugar, she sighed. "How did you know? I didn't know what I wanted, but I do now!" She sipped and more colour flooded into her cheeks. "I've had nothing to eat all today and all day yesterday. George is so worried," she added with pride.

"No need for worry," Emily said and stopped when Janey gave her a warning glance. She left Sadie with the glass between her hands, supping greedily at the drink.

"They don't know," Janey whispered, and giggled. "Isn't it wonderful? I shall have a grandchild!"

"She's a pretty thing," Emily ventured. "Is George happy?"

"As happy as he can be now Emma is married, and he'll settle down now that Sadie is pregnant."

"He wasn't settled before this? Emma thinks he's forgotten he was sweet on her."

"He loves Sadie, make no mistake of that, but you and I know it's second best. After Hiroshima, he wrote to me and said that life was too short to waste time longing for what he knew he could never have, and he had met a very sweet girl who loved him, so he was going to be married as soon as possible, and I mustn't be hurt if he didn't bring her home first."

"The baby may be the answer," Emily said, and her sister looked anxious. "Time will tell," Emily said softly. "Now we have a horde of hungry mouths to feed, so let's get started."

Janey smiled. "I remember Mother with her lemons. I'll make pancakes and no one will notice that Sadie eats them with lots of lemon! She needs building up. I never saw such a thin girl."

"They call it fashionably slim now," Emily said.

"The meat and vegetable pie has turned out well and there is mashed potato with chives and butter and lots of carrots and mashed swedes," Janey said. She called up the stairs to George, who had left them all, saying nothing to Emma and telling his mother that he would unpack. He had not returned to the family. "George? Come down and put in the extra leaves in the dining room table," she said. "George ought to be told before he goes down memory lane," she said wryly.

Slowly, he came down and looked about him. "Sadie is with Bea and Emma, and Dwight and Paul are putting food in the big larder," Emily said. She looked at Janey, who took a deep breath and told him that they thought Sadie was pregnant. He took the handle that wound the table top open to receive the added mahogany leaves, and let it slip to the floor.

"Are you sure?" His face held a mixture of emotions, disbelief and a kind of pain, and then as if something was dawning and beautiful, an elated smile filled his eyes as the news hit him that he was to be a father.

"I rang Dr Sutton," Emily said. "If you want to see

52

him he can be there after you've eaten, and he can tell you both for sure."

"Have you said anything to Sadie?"

"Take her to the doctor for a check as she hasn't been well, and let him tell her." Janey laughed. "We promise to be surprised when you bring us the news. We're good at that."

"Get on with the table," Emily ordered. "We can't eat off the floor!"

They saw his beaming smile and Janey shook her head. "The pie won't spoil and you'll never get through supper without blurting it out," she said. "Take her over now, and use my car as it has a heater."

"I'll fetch her coat," he said, and Janey called Sadie and told her that George was worried about her and wanted her to see the family doctor, before Dr Sutton joined his family for Christmas.

"Paul is a doctor," protested Sadie.

"Paul deals mostly with the mind," Janey said. "George has brought your coat down and has warmed up the car." She bundled the girl into the fur coat and gloves and waved them away.

"What gives?" Dwight asked when he heard the car engine.

"Nothing but a check-up with Dr Sutton for Sadie," Janey replied.

Paul gave her a grateful look. "Good," he said simply, and Janey suspected that he knew of Sadie's condition and wanted nothing to do with her professionally because George had been in love with Emma. It might be awkward if George resented any contact with Paul who had married the woman he loved. They were two separate families now.

"Do you want the additional leaves put in?" he asked, bending to pick up the cranking handle.

"Please, Paul. George didn't have time to finish it."

Janey stirred the gravy to prevent a skin forming on the

top and Bea made hungry noises and wanted to steal a spoonful of mashed potato, but Dwight slapped her wrist lightly then kissed her. "You may be eating for two, but we all want a meal, so you can't eat it all," he complained. "I wonder how long they'll be?"

An hour later the car arrived, and Janey tried to hold back and look nonchalant, but one look at George's face was enough, and when he told them the news, Emily and her sister gave a very good imitation of astonished joy.

Bea kissed Sadie's cheek. "The sickness is the worst," she said. "I existed on plain cracker biscuits and mashed potato for weeks, but now, I'm hungry! Please, when can I be fed before I die of hunger?"

George watched his wife eat mashed potato and a small pancake covered with lemon juice and Emma gave a sigh of relief. She had seen the agonised glance he had given her when he arrived, and the fact that he'd avoided her made her unsure of how they would be when they had to meet, but the news had changed all that and she sat easily, talking to her companions while he gave Sadie his full protective attention.

"The rather bloody bundle in the kitchen is a joint of beef that the good doctor sent," George said. "Patients seem to have brought much more than he can eat and so it's up to you what you do with it. You need a big refrigerator like they have in the States."

"We'll pickle it," Emily said. "I have some salt petre and a block of cooking salt and there are bay leaves and onions and it will keep sweet and be just right for the New Year."

"You'll have to eat a British classic," Paul said to Dwight. "Boiled beef and carrots, with dumplings if we speak nicely to the aunts."

"Sounds like real covered waggon food," Dwight said. "They did all kinds of food preservation on the trails."

"Catch me a buffalo," Bea said, her eyebrows raised in amused mockery. "Don't get him started on his ancestors who struggled and died for America. It's a wonder that he was ever born as they ran out of virile men and the women must have lost a lot of babies being tossed about in those awful waggons over rough country. I don't think he has Indian blood but strange things happened out thar on that thar trail."

Everyone laughed but Sadie. "Please don't," she said in a small voice. "I feel low enough as it is. I think I need my bed." Janey was surprised: the girl had eaten well, had second helpings of pancakes and had laughed with Paul and George, who seemed to be getting on well together, but now her voice took on a whining note and she looked as if she felt neglected.

Emily picked up dishes from the table and helped Emma carry them to the kitchen and the others followed until the table was clear.

"C'mon, Honey, we wipe and the others wash and put away," Dwight said firmly when he saw Bea look towards a comfortable chair. "You ain't sick and the exercise is good for you after all that food."

"You are a heartless man," she said and hugged him. "I am carrying your child sir, or didn't you guess?" Hastily she put a finger over his mouth. "No, we don't want to hear about the women who had babies while climbing mountains and then baked a dinner for a hundred men."

"You exaggerate," he said and smiled, his pride and pleasure of possession showing. "Bet you couldn't do that."

"Who'd want to? I expect to be cossetted. Sadie has got it right. She came over faint when she saw the washing up," she added dryly.

"So don't get ideas," he said. "I didn't marry a useless doll," he added in a whisper.

"Who promised to dry?" Paul called. "I've been detailed to stuff the turkey for tomorrow and I'll need Emma's help and advice in the pantry."

"It's cold in there, Bud." Dwight grinned. "Leave the

55

door open and we can check that you are really stuffing the turkey."

"Don't be coarse, dear," Bea said, knowing that Dwight hated being called dear. It reminded him of an unfavourite governess he'd suffered when he was five.

"Don't call me that," he growled.

"Sorry," she said airily. "I thought all pregnant wives called their husbands 'dear'."

"You are not a wispy blonde."

"I am blonde," she said, her cats eyes glowing with a provocative glint.

"Not inside, you're not," he said cryptically. "Start whining like her and you get your butt smacked hard."

"Worth a try," Bea said and looked pleased.

George had gone to the bedroom with Sadie and came down for a glass of water, then a dry biscuit, and then a stone hot water bottle. He listened wistfully to the muted companiable laughter and the clatter of crockery, and Janey told him firmly to leave Sadie to sleep and come down for coffee.

"Sleep is what she needs and when the sickness is over, she'll feel and look as well as Bea does, so just leave her in peace, George. I know you are anxious and it's been a shock, but a very pleasant one," Janey said, tenderly. "But you mustn't forget that it isn't an illness – it is the most natural thing in the world."

"Thank God for sensible mothers," he said with a sigh of relief and grinned. "Do you mean that Sadie will not break in half if I leave her for five minutes?"

"She will need you close to her for a while, as she is in a strange country and feels ill just now, but later, she must do things for herself and not depend too much on you. I'm not being hard but you have to make sure she is well and independent when you go back to work." She looked serious. "We all suffer at these times but some women are naturally more . . . dependent than others and Sadie has been sheltered at home with her elderly adopted parents. She needs your support but not your constant attention."

"George?" a weak voice called.

"I'd better go," he said. "Promise me this doesn't last?"

"It has no need to last," Janey said.

"I heard some of that," Emily said as she poured hot coffee made from fresh beans that Dwight had brought. The aroma was tantalising and Janey hoped that George would be lured downstairs by it, but Emily had the brown teapot full of her usual strong and stewed tea, with the whisky bottle and sugar at hand to lace it well.

"Who does she remind you of?" Janey said shortly.

"You see it too?"

"I remember Mother dancing attendance on Uncle Edward's wife who was always too weary to wash and iron and cook for him. I know she had diabetes but she played on that and when she was treated for it after insulin was discovered, she didn't improve in her dependent selfishness although she managed to have enough energy for her own pastimes."

"She's young," Emily said, seeing that her sister was upset.

"That's what Mother used to say," Janey muttered. "If only—"

"That's enough of that. What's happened has happened and she'll make him happy," Emily said firmly. "In time Alex will like her too, although he prefers strong women."

"You noticed that too?"

"He never says much about anyone but by now I do know him well and respect his judgement. Sadie might be difficult to take for any long period!" She sighed.

"She may have to live with us when George is away," Janey reminded her glumly. "She may find me a difficult mother-in-law."

"Tea or coffee?" asked Emily.

57

"Tea as we had it years ago?" Janey said and tipped a good slug of whisky into a huge thick cup. "Nothing like it for comfort."

The log in the fire broke in half as Paul poked it with the long iron rod by the fireplace. "Why is it that men always take over when it comes to poking the fire?" asked Emma sleepily.

"Time we went home," Dwight said. "It's quite late for this neck of the woods and it's Christmas Day tomorrow."

"I'm not tired," Bea protested.

"I haven't noticed any night clubs around here," Dwight said, caustically. "You are supposed to be pregnant and frail," he added, laughing and glanced at George who was sipping coffee as if he needed it. "I've never seen a woman so energetic, and I mean energetic."

Bea blushed. "Not time for bed yet," she said primly.

George made a rude face. "Some men have all the luck. Do you think that Sadie will be, well, less wishy-washy soon? It's been a few weeks now."

"You have to beat them," Dwight said, eyeing his own wife with pride. "Be firm and don't give them an inch! Ouch, that hurt," he said when Bea pinched him. "OK, I give in Honey. What do you want to do?"

"I want to go to midnight service," she said and everyone was silent.

"You're kidding," Dwight said at last. "I doubt if you even believe in God."

"I'm not sure that I do," she agreed. "But it's Christmas and if it is true, I want to be a part of it, just for tonight."

"I'd like it too," Emma said. "We've time to stoke up the fires in the cottage and be ready for bed when we come back. It isn't far to the church in Newport."

"Not me," Emily said.

"Nor me or Alex, who is already nearly asleep, and George can't spare the time," Janey said. "See

58

you all tomorrow and we'll need some help with the dinner."

The road was covered with thin frosty rime and the houses were dark and silent as if everyone was asleep or in church. The only sound was of church bells, triumphantly ringing now that the threat of invasion was gone and bells were permitted to be rung again, in joy now and not in dread.

I wonder if the chidren have hung up their stockings? Emma thought, and knew that parents would have a hard time filling them this year, even if they had money enough to buy good toys.

The church was lit by candles and the old crib by the altar screen was as Emma remembered it from childhood. The chipped oxen were badly in need of a lick of paint but this year, nobody had mislaid the baby Jesus.

Bea led them confidently to a pew three rows from the front from where they could see the vicar and follow the service. The organ played softly. Less bold members of the congregation sat behind them and the church was nearly full. Emma watched the cross over the altar and saw the glint of stained glass windows no longer forced to be hidden by dark black-out drapes.

The service went on and Emma's hand was firmly held by Paul while Bea on her other side sat close as if needing her support.

The grey walls and vaulted ceiling seemed to drift away and Emma saw again the bare boards of an emergency surgical ward packed with German prisoners, with the British soldier guarding the door, sitting relaxed when the patients were permitted to hear the distant carols, sung by nurses dressed in dark cloaks with the red linings turned outwards for the candle lit procession round the wards.

Bea tensed as the organ began a fresh hymn and when Paul looked at their faces he saw two girls with tears streaming down their faces unchecked as 'Silent Night' filled the church. Emma smelled the musty odour of stale bodies and dirty uniforms and heard the sharp breath of a boy of fifteen with shrapnel in his chest. She also heard the soft refrain from a harmonica, beautifully played, with tenderness and anguish, by one of the prisoners, as the rest of the ward sang very softly, '*Stille Nacht*'.

Dwight handed Bea a large handkerchief and Emma took the one that Paul offered her, and both of the men looked grim, each with his own thoughts, that the promise from the pulpit of peace on earth, goodwill to all men, did nothing to erase.

"My feet are cold," Bea said when they filed out of church and made for the car. She smiled up at Dwight and he cuddled her as she walked.

"You OK Honey?" he asked softly.

She felt the tears forming again and dashed them away. "If you speak like that again, I'll call you dear," she said, then buried her face in his greatcoat.

In the car, he tried to see her face, sensing something strange as if she was confused. She giggled weakly and took his hand to rest under her coat on her swollen belly. "What is it, Bea?"

"It, as you called it, is your offspring," she said softly. "Can you feel it? It liked the service, but got a bit restless, and now I feel tiny hobnailed boots kicking me!"

"He's going to play football, American style," Dwight said with delight.

"No, all our well-brought-up gels play lacrosse," Bea said firmly.

"Only the ones in snobby schools," Emma said from the front seat.

"You shut up Emma Dewar," Bea said complacently. "You're only jealous." She sighed. "I enjoyed church," she said. "Had a good cry and washed my soul." Her voice broke. "But never ever learn to play the harmonica, any of you."

"Or sing 'Silent Night'," Emma added.

In one way they felt very close to their partners, but

in another, they were miles apart in their past memories and they had no need to share them.

"Christmas will be better when we have the baby and can do silly things," Bea said, hopefully.

"Sure Honey," Dwight said. "Next year it will come right."

Chapter Six

"Do you mind wearing them?" Bea sounded anxious.

"They are lovely," Emma said, holding out one foot on which she had fitted a shoe. "Your present isn't new either, but that jacket will be fine to hide the lump. It was too big for me, so I never wore it.

"Pa hasn't been away lately and Miranda gets most of the perks now he's married to her, but I wore those shoes only once and now the heels are too high for an old preggie woman."

"I like the shoes you have on now," Emma reassured her. "With your slim ankles and high insteps they look good, and the leather is just the right colour for that skirt."

"I shall have to wear something looser. Junior doesn't enjoy being zipped in too tightly, and I get a bit uncomfortable too."

"We'd better go over to the house and help with the dinner," Emma said. "I've got their presents, such as they are this year, and I must show Aunt Janey the shoes. She loves fashion."

"We can walk. The men have gone ahead to chop wood or do what ever the aunts want. Dwight said not to be long. I must pick more parsley. Do you think Sadie will share my cravings?"

"I hope so for George's sake. At least turnips are cheap!"

"Well, if she craves for caviar, or for many more lemons, she'll be unlucky here," Bea said heartlessly. "I wish I liked her."

"Give her a chance. She's not at her best just now. She must be nice if George fell in love with her."

"If she whines too much and George gets fed up, be careful, Emma. He still carries a torch for you and this is only a blip that could have worked if he'd stayed away, because she's very pretty." Bea pulled her scarf up over her face and shivered. "I know exercise is good for me, but I do feel the cold now."

"They'll be fine," Emma said but sounded unconvinced.

"Trouble with her is that she has no sense of fun. Glamorous when she's feeling well maybe, but humour, *Non! pas de humour.*"

"I did notice," Emma said. "Fortunately they leave with Janey and Alex tomorrow, Boxing Day, and I shall not see George again for ages as we return to London as soon as we have sorted out the sale furniture."

"We return with you, too," Bea said firmly. "I remember you saying you wanted us to live with you and you couldn't do anything without my priceless talents when it comes to arranging furniture," she added sweetly.

"Who invited whom? But I do need you to help us plan the house and the clinic."

"I'll do my best. You've no idea what that will do for my morale. I feel a bit useless, and each day I get a lot bigger. I think I am nurturing an elephant who kicks," she said, holding her abdomen.

Emma gave identical silk scarves to the aunts, presents that one of Paul's colleagues had brought from France and sold to him, and Dwight produced boxes of crystallised fruit and biscuits.

Emily looked embarrassed. "I don't know if you will wear this, Bea, but I asked Miss Price to make up some material I bought in the early part of the war before rationing came in, using a Vogue pattern she has for maternity wear."

She shook out the panne velvet that gleamed softly in

the dim sunlight, the soft almost crimson dark rose pink gentle on the eyes and the texture expensive and elegant. It was a suit of two pieces, a smock that draped well and had a froth of Emily's hand-made lace at the throat and a skirt that Bea held up, obviously puzzled. "It's got a hole in it," she said.

"It's made for women just like you who like a slim fitting skirt even when they are expecting," Emily said. "The skirt is cut away to go *under* the lump and can hang straight and the waistband is on top so that it's fixed. The smock covers everything we don't want to see. The skirt is strengthened by an under skirt of stiff taffeta rayon to keep the shape. I'm afraid I couldn't get anything better for the lining."

"It's wonderful," Bea said. "Is it a bit big for now? I shall wear it to death next month. I'll try it on and if it's all right now I shall wear it today."

"The skirt is adaptable," Emily said, her pleasure making her cheeks pink, and Bea went up to Emily's room to try it on.

Sadie looked sulky. "Are you going to make me one?" she asked. "The material is just wunnerful and the colour would suit me too."

"We can cable your folks to send out some clothes," George said.

"Not like that," Sadie said and Emma hastily followed Bea to help her with the fitting.

"It's gorgeous," Bea said, turning to look at all angles in the triple mirror. "I dreaded being like some women I've seen who have their skirts riding up so much in front that their knickers show when they sit down. It makes the lump seem even bigger. Quite obscene, but this has style and dignity. How did she know? I must ask Pa for pretty material from Switzerland and have the dress maker make some more. In this, I can even go to a cocktail party, and Pa will be very pleased as I said I would be incommunicado for nine months."

"Calm down and try not to say too much in front of Sadie. She already feels left out and I think she does a very good line in sulks, so take it off and eat dinner in your other clothes in case Sadie drops gravy on it . . . accidentally."

"Back to the kitchen," Bea said, and they worked hard to get everything ready for the meal, even decorating the table with sprays of holly and some late chrysanthemums. Dwight was grinning, and listening to Emily and Janey reminiscing about their childhood. "It can't have been that good," he said.

"Christmas was, even if there were bad times in between," Janey said. "A big family has it's ups and downs and petty jealousies but Mother tried to treat us all alike and made sure we each had a present that we wanted."

"Sounds great," Dwight said. "We ought to have a big family Bea. Out West there will be room for as many as we like."

"So you are going to have the next one, are you?" Bea asked sweetly.

"I don't want a big family," Sadie said. "I wish we'd waited for a while. I want to go places and see England without feeling ill all the time."

"You weren't sick this morning so the worst must be over," George said, helpfully, then saw that this was not the right thing to say. He made it worse. "I know you have to rest and take care, but look at Bea. She is fine now and full of energy."

"I have a delicate constitution," Sadie replied defiantly. "I just know I'll feel ill for months and get ugly." Her eyes filled with tears that found no sympathetic reaction from the other women, so she decided to smile when she saw that sulking did not work and George was eyeing her with a hint of less than adoration.

Emily began to collect the plates while Janey brought

in the Christmas pudding that she had made with dried fruit carefully accumulated over the past three months.

"Will you try this or have stewed fruit?" Emily asked Sadie, ignoring her pregnant state and determined to limit her concessions to the passing weakness of the obviously spoiled girl. Poor Janey, she thought. She'll have Sadie and her sulks undiluted if she has her to stay alone while George is away.

"The pancakes were nice. I'll have some of those," Sadie said.

"There aren't any," Bea said firmly, before Janey could rise from her chair and offer to make batter and cook pancakes, when there was plenty of other food available and Sadie knew that none had been made. Bea gave a sweet smile. "You seemed to enjoy the turkey, so you must feel better. You can have pancakes later. I'll show you how to make them so that you can have them every day. That is, if you make your own, and if you can find lemons to go with them," she said with a trace of bitter lemon in her voice.

"That's good of you Bea," George said, missing the edge in Bea's voice. He smiled tenderly at his wife. "Try some pudding. It's special for Christmas over here and very good with the brandy butter that I made."

"Who made?" Dwight asked.

"Well, I added the brandy and pointed out the lumps you missed."

Emma regarded Janey with interest and hoped that she would be firm with her new daughter-in-law. She didn't envy her having to put up with Sadie, but it looked as if they might be living together in the house in Hampshire for a while.

Sadie rested on her bed all the afternoon and the others dozed by the fire, with Bea half-asleep on a chaise longue. There was an air of peace and Paul used the time to read the notes he'd made about the house.

"I have to get back," he said at last. "Tomorrow

morning, I ought to catch the early ferry and be there to make sure that Mrs Coster has finished cleaning and locked up, before I go back to Tommies."

"I'll have to leave too, Hon," Dwight said. "If you give me a key, Paul, I'll send some of our stuff over to Kensington and you must let me know what we'll need if we are to sleep there." Dwight looked at Bea. "You'll stay with Emma until we have it all fixed in London? Can't have you doing too much."

George listened and said little.

"I'll bring Bea back by train in a day or so after we've checked what furniture we want, and arrange to have it sent by carrier," Emma said.

"What about new furniture?" asked Bea.

"Have you see the awful Utility tables and chairs? And the beds are just struts of wood with hardly any springs," Emily said.

"The old things may be worn but they are strong and comfortable and you don't have to give up coupons for second-hand items. Keep your dockets for a cooker and refrigerator and things for the clinic, like waiting room chairs," Janey advised. "Utility furniture would look lost in big rooms, and you will need large pieces." She sighed. "I wish we could stay but Alex wants to go home and we must make sure that Sadie is comfortable while she is with us."

"Is that all right, Mother?" George asked.

"What do you mean? Of course you and Sadie must stay with us until you find a place of your own," Janey said.

George shrugged. "Thanks Mother. If she was not having a baby, she could have followed me in hotels and we could have had a great time, but now, she will be lonely if I have to leave her with strangers." His eyes darkened and his voice held a pleading note as if he knew that Sadie was not one of Nature's saints who bore adversity without moaning.

"Sadie is your wife, George. She will be the mother of

your child and that is enough to make sure she is welcome and loved in our home," Janey said.

He bent to kiss her cheek. "I'm a lucky guy," he said, but didn't say why. "Any one for a walk? I've eaten far too much." He looked at Paul and then at Emma, his glance lingering on her face.

"Not Emma. She is helping me with my mending," Bea said.

"Come on," Paul said, and George reluctantly followed him out to the garden.

"Since when did I do your mending?" Emma asked curtly. "I need a walk too." She saw that Bea had shuttered her eyes as she did when her thoughts were private. "Don't get all po-faced, Bea. I know what you're doing and I don't need a chaperone."

Lazily, Dwight unwound his legs from the deep armchair and came over to Emma. He winked at Bea and then kissed Emma firmly on the lips. "Any better? If you need someone to flirt with other than your husband, then I'm here and Bea is in no state to object." He wagged a reproving finger in front of her eyes. "George is a no-no and dangerous. Sadie is a dawg and I hope he goes away soon and you never see him. He's a nice guy but he hasn't thought this through beyond her pretty face. That marriage will hit the fan."

"My, my, what a speech!" Bea said. "I'll let you off this time but keep your hands off my best friend."

"Love you," he said lightly. "Come and help me pack," he suggested and pulled Bea up and into his arms. "'Gee, it's good to have a girl so big and fat,'" he sang in a Hoagy Carmichal gravelly voice. "'That when you go to hug her you don't know where you're at' . . . Emma's far too skinny for me. You wearing a Mae West, Honey?" He swore softly. "Don't hit me, ma'am, you'll wake Sadie." He turned to Emma. "You'd better come too and pack for Paul. We start early tomorrow." He grinned. "We have to keep you under wraps in case the big bad wolf comes after you."

"Thanks," Emma said. "It's a bit sad as I'm fond of him, but I know you are right."

Dwight disappeared into the kitchen where the two sisters were talking and came back holding a parcel. "I said goodbye to my girl friends and told them that as we were getting up early tomorrow, perhaps we'd have an early night and eat in the cottage tonight." His guileless smile fooled nobody. "Cold turkey is good for the soul, Emma," he said, cryptically. "And there's some in this parcel, too, for supper."

Bea looked at the kitchen door then smiled at Emma. "Come on, we'll say goodbye to Aunt Janey and tell Emily that we'll pick her up at eleven, when they've all gone, and we can drive out to West Wight to see the furniture."

Dwight buttoned the coat high under Bea's chin and pulled her hat down further. "Warm enough, Honey?" He linked arms with the two young women and sang as he escorted them to the cottage.

"It's warm," Bea said, and took off her coat as soon as they went into the cottage.

"Emily told the boy to light the fires as she thought that we'd want to be here this evening."

"He works on Christmas Day?" asked Emma.

"A small matter of sausages and a turkey drumstick helped," Dwight said. "He and his sister live at the farm and depend on odd jobs for a living. They want to emigrate to find a better life and if I wasn't depriving Emily, I'd tell them to make for my parents' ranch, as he's honest and a good worker."

"And you said you'd help with their passage?" Bea asked, raising an eyebrow.

He shrugged and looked embarrassed at being found to have done a good turn. "It would be worth my while. You don't want to lose all your best young people to the

69

Antipodes on cheap assisted passages. Give the US a few. Come on, it's time for the news."

He switched on the wireless and let it warm up. Crackling noises from the large brown bakelite and mahogany wireless set gave way to stilted speech and the Oxford accents brought them news of church services all over Britain, giving thanks for the first Christmas after the end of the war, and prayers for a bright future, then news of men on remote Pacific islands, being brought home, after continuing fighting as they had not heard of the end of the war until the Navy sent in boats of marines to spread the news. Some marines were killed while on this errand of mercy, as the other side thought they were re-inforcements and fired on them.

Dwight relaxed at last, as if he had been expecting something more that would affect him badly, and Emma made tea.

"I can't believe it's all over," Dwight said. "Maybe we can go home soon."

"There are plenty of pieces to pick up," Emma said. "It takes time, Dwight. How can you tell a man who has lost an arm and has a permanent injury in his chest and chronic asthma, that everything will be fine and he'll get a job easily? It happens in hospital and the almoners have a hard time trying to arrange something other than emergency clothes for them. It's difficult to make sure that civilian casualties obtain a pension for wartime injuries."

"We'll be reminded of it all again when we get back to Town," Bea said. "Some of the bombed sites are very ugly and the shops are almost empty. Is there room to grow spinach and potatoes where you live?" she asked. "I heard the announcer say that potatoes might have to be rationed next year as the last crop was bad. I hate rice, so we'd better grow our own in whatever garden there is."

"Remember me?" Dwight gave her a rueful glance.

"We may be back in the States by potato harvest time," he said.

Bea's mouth was dry. "Early potatoes are dug in the spring," she said, slowly. "About the time my baby comes in May." She smiled hopefully. "Can we wait for the main crop, much, much later?"

Paul came in and shut the hall door behind him. "I hope you told George to leave your wife alone," Dwight said, laughing. "Little honey pots we have, Paul. Got to watch them. I was hinting that we ought to go back to the States as soon as my stint here is finished, and that could be when I want to make it happen, or so I was told."

"The weather forecast is for gales in the Atlantic, for weeks and weeks and weeks," Bea asserted.

"I'm a good pilot and so are a few other Yanks," Dwight replied. "You flew out with Emma that time when I was hurt and she went to visit her uncle, and now they have better ones for passengers." Emma sensed that he had a battle before him. "You enjoyed it, didn't you Emma?"

"I was thrilled to meet my Uncle Sidney," she said non-committally.

Paul coughed gently. "I think that now might be the time to talk this through."

Bea groaned. "He's put on his psychiatrist's hat," she said.

"I called your gynaecologist, Bea. Remember the x-ray he thought was a good idea?"

Dwight leaped out of his chair. "What's wrong? Tell me for God's sake! Get a second opinion!"

Bea was pale but calm. "Do be quiet, darling. Nothing is wrong. I feel wonderful today and I think I know what Paul wants to say." She eyed Emma accusingly. "You know, don't you?"

"Only what Aunt Emily thought," she answered cautiously.

"The x-ray shows twins," Paul said.

Dwight sank back into the chair as if suddenly deflated. *"Twins?"*

"Two babies for the price of one," Bea said calmly. "I knew there were more than two football boots in there, and already they are fighting each other!" She saw alarm and disbelief in her husband's eyes and remembered that it was only very recently that he'd been treated by Paul for impotence after Hiroshima and the mind is a fragile piece of equipment.

"They look fine and healthy," Paul said crisply. "The consultant said eat well but try not to eat too much fattening food, Bea, and have checks every week for a while."

Bea began to laugh but Emma sensed that she too was thrown by the news although she had suspected it might be twins.

"You can laugh just now?" Dwight asked. "You really think this is something funny?"

Bea's eyes sparkled. "You certainly made up for lost time," she said deliberately. "But really, darling, you didn't have to prove your virility as much as this!"

Slowly, he smiled and an expression that held male pride and a growing excitement suffused his face. "Gee, Honey, we sure are fertile."

"Maybe," she said with a mockingly stern look. "Just don't come to think it was all *your* idea, and I was just a female brood thing for my husband's pleasure. I shall be as niggly as Sadie now and you will wait on me hand, foot and finger!"

"I'd divorce you if you were like her," he said, coming down to normal swiftly.

Bea hooded her eyes and Emma knew she was scheming. "I'll have to see the gynae man again soon, I suppose. Did he say anything about exercise? . . . Travelling? Lifting and things like that, Paul?" She contrived to appear fragile and brave.

He exchanged amused glances with Emma, then said

soberly, "It is important to be mobile but not to have vigorous exercise or go into any dangerous situation that could be avoided, for your own peace of mind rather than being in any real danger of losing the twins. Air travel in a plane that isn't completely pressurised in the right way could be a risk now."

"Could it?" she said, her eyes widening as if she was very ignorant of all medical matters.

As if she doesn't know the affect she's having on Dwight! Emma thought with admiration. She should have been an actress.

"You'll have to stay here until they are born," Dwight said, urgently, sitting on the floor by her feet and holding her hand as if she might break.

"But you wanted to go home," Bea said. "So many people would be disappointed and I'm sure it would be all right."

"Forget that! You stay here and make sure you are looked after. Gee, Emma, what a good thing we're staying with you from now on until it . . . they are born!"

"Whatever you say, darling," Bea said humbly and bent to kiss his cheek.

"Cocoa, anyone?" Emma asked hastily, before Bea could look too much like the triumphant Siamese cat she resembled. "Or coffee and . . . cream, Bea?"

"Cream, please," Bea said and helped herself to sugar.

"What a clever girl you are," Emma said dryly. "Two babies and getting her own way without even trying hard, all the time," she whispered as she bent over the tray. "Miaow!"

Dwight looked at them in puzzled wonder. "What's funny?" he asked.

"Overwhelmed by the news," Bea said. "Over the moon."

"It sure is good. I must send a cable tomorrow to my folks and tell them we shall stay here to be quite safe."

"You do that," Paul said and sensed that the two girls

73

were on the verge of hysterical laughter. "Check the fire in your bedroom as Dwight and Bea ought to get to bed now." He yawned. "That goes for us all. We have a full day tomorrow, one way and another."

"Sorry if you disapprove," Bea said when Dwight was upstairs. "But I am being sensible and not just Sadie-selfish, aren't I?"

"You are doing fine," Paul said. "If you do as your gynae man says and don't get stroppy with Emma and me, we'll keep you safe, Bea."

"Thanks Paul." Her voice was suddenly husky. "I'm so happy I could burst," she said.

He eyed her swollen body with mock alarm. "Not here, not over the carpet, please," he said, and she wandered up the stairs to Dwight, smiling.

Chapter Seven

"I've had a look at the car and it seems fine," Paul said. "Aunt Emily's friend bought you a bargain and I really do need my car in London now." He kissed Emma and she felt again the depth of the warmth they shared and her love for him. "Emily will be a bit lonely, when we've all gone," he said.

"She will breathe a sigh of relief, and get on with her own life," Emma said. "After a lifetime of hard work for others in the family and doing war work, she enjoys solitude and her job at the surgery is interesting but not what you might call strenuous like the one at the British Restaurant. She thrives on work and even if some people think she is too old to do anything outside the home, she says as always, 'You're only as old as you feel,' and gets on with it."

"It's important that she meets a lot of people and can give good advice. Your aunt couldn't exist without that," he added, smiling indulgently.

"She's coming with us today, as she knows where the furniture has been stored and has a key to let us in if the caretaker isn't there at the farm. It should be interesting as both the manor and the manor farm have been sold to wind up the estate of the last of the family who owned it all."

"I wish I could stay. It sounds a good day," Paul said wistfully. "At least George and Sadie will have gone and they can cast a blight on Alex and poor Aunt Janey until George finds a house to rent in Bath." He regarded Emma with a level gaze. "I'm glad that he is being sent to Bath.

75

The War Ministry in London would be a bit close. You don't need Sadie as a neighbour and I certainly don't need George."

"I don't need either of them," Emma said. "George is married and so am I, and even if I hadn't married you, he would have had no chance," she said, tenderly. "It's a pity he felt as he did about me as I'd like him as a nice amusing cousin, but that's impossible, isn't it?"

"Impossible!" He kissed her again. "Ferries sometimes leave on time and we have the cars to load. I'll take Dwight to the ferry and his driver will pick him up on the mainland. Aunt Janey will drive George and Sadie and Alex, and I'll leave them in Portsmouth and go on to London alone. Be good and don't buy a whole manor house."

"Goodbye Dwight, my love," Bea said dramatically from the window to the departing car, then sank back into bed again and pulled the covers high under her chin.

"You don't look sad," Emma said.

"You don't either," Bea retorted. "Confess! We are looking forward to being three independent women together and having time to riffle through the junk out there all day if we want to, and not be told to hurry up!"

"For a moment this morning, I thought that Dwight would refuse to leave his lady wife, who is suddenly so precious and fragile," Emma said. "Do they shoot deserters from the American Air Force?"

Bea giggled. "He's never had twins and he feels a bit limp at the thought. Not like me," she said, and swung her legs over the edge of the bed. "I'm hungry."

"Can this be the pale pink person who nibbled at a piece of toast just to please Dwight, and sent him off thinking that you need extra special care or you might go into premature labour?"

"He will call his family, today," Bea said shrewdly. "With that picture of me in his mind, he'll be firm and tell them that there is no way that we can fly over the pond so that his children can he born American!"

"You don't change!"

"That is good for all of us," Bea said softly. "Things change but we must stay the same, Emma."

"That's not altogether true. If you look back, you'll see that we have changed but I think we have learned a few things on the way," Emma said.

"We had enough sense to choose the right men for husbands." Bea looked thoughtful. "Guy was important, if only to let you see a set of values that many men have and take for granted, but ones that you would find hard to accept, after working in a responsible job in hospital and having to make decisions. You would have found him and his family intolerable and been sucked under, if you'd married."

"I hardly think of him now," Emma said." I should feel more for him, as he was sweet and loving," she conceded.

"But selfish," Bea said.

Emma shrugged. "He did expect me to do as he wished, even when I had other ideas."

"But Paul lets you have your own way? Surely not all the time? It isn't in the nature of the beasts. I have to give in when Dwight really sets his mind on something, but I can influence him, too, like last night, when I made sure that I can have the babies here. Its fun getting my own way and convincing him that it was all his own idea!" she said and smiled as if her thoughts were sweet.

"I'll scramble some eggs that Dr Sutton left for us. Get dressed and we can be ready to collect Aunt Emily in an hour."

Emma felt somewhat smug. Dwight did like his own way sometimes unreasonably, even if he was sweet about the outcome, and Bea liked a little drama in making up after a half-hearted fight.

Paul discusses everything. I've never felt forced into

anything I didn't want to do, Emma thought. In fact he makes me decide everything that concerns my work and happiness. She beat the eggs with the wire whisk, then reached over to turn the toast on the grill.

But was it her intention or Paul's that had made conversation with George impossible? Last night she had exchanged only a few words with him. Paul had been there all the time and George stayed at a distance.

"Even I can't eat all that," Bea said when Emma brought the dish of eggs to the table.

"Don't even try. I want some for egg sandwiches for lunch. We have scones and jam and I'll take a bottle of lemonade, and some coffee in a flask."

"Good! I'm going to love living with you."

"You can do a lot of things to help when you are queening it on the sofa," Emma promised heartlessly. "We don't have passengers on our ship." She giggled. "I admit you are in no shape to climb the rigging."

When they arrived at Emily's house she brought out rugs and more food, and a hot brick that had been in the side oven over night and now was swathed in thick flannel to keep the heat in and the cold out, and to prevent burning any skin in contact with it.

"Be careful and don't unwrap it," Emily warned when she planted it on Bea's lap. "It's a long way over to Yarmouth, and you need the extra warmth."

"Bliss!" Bea was purring like a contented cat. "I shall recommend you for a medal. I shall emerge with a lovely smell of singed flannel." She tucked an extra cushion into the hollow of her back and settled in the back seat, while Emily sat in the front passenger seat with an air of anticipation.

"Look at these," Emma said and gave Bea a sheaf of papers with sketches and diagrams on them. "When your father sold us the house, he gave Paul the plans of the rooms. The measurements will be useful when we try to match furniture with rooms. I brought a long measure and a yard rod, so we can pencil in the dimensions of the pieces in the rooms we think suitable."

"You think of everything," Bea said. "I'll bet you have at least six pencils."

"Damn!"

Bea laughed. "We can't do without each other. I brought not only pencils but a red one and a green one and an eraser."

"You've seen the plans?"

"Last night, and I think the house is intriguing. You really have bought it and paid for it?"

"Paul had money he would have had to use if he bought a partnership in general practice, and I had the money from the cottage that Guy left me, so we had no problems there. Why do you ask? It's all signed and sealed and legal," Emma said. "Don't try to scare me, Bea."

"Sorry. It's just my suspicious mind, knowing my devious father."

"Paul had the deeds examined carefully and the title to the property proved, so your father has done nothing wrong," Emma said. "In fact we bought it for far less than it's potential value and your father was very generous."

"He's very fond of you, Emma, and I'm sure would do nothing to hurt you financially, especially now that he's married to Miranda who keeps him on the straight and narrow and does him a lot of good, but I have a feeling that when you have it really well-furnished and attractive, he may regret selling and want it for himself. He needs a bigger place in London now as the apartment in St James's is really a bachelor flat. Looking at these papers makes me think that his long-established habits would make him look over the transaction later, to make sure there was no loophole in law that he could use for his own ends."

"He couldn't turn us out! We *do* own the property."

"Of course he couldn't! Obviously Paul has been careful and Pa wouldn't dare hurt you. Forget what I said. It's just that knowing my pa, he couldn't resist *thinking* about the possibilities, like a cat sitting by a goldfish bowl and just watching. He *might* toy with the idea of trying to make you an offer that you couldn't refuse, and might want to buy it back."

Emily, who had listened in silence, now said, "Paul isn't a fool and it would take a very hard man to get the better of him if he decided that he wouldn't do as asked."

Emma nearly stalled the engine. "Paul isn't hard or a fighter."

"I'm not saying he is. There's a difference between being hard and tough and ready to fight, and being sure of what you want and strong enough quietly to hold on to it."

Bea chuckled. "Full marks to the lady in the front row. It's nice to have my own opinion endorsed. For a start, he'll never let you go. He'll care for you for ever and if anyone ever tries to make you suffer, I'd love to be there when he really piles into him."

"Well, I haven't noticed any dragons chasing me lately," Emma said, laughing. "And Paul has no lethal weapons."

"Don't you believe it. He can read minds. What better weapon can he want?"

"That's his job," Emma protested. "It isn't something you are born with like Aunt Emily's fey periods when she sees twins and Sadie being pregnant," she teased.

"That wasn't anything but observation as far as Bea was concerned," Emily said. "It was the size of her!"

"You said that another pregnant woman would be in the house," Emma said quietly. "Sadie arrived, sick and tiresome and you wouldn't say any more about her."

"Time enough for that," Emily said. "Look out at the fields. I like to see the rabbits running now that the stubble is burned off. Poor things, they are easy targets when they have no tall grass to shelter them, and the hedgerows don't hide them."

Emma smiled. What a way to change an embarrassing subject! Emily never felt anything for bare fields, or for rabbits unless they were fat and good for the pot. She went on, in a conversational tone. "It looks as if they had to work hard at the ricks to get them thatched before the rain set in or the hay would not look as good now," she added as if that was of great interest. "Your grandfather often bought sweet hay from that farm."

"All right, we'll leave Sadie as a subject of interest," Emma said dryly. "Which way now? You have been here and know the way."

They had driven along the Military Road along the coast of West Wight, and the sea on the left was as blue as it was in summer, with the white cliffs of Tennyson's Freshwater in the distance. Remnants of gorse and darkening bracken, even in winter made a haze of colour unchanged in peace and war, and Emma felt a warm familiar pride in her Island.

"There will be harebells on the cliffs again this spring," Emma said almost to herself. Flowers were as evocative as music, she thought and smiled almost guiltily. Harebells had been the flowers crushed beneath them when Phillip, her childhood sweetheart, who had come back from near death as an RAF navigator, thought she would let him make love to her on Tennyson Down. Buttercups too, she remembered wryly; crushed gold and blue, and bitter disappointment for a sweet and good man whom she had never wanted in that way.

For Guy it had been the pale dense blossoms of mock orange, which she had always known as syringa, sprays of which she plucked each summer even now, loving and hating the heavy scent and the cool waxen beauty.

"Wake up, Bea," Emily said. "I think we are there."

Emma nodded and said she'd park the car by the barn and ring the bell of the farmhouse to ask if the caretaker

81

was there. Mentally, she shook herself. It was being in the countryside that she loved that made her think of the association of flowers. Even Arthur, the lord of the manor in Surrey who she had nursed and who had wanted to marry her, had his own flower that would bring him to mind each time she saw it. She smiled. Not one he'd appreciate, and very unromantic. It was the coarse yellow weed that a girl had said would poison her horse if she let it feed in his field.

"Excuse me, but we have come to check the furniture for Mrs Sykes," Emma said to the woman who opened the door.

"He locked it all in there," she said, pointing to the barn. "Anyone would think it might be stolen," she added resentfully. "When you've seen that lot, come to the house and I'll take you into the manor. There are a few bits in the dining room that Mr Cooper thought might be too big and said you'd decide."

"Did Mr Cooper pay for them?"

"It's all paid for but he said he'd take off your hands any you don't want." Her manner softened. "Just as well he locked the door, I suppose. No one from round here would steal anything but when the storm died down and the ferry started up again, a few dealers came over from the mainland nosing about the manor and I didn't like the look of two of them. They complained that the sale ought to have been postponed as the weather was bad, but I told them that locals came first and locals had bought the best of it."

"What happens to the estate now?" Emma looked up at the crumbling facade of the farmhouse and the empty windows. "Do you live here?"

"Worked at the manor for years but the family here died out and even the farm will go now as a separate sale, so I have to go."

"Where will you live?"

"The old owner gave me a cottage some years ago

82

when he knew he would be the last one here, and I have enough to live on with my husband's army pension and a bit I had left me."

"It will be hard to leave this house," Emma said. "It must have been beautiful." Impulsively, she said, "Did they sell the things that you used here? All your bedroom furniture, for instance?"

"It's all in there," she said, sadly. "They said it was all to be sold, but I'll need a few sticks and pots as the cottage isn't furnished."

Emma remembered the blue china dishes that her grandmother valued and that Emily still treasured. "Come and show me which are yours and you must have your own familiar things round you," she said firmly. "I wouldn't feel comfortable taking them from you, so don't think I am being kind," she added when the woman began to protest.

"Aladdin's cave," Bea said when the doors were thrown back. "We have work to do. What a good thing they put sale tickets with numbers on each lot. We can start from there." Emma dragged a comfortable chair up to a huge dining room table and Bea sat in state, with plans and pencils.

Emma found Mrs Barton's furniture and a boy from the farm came with a cart to take it away. She included whatever kitchen utensils she might find useful, some odd china and a few knives and forks, a comfortable chair and a job lot in a packing case. Emma knew she would never use the odds and ends and faded lamp shades unsuitable for the Kensington house, but Mrs Barton was overwhelmed and and inspired to offer tea when they were ready for it.

"Good riddance to that lot," Emily said. "Can't think what Bert's boy was thinking of to buy that rubbish."

"I think he was told to buy anything that wasn't nailed down," Emma said. "What we don't want, he can sell again for his own profit, if I know that family."

"He'd get on well with Pa," Bea said.

Long heavy curtains were festooned over the walls of horse stalls and huge carpets were rolled up and stacked by the furniture. "I hope Paul's treasure, Mrs Coster, likes cleaning carpets," Emma said. "It's impossible to gage if they'll do, but we'll take them all."

"Some of them are valuable," Bea said with the eye of one who knew quality. "Find an expert cleaner and they will come up as new, or better still, elegantly shabby, so that people will know they are really old and valuable." She pointed to a walnut writing desk. "Measure that, Emma. I have just the place for it in the morning room, and the tallboy will fit in there too."

"Plenty of chairs, and some look really comfortable," Emma said with growing excitement.

"Must have been a very old family," Bea announced. "They never throw anything away over the centuries, and whoever sold this must have been mad, but if it was sent to auction by a farm agent who knew nothing about antiques, and there were no dealers in competition, then they had to accept what was offered. That is Queen Anne and I know Chippendale when I see it." She walked slowly round the barn and stopped. "Halleluia! We've struck gold. You shall sleep in a half-tester bed, Duckie," she told Emma. "Do you think Queen Elizabeth slept here?"

"We can pretend at a wonderful history, but I don't think I want it."

"Good mattress and lovely hangings. If you don't want it, may Dwight and I use it? I shall have my babies delivered in it and be like medieval Royalty."

"They had hundreds of people watching," Emma said. "Not very private in those days and not very clean either."

"Dwight will adore it and we shall make passionate love with the curtains drawn," Bea said with glee.

Gradually the plans were covered with numbers as they decided on where each item would go and the whole house took shape in their imaginations.

Mrs Barton called them and they went into the manor house. The huge hall, still with coats of arms high on the dusty walls, looked bare. A single-bar electric fire glowed under a huge oak beam in the vast grate but the room smelled damp. "Look round if you want to, and then come over to the farmhouse. It's warmer there. You said you've brought some food, so I'll make a cup of tea to go with it and you can eat it there as I have a few chairs and a table that the agent wanted left for when he deals with a buyer for the farm. You'll have to excuse the bed in the kitchen. I live there all the time now until the farm is sold, when they won't need a caretaker."

A huge black lacquered cabinet stood in a corner, with a smaller one by its side. "What's this?" Bea asked.

"Great ugly thing! I wouldn't give it house room and Mr Cooper agreed and said he thought it was a white elephant that you could leave here for him if you didn't want it. He is ready to take it off your hands. Nice man. My father knew his father in the old days."

"Matching linen press too?" Bea sighed and ran a finger over the golden dragon on the door. "I doubt if Dwight has anything like this on the Ranch. They may be wealthy but I think his family have more earthy tastes and would never buy chinoiserie." She laughed. "I really would like to meet kind Mr Cooper who is willing to do you such a favour! No wonder the dealers were hopping mad to miss this sale. If you don't want it, Emma, I'll have it shipped to America."

"You can have the bed," Emma said. "These will make a great impression on rich patients and I know that Paul will like them."

The farmhouse kitchen was warm and the old kitchen range glowed with black lead and care. Bea sank into a chair by the stove and Emily eyed the range with envy. "It's just like the one in our house when we were children," she said.

"You still have open fires and a Yorkist stove as well

85

as a very good modern gas cooker," Emma pointed out. "This must take hours to clean."

"It does, and they haven't had enough maids here for a long time to do everything properly, because of the war, but I'll miss it," Mrs Barton said, and helped herself to another of Emily's sandwiches.

"I've listed all the furniture and the van will collect it all and get it out of your way, Mrs Barton. They said they can come tomorrow and it will go on the late ferry and be parked until we are ready to receive it in London the day after that."

"And we do want the cabinets," Bea asserted.

"I've listed them for the removal firm," Emma said, so that there was no way that they could be 'forgotten' and left as a bonus for Bert Cooper's son. "I'll telephone them as soon as we get back and they can call in for the list before they come here." She named the firm that would collect and said that the firm recommended by Mr Cooper was not suitable for delivering on the mainland.

"It isn't that we don't trust him," Emily explained. "We just wouldn't want to put him to any more trouble."

"Exactly," Emma agreed.

"The pieces we don't want, he can sell, but first take your pick of them and put them aside so that he doesn't take the lot," Emily said. "There's plenty there to pay him for all his trouble and more," she added. "So he's got no cause for grumbling."

"Everyone happy?" asked Bea and shivered. "Let's go back to a warm house. This is a wonderful place, but I'd hate to live here except in summer. It's draughty and sad and I hope it goes to someone who can heat it properly and use it for a school or a large family."

"It's big enough for you," Emma said.

"Very droll! I have no urge to produce a football team, even if Dwight is keen."

Chapter Eight

"They said the carpets should be dry today," Emma said and she peeped into the rooms from which everyone had been banned for several days while the carpet cleaners worked and left the carpets laid flat but damp.

"Good! I'm tired of coming in through the tradesmen's entrance and up the back stairs like a tweenie maid," Bea said.

"Ah, but when you get upstairs, what do you find?" teased Emma. "One really nice sitting room with the only carpets clean enough to use at once, which I have to share until the other rooms are done, and a bedroom with that terrible contraption of a bed that you fell in love with. I notice that Paul and I have the bedroom with bare parquet and small rugs and no window curtains."

"It's only right," Bea said complacently. "Paul told me once that he has a theory that babies do hear sounds before they are born and they react to their surroundings. Any tensions the mother suffers react on the baby. My babies are being exposed to me being used to luxury and I play music to them when I have my afternoon nap."

"Benny Goodman and Edmundo Ross? No wonder they kick," Emma said.

"I give them a little American swing, just to be fair," Bea said.

"Do you think 'Rock Around the Clock' is safe? I seem to recall being thrown over a Yank's shoulder when he taught me to dance like that."

"I hate to think what vibrations Sadie's baby is hearing," Bea said.

"She's a lot better. Aunt Janey says that now she has George to herself, she is almost human, the sickness has gone and she has an appetite."

"Which being translated means that George no longer looks up when you come into the room and goes pale green round the gills."

"That's not fair. I hardly spoke to him and they weren't with us for more than a day."

"Five minutes is long enough for any woman to test the water," Bea said enigmatically. "She knew at once that he wasn't completely hers."

"The baby will bring them close," Emma said hopefully. "I do want him to be happy."

"He will be if you aren't there," Bea said, and laughed. "I can't imagine Paul taking you to Bath to visit them. It's a pity, as I like Bath and it was on my list of places that Dwight would drool over, as the buildings are so old and beautiful and he's interested in Roman remains. You and I could have looked at the fashions in Milsom Street while he went down damp passages to look at stones and old hypocausts."

"We can't do everything together," Emma reminded her.

"While we can, we will," Bea replied. "I'm not clinging to the past, Emma. I look forward to a wonderful time in the States but I am more relaxed now that I know I shall have my babies here."

Emma closed and locked the doors to keep the rooms empty. "We'll give it another day to dry out. I think the carpets smell a bit damp and we can send for the main furniture at any time. There's no real urgency for us to move in the furniture as Paul is still at St Thomas's."

"I must let Dwight know when we need some muscle. He has a couple of men who want somewhere cheap to stay in London for a day or so when they are on leave, and he offered them the basement here in return for moving the heavy pieces."

"Not exactly the Ritz," Emma said. "Has he seen the rooms down there?"

"Dwight looked over the whole house before he went to Germany," Bea said. "He made me promise not to lift more than a feather and said the basement would be fine for odd visitors or hired staff as there is a stove and four iron bedsteads like the ones we had in the emergency wards in Surrey. There is also a separate entrance through the area steps and no need to come into the main building unless they are invited."

"Of course! Someone said it was used by the local Air-Raid Warden and his crew," Emma said. "They must have sent up a prayer of thanks the night the terrace of houses was bombed and this one escaped, but the basement is solidly built and must have made a good air-raid shelter."

She followed Bea to the only room made habitable enough for them to sit in comfortable chairs and look across at the park. "I wish we had the telephone," Emma said. "I find I want to ring Paul and tell him the latest developments here . . . and just to talk."

"Not getting broody like me?" Bea asked with a mischievous smile.

"No." A degree of uncertainty crept into her voice. "I've never cared much for children," she said. "I doubt if I'd be any good as a mother and I'm in no hurry to find out."

"*Je crois*," Bea said, cynically. "You are made for it. I was the one who blenched when babies were mentioned, and look at me now."

"Looking absolutely blooming and ready to go out tonight," Emma said. "Paul will meet us there as he can't be away from Tommie's for more than a couple of hours."

"Miranda said that Pa's chauffeur can collect us and

bring us home, so Dwight can't tell me that I'm doing too much."

"Not as risky as flying to America," Emma said.

Bea chuckled. "His folks are thrilled at the idea of twins and now want me to stay wrapped in cotton wool until they are born, so no more talk· of going over there to deliver. Dwight talked to them when he was in shock I think, and it was catching."

"Does he still think you are Dresden china?"

"He has doubts. When we made love last, he thought I was strong enough to swim the Atlantic," Bea said, as if the memory was good.

"You are having checks?"

"Yes, and I'm booked into Beattie's private wing."

"When?" Emma looked away from the view of bare trees and the distant paths leading to the Peter Pan statue. "I didn't know you'd got as far as that."

"Don't look so worried. I'm fine but I may have to have a Caesar as the babies are a bit entwined and one could come as a breech presentation."

"Does Dwight know?"

"I have said nothing as it isn't certain what they will do, and you mustn't say anything as he will think about it too much, and for a flyer, that isn't a good idea."

Emma nodded agreement and neither referred to the temporary breakdown Dwight had suffered when he convinced himself that he alone had dropped the bomb on Hiroshima. "I shall tell Paul," Emma said.

"Bless you. If you know, and he keeps an eye on me, I'll feel safe. Just now I feel restless and the twins say they want to go walkies."

"Having puppies?"

"They wouldn't fit into the baby clothes. Anyone would think I am going to have at least six babies. Everyone has been far too generous with very difficult to get gifts. The latest is a twin cot, made of sweet smelling pine that a craftsman in Dwight's camp made. It's being trimmed with a white cotton lining and has rockers," Bea said, and her pleasure was apparent. "Real American covered waggon stuff!"

"You'll have to wear a frilly apron and calico bloomers," Emma said dryly.

They walked out into the misty winter sunshine and followed the paths to the lake. Ducks made squiggles on the still water as they dived and surfaced and shook their feathers. "I prefer water with more lively movement in it. Lakes are too static and not my favourite scenery. I miss the gulls," Emma said, so they left the ducks and walked across to the Peter Pan statue.

"One nanny I had brought me here, but she was more interested in a soldier who came and sat on the seat next to us and she didn't tell me anything about it," Bea said. She touched a small stone mouse and then a squirrel on the carved base of the stone tree. "What fun to sculpt that and what stories I can tell the twins when they come here."

"It's a wonderful statue," Emma said gently, but she knew that when the twins were old enough to notice Peter Pan, they would be far away on the wide open spaces of the ranch in Texas. "He never grew up."

"Wonderful for him," Bea said. "Everlasting fun and no responsibilities."

"Sad too," Emma said." Did he know what he was missing? Grown-up food and music and love and independence? He must have seen his friends grow and change and leave him alone."

"He's right for children, who never bother about the future," Bea asserted. "Given the chance, he would have been a friend to me if I was brought here to talk to him." She looked fierce. "My children will never be left out of anything. I shall make sure they have really happy lives."

"You needn't try too hard and swamp them. Just being the children of you and Dwight will rub off on them and they'll be fine." Emma laughed. "Here we are, looking at Peter Pan as if he could give us some answers, and planning your unborn family's future. What schools have you chosen?"

"Idiot! I daren't mention that to Dwight or he'd be doing just that, enrolling them in an expensive academy before they are born. Maybe they'll be girls and want to go to the local school with all the children of fathers working on the ranch."

"You could try to teach them poetry as well as music while you have them captive in there," suggested Emma. "Come on, it's getting cold and you need a rest if you are going to be bright and relaxed tonight."

After a cool bath, Bea brushed her hair. It was still long and Dwight refused to let her have it cut short as fashion decreed. "Look," she said bursting into Emma's room. "It's coming out in handfuls!" She displayed a few blonde hairs on her brush.

"Don't brush it so hard," Emma said. "If you think you're lacking vitamins, ask Paul what he suggests. I know that pregnancy takes a lot from the mother and this might be an early sign but one that you can do something about. It's glossy and thick and looks all right to me." She grinned. "Don't suggest having it cut. I heard the last argument about that!"

"Hell! I want it short and I hoped you'd back me up."

"It's a good thing to leave it, now that everyone else is having long hair cut off. It's a reaction to the lack of hairdressers during the war and the pressure of fashion designers who are in cahoots with the expensive beauty parlours that are cropping up. You say you like to take attention from the lump, so what better than a flower or a pretty piece of jewellery in your hair tonight."

Bea giggled. "Better stick to a black velvet bow. Dwight told me what the various flowers mean in the hair of women in the Pacific Islands, and some are a bit rude, so I'd not want to be misunderstood by someone who has been out there."

The car arrived early and they were driven slowly to The Bagatelle where the reception was to be. The coffee velvet chairs and carpets and gilded tables were as Bea remembered them from long ago and she was amazed to look back and think how much had happened since she was last there, on the fringes of a Royal party during the London Blitz, when Edmundo Ross played Latin American music for the young Princess.

The rose velvet suit was perfect, and the fact that Bea was pregnant didn't register with many people as she had a slim lower silhouette and her skin and hair were flawless. Emma thought she had never looked so lovely.

Paul arrived in a hurry and stayed for an hour, long enough for Emma to ache for him, and long enough to form a deep discontent at their parting. "Must you go so soon?" she asked wistfully and knew that she had never felt so deeply for any other man.

"We'll soon be together most of the time, in work and at leisure," he said tenderly. His smile was lopsided as if he couldn't trust himself to show what he felt. "Why do I love you so?" he whispered. "If I come back with you tonight, I'll never do my night round. Have fun, but not too much," he added, with a warning glance towards a couple of hopeful-looking French businessmen who were there to talk vineries with Bea's father.

"Don't worry," said Bea who had appeared with her one permitted glass of white wine in her hand. "My Pa has eyes like a hawk and now I'm safely married and in no state to flirt, he misses nothing. He guides away anyone saying more than good-evening!"

"Where's Miranda?"

"In the latest play, but Pa says she's being good about her diabetes and looks well. I must make time to see the new show and talk to her again, when Dwight can manage a weekend off. He comes back from Germany soon and I can't wait to show him our rooms."

The French guests were talking about the charity scheme that sponsored girls and boys of about ten years of age to come for a holiday in England, away from their war torn cities in Holland and France.

Paul nodded as they told him details and he suggested that attention to their diets was as necessary as a change of scene. "They sent some Dutch children to the Isle of Wight in October and they thrived on fresh fruit and vegetables and good soups and fish and milk. Some had eaten nothing but potatoes and porridge and a bit of dried fish, and a little cheese, for months as the Germans had taken all the wheat and fresh supplies during the occupation, and with stringent rationing, many starved and died. They were even reduced to eating the flower bulbs that usually were sold for their living."

"I remember Aunt Emily telling me about it," Emma said. "It was heartbreaking to see some of them with thin legs and arms and no colour in their cheeks, and she wanted to help by cooking for them, but they were put in a holiday camp all together with staff and an interpreter. They had a band of helpers there who did very well, amusing and feeding them, and sent them home a few pounds heavier, carrying all the fruit they could manage for their families."

"The Isle of Wight?" A man introduced himself as a news reporter and cameraman. "I was there in the autumn to help with a programme about two people walking round the countryside as part of a national programme." He laughed. "It's strange even now to think of making a film about Britain, when for years we've kept every scene off the news and made sure that the enemy had no fresh photographs of the country. When we made this film I kept looking over my shoulder in case the police wanted to see what I had in my camera."

"That's right," Paul said. "A lot of beaches and coasts

were considered classified material and some innocent people taking what they considered holiday snaps, were in real trouble until peace was declared. I was refused a pass into the Island until Dr Sutton, a highly respected local doctor wrote to the chief of police and told him that I was an innocent embryo doctor who might bring his skills to the Island," Paul said and grinned. "It was understandable caution as they were building parts of Mulberry Harbour there, before D-Day."

"Has the film been finished?" Emma asked.

"Yes it will be in the cinemas now, with two well-known BBC personalities in it: Ronnie Waldman and Doris Arnold."

Bea looked tired and Paul told Emma to take her home. The car was waiting within five minutes of Paul mentioning it to Bea's father, and Emma and Paul had to make their good-night kiss brief.

"It was good to see a few bright lights and fresh faces again," Bea said, and sighed. "I must ring Aunt Emily tomorrow to tell her that the suit was wonderful and I felt human in it."

"But you'd had enough?"

"I feel heavy and I think I shall vegetate for a while," Bea said, and sank into the back of the car while the driver took them home a long way round, past beautiful buildings, unscathed by war, but also by weed-covered bombed sites, the ruins blurred by rogue bushes of buddleia.

Emma put hot bottles in Bea's bed and helped her to put the velvet suit away. A small electric fire made the room warm and Emma brought supper into the bedroom.

"You've no idea how good it feels to wake in this room and know I am in England," Bea said. "Just passing through Piccadilly tonight with lights once more and Eros back on his rostrum, shooting his arrow into Shaftesbury Avenue, made me feel almost tearful." She smiled. "Miranda has been so good for Pa and he seems

95

to be really fond of me now. He told the driver to bring us back through the West End and it was worth seeing the lights and people walking and talking as if there had never been a war."

"I saw at least four women in the New Look and one had a black Renoir bonnet that I know would suit you as you have long hair," Emma said. "They sell them in Oxford Street and have huge hatpins with bobbles on them as big as ping pong balls."

"Tomorrow," Bea said sleepily. "The twins enjoyed the wine and they say it's time I went to sleep."

Emma went down to the room where a mass of curtains fresh from the cleaners waited to be sorted out and altered if necessary, before they were hung. She measured and tacked hems and when she looked up it was after midnight and she yawned. The house was quiet and the distant hum of tram wires and sparse traffic on the roads was soothing. I am happy here, she decided. This house has no bad ghosts and it welcomed us from the first day we saw it.

She closed the door of the room behind her and wandered through the hall and up the shallow stairs to her bedroom, looking in each room she passed to see which curtains on her new list would fit. The required measurements were on the doors, neatly documented with the lot numbers of the furniture, so that the right pieces could be put in the right places with no fuss.

She smiled. Bea was surprisingly efficient and said that she could at least organise and bully the removal men, but her help had been enormous.

One room had faded *Toile de Joie* wall coverings, just right for the pale green damask window drapes that were the right length for the windows. Another needed fresh distemper over old paper to clean it up until they could obtain new wallpaper that wasn't monotonous or hideous.

The small room next to the room that Emma and Paul would use was bright in the moonlight that streamed through the uncurtained windows. Emma paused then went in and sat on the wooden window seat. The night was cold but the room seemed to emanate warmth. The moon was a lamp that had survived war and blackouts and tonight gave a soft and friendly light, unlike the times when she had shone relentlessly bright over cities, making it easy for bombers to home in to targets.

"Dangerous Moonlight," she murmured. She recalled sitting in a shabby cinema on her day off, alone as none of her friends were off at the same time, miserably eating a rather hard peach and feeling tired.

She remembered little of the film except for Sally Grey and Anton Walbrook sheltering under a grand piano during an air raid in Warsaw and his voice, soothing and very sexy, saying that moonlight was dangerous . . . and he didn't mean the air raid, she thought wryly. And music that would for ever bring back the memories of war, the sweeping bitter-sweet cadences of the Warsaw Concerto, and the poignancy of uncertainty, impermanence, excitement and loss.

Tonight the memories were soft and she was aware of the house as an entity. If Aunt Emily was here, she'd love the atmosphere. If there are ghosts, she'd find them sweetly scented of lavender, Emma pondered. She could smell lavender. A built-in cupboard was unlocked and as she opened it she smelled it again and found a few seed heads and a piece of mauve ribbon on a shelf.

A linen cupboard, Emma thought. She looked at the wallpaper inside the cupboard, always a giveaway as to what paper had been used in the room at an earlier time. There was a band of rabbits and fairies and a hint of moonbeams on a frieze half-way up the wall, well away from tiny grubby fingers.

"It was the nursery!" Emma shut the cupboard door. "Not yet," she whispered, but she felt strangely at peace. For the time being, it could stay empty and shabby and the floor could wait for sanding and new rugs. She wouldn't use it until it was time to get it ready for the purpose for which it was intended and obviously well used. A rocking horse over there, and a playpen there by the window, she dreamed and almost saw.

"Bea can use the other one next to their bedroom, but this is mine," Emma murmured, as if she had a guilty secret.

Chapter Nine

"Where have you been?" Bea eyed her husband with less than pleasure. "It's early and yet you have been out for ages." She walked slowly into the kitchen and waved away his help. "I can do it," she said, pouring coffee. "At least I will when I've spent a penny. This is becoming boring," she added as she left for the bathroom. "The little devils are pushing on my bladder again."

Dwight put the coffee pot back on the stove on an asbestos heat diffuser and waited. When Bea came back, he said, "Don't sit down, honey, I want to show you something I bought for the house."

"At six o'clock in the morning?"

"They like you to be early at Covent Garden or the best buys have gone."

"We have flowers," she said, pointing to the huge vase of freesias and daffodils that he had bought the day before.

"Not flowers," he said smugly. "What every prosperous consultant needs, to show a little snob value."

"Couldn't you sleep?" Emma asked as she joined them, wearing her dressing gown.

"Wonder Boy is hooked on Covent Garden," Bea said. "I'll buy him a porter's hat for his birthday."

"C'mon," Dwight said impatiently. "I want my breakfast, but I've got to show you this."

Outside the front door, newly painted a dark racing green, with a lion head brass knocker and a deep letter box, stood two green wooden tubs in which very formal long slender trunks supported rounded heads of dark green leaves.

"Bay trees!" Emma said. "They must have cost the earth."

"But good?"

"But very good," she said. "They put the seal on this house but you must stop spending so much money on us," she reproved him. "Do you know, I have always been awed by houses with tubs of bay at the door. Reminds me of the dentist we had at home, so I hope they don't frighten the patients away."

"They do make the place look solid and expensive," Bea said. "Pa likes bay and had a tree by the apartment until it died during the war, so it isn't true what they say, that the wicked flourish like the green bay tree! He flourished but the bay tree died."

"I want to take a picture, with you all in front of the door," Dwight said.

Emma and Bea both backed away. "Not like this, you don't!" Bea said. "Get dressed Emma, and we'll eat before he gets any other odd ideas. A picture of me, like this?" She smoothed her swollen abdomen and sighed. "Was I ever slim and svelte?"

"You look great, Honey."

"That *is* my problem," she replied soulfully.

The newly-painted kitchen was bright and every gadget that Dwight had installed worked well, to Emma's surprise, but she wondered if she would use the electric mixer from America that groaned in an unnerving manner and made more washing up than if she did the job by hand in the same time it took to assemble and mix and dismantle.

Paul sat down and lifted toast from the chromium plated toaster that now had a place of honour on the breakfast table. "We need one like this at the cottage," he said. "I seem to recall burning half a loaf in an attempt to have one nicely-browned slice and when

100

we have no fire and a toasting fork, this would be excellent."

Emma put the last of the bread in the toaster. "I'll make soda bread or Scotch pancakes later. I never thought that bread rationing would be so galling. I use a lot of bread for cooking and we seem to get through a loaf at breakfast. No more steamed bread puddings," she said. She glanced at Bea, who was piling home-made apple jam on to her toast, and decided that she needed to have another blood pressure check, as her face was flushed and her ankles had thickened during the past few days, but Bea had refused to visit her obstetrician the week earlier, saying she was far too tired.

"Gotta go," Dwight said. "I'll finish packing and if the driver comes, say I'll be with him in ten. Don't come up, darling, I'll say goodbye here before I leave."

"I have two patients this morning," Paul said, then turned to Bea. "It's far too warm to rush over to see Miller. I'll take your blood pressure and Emma can test your urine. We can telephone that everything is in order and that you don't need him as yet."

Emma smiled. Paul was so good at making patients feel they had a choice, when in fact there was no choice but what he wanted them to do. "Thank you, Paul. You must have read my mind," Bea said dryly, not fooled for a moment but bowing to the inevitable. "I'll produce some wee for Emma to cook in her nice little clinical room and you can listen to my pounding blood."

"Is it pounding?" Paul asked casually.

"Some," she replied shortly, and gave him a look that conveyed the message that Dwight was not to be told.

Dwight returned and kissed his wife, searching her face for signs of stress. "*Au revoir,* darling," he said. "I'll be back in three days. It's only a short hop to Antwerp for the conference this time. Give me a hand Paul, will ya?"

Paul picked up the valise and raincoat and Dwight carried his larger bag and an attaché case. Outside,

101

Dwight stopped. "Take this card," he said urgently. "If I'm needed in a rush, they'll radio me and I can be back within three hours."

"Can you leave a conference of Heads of State and Senior Forces Personnel like that?"

"If necessary," Dwight said firmly. "I got my priorities right some time ago." He grinned. "I have one devious bitch of a wife who fools me some of the time, but now I know when she's lying. I went to see Miller and he told me he would have to operate and he said he'd taken it for granted that Bea had told me. I think she asked him to say nothing to me personally as I was away for long periods and must not be worried, but he saw one very determined husband, who incidentally is bigger than he is," he added complacently. "And he gave me the details but said I must carry on as normal as he didn't know when he might have to do the snatch, as he called it. I can be contacted, and I want to be here."

"That's a relief. I shall check her blood pressure this morning and be in touch with Miller. I think that a few days in hospital might be a good idea. She's doing too much and is restless. If she is admitted, don't panic, as it will be just a precautionary measure and means she is under observation twenty-four hours a day."

The driver sounded his horn and Dwight ran for the car, shouting his thanks as he ran, and adding, "You take the pictures of Bea and Emma."

"You were a long time," Bea said to Paul when he came back into the house "*I'm* the one he says goodbye to."

"He was talking about taking a picture of you and Emma by the door," he answered mildly. "I *do* know how to hold a camera but Mr Know-all needed to tell me." He saw her relax and giggle.

"Take two, one not for publication, showing all my girth and one of me modestly standing half-hidden by Emma and a fern or two as if having babies is fun!" Bea said.

"I thought you were dead against having a picture of you taken when heavily pregnant," Emma said.

"I've decided to be nasty! When the twins play up, I shall show them what a sacrifice I made of my figure and beauty to have them, and if Dwight has ideas of nine children, he can feast his eyes on the picture and adopt a few."

"Pictures, then blood pressure," Paul said.

"Yes sir!"

The pictures were taken; some of Paul and Emma, Bea and Emma and Bea alone, posing so that she looked her worst. "That's for my pa," she said. "It should encourage him to spoil his poor misshapen daughter and give her lots of lovely goodies from Switzerland," she said calmly. "I suppose I can't have one taken with Paul taking my blood pressure and looking aghast?" She sighed. "Thought not, but it would shock everyone nicely."

"You are only a month away from the birth," Paul said, after he'd taken her blood pressure. "One head is obviously well down now, which makes you want to pass water frequently. It means that although you aren't in labour, it's starting to happen in there, all lining up to see who will be the older twin." He regarded her with sympathy. "You are very tired." She nodded. "I think you need a rest to give you the energy you'll need later if they are delivered normally. If you have a Caesarian, you should be in bed at Beatties at bed rest before it's done."

"I do feel tired," she said.

"You can rest in bed here, if Miller gives the OK."

She smiled, hopefully. "I don't want to go to the Wing yet."

"Or," he said as if she hadn't spoken, "you can be admitted to Beatties for a rest and not have the anxiety of your membranes breaking and flooding the bed. You are carrying an awful lot of water, Bea."

She stared at him. "I suppose that could happen. I

thought I could get to a bathroom if it started leaking," she said. "Yuck!"

"Niagara Falls," he said, nodding wisely. "Not many leak, they just gush."

"And you, Paul Sykes, are a devil! You know I couldn't bear to gush all over the lovely bed or those Persian rugs."

"So what have you decided?"

"Arrange for my tumbril and I'll drape myself in thick towels in case it happens today."

"Good girl," he said and kissed her. "I'll ring Miller and Emma can pack a bag for you and drive you to the private wing."

"At least I escape screaming sirens and ambulances," Bea said.

"It is a little more dignified this way," he agreed.

He telephoned the news that Bea's blood pressure was raised and the urine specimen showed traces of albumen and acetone. The newly installed phone helped to eliminate the frustration of bad communications, and just now Paul was doubly thankful for it.

He glanced at his appointment diary. Patients were booking with him for consulation with increasing frequency, referred by doctors who had heard that the new man was very good, and he knew that he could concentrate entirely on psychiatry if he wished.

"They expect you as soon as you can make it," he told Bea. "No rush but you might as well get settled in while Emma can help you as my patients this morning are both men, but I need her to chaperone me with a female patient this afternoon."

"Is that a hazard of psychiatry?" Bea wanted to know. "What fun!"

"It can be fraught," he said briefly. "Why did you think I married Emma? I need her protection."

Bea giggled. "You may need Dwight or some other male to be with you sometimes. You can handle females."

He looked puzzled. "Can't be as bad as that time when a rather queer gentleman came to casualty demanding that the poor casualty officer should examine him very intimately. He turned white every time he saw the patient and finally asked the casualty sister to take over when he came in for the third time, complaining about pain in his scrotum."

"Not Butch Irene?" Emma asked." She was enough to scare anyone male or female. She took size eleven shoes and had arms like a wrestler and had worked in the VD clinic."

"She really is a woman, but a bit anti-men. It did confuse people a bit as to her gender but she frightened the pest away."

"When I sit in with Paul and one particular patient, I have to make sure I need never leave him alone with her for a moment. It's amazing how many excuses she can make for me to leave the room, so I have glasses of water, extra pillows of all sizes for the couch and spare handkerchiefs ready now." Emma laughed. "She finds my husband quite irresistible."

"I'm hoping she'll leave me and go to another clinic, but she does have real problems and I think I am helping her," Paul said.

"I'll be home for lunch," Emma said.

It was strange to drive up to the entrance of the private patients' wing at the Princess Beatrice Hospital, after all the time they had worked and sometimes suffered at Beatties. It was even stranger to have Bea's bags taken by a polite porter and to be whisked up in the elevator as an honoured patient plus companion, instead of heaving one's own baggage up the back stairs and into the nurses' home.

The pale blue walls and vases of bright spring flowers were as Emma remembered them in the entrance hall, and the Obstetric Wing had the smell of antiseptic and expensive talcum powder that could be in no other part of the hospital.

"Home from home," Bea said bleakly. "I even recall that window overlooking the car-park. The blackout curtains never fitted well and we had trouble with the Air Raid wardens."

"Nice ones now," Emma said. "Roses and butterflies and no need to close them at night."

The pretty room with a pink bathroom en suite was furnished simply but well, with two comfortable chairs, a mahogany bow fronted chest of drawers and a firm mattress on the bed. Fresh curtains and matching bedcover reminded Emma of the Home on the Downs in Bristol where their nursing careers had begun together.

She hoped that Bea had not noticed the similarity, or if she had, did not object to sleeping in a room so similar to the ones that the residents of the Home had for their declining years.

"At least I don't have to wander down Green Alley to pee," Bea said and they laughed, remembering the communal ablutions unit with baths and lavatories on each wing of the Home, covered from floor to ceiling with green tiles.

"I always wanted a room like this when I was so tired I could hardly move," she went on. "Our own rooms were quite good but in a kind of defiance against the rules there, I had a fantasy of taking a lover into one and Sister Cary discovering us *en flagrante*. No, leave the case. It will give me something to do if I unpack it myself. I shall expect you to ring me tonight." She pointed to the telephone. "Take the extension number and *use* it. I shall need to talk."

She gave Emma a dismissing hug. "Get back to Paul and prevent his female patients from devouring him." For a moment she looked as if she might cry, then smiled, her old half-forgotten cynical pose in place and intact once more, as it had been over the traumatic years.

106

"Anything I can do?" Emma asked feebly.

"No, you were right Dewar. There are some things we can't do together. Birth is a private affair. I don't even want Dwight here now. If I was religious this would be the time for confession and absolution. I'll have a nap and I expect Sister will be in to see me, so, on your way and think of me."

Emma found the Wing Sister and to her delight recognised her as a nurse trained at Beatties who had been in two sets above her. She also recalled that she was warm and efficient and that Bea liked her.

Sister Booker laughed. "Shuter was the last person I'd say would welcome twins."

"She and her husband are ecastatic," Emma said. "You'll really like Dwight. Believe it or not, Bea has found a man who truly loves her and manages her when she gets stroppy. Quite a hunk, too." She glanced at her watch. "Must go now but maybe we can have a chat some time?"

"That's a must! I'll pop in to see Bea now," she said. "They may want her in theatre tomorrow."

"Can it wait a day until Dwight comes back from Antwerp?"

Booker made a note. "I'll mention it to Himself," she said. "But her last tests showed a bit of foetal panic and she may be worse now, so the twins could want to be out as soon as possible. Leave your phone number."

"Safely installed?" asked Paul, when Emma had returned from Beattie's.

"I think so. I'm glad she's there now. It's a safe cocoon where she is relaxed and wants to be alone. As I haven't done midder, I would be helpless, or worse still, do the wrong thing."

"I thought we'd go to the cafe round the corner for lunch," Paul suggested. "We really do need a maid or someone," he said and shrugged. "Someone between a char and a housekeeper but not to cramp our style and interfere. I couldn't bear to have a stranger here, expecting to be with us all the time as family."

Emma laughed. "I'd settle for a good charwoman like Mrs Coster to come three times a week and do nothing but clean. I like cooking and seeing to the clinic, but I must admit that I've worked far harder in the past and have time on my hands now that we have the house more or less straight. When we take a patient in, if that's inevitable, but not what I want to happen, we'll need a night nurse; not fully trained but an auxiliary."

"I hope we can keep away anyone needing to be admitted. If they are that bad, then they'll need a nursing home with lots of round the clock staff, and if not, they can be treated as outpatients."

Emma regarded him with interest. "You seemed set on having bed patients when we talked to the aunts on the Island. What changed your mind?"

His smile melted her heart. "I lied," he said. "You need to learn to enjoy having leisure and not having to care for everybody. I want to be really selfish and keep you to myself for a while." He grinned and kissed her." The thought of disturbed men or women in this house was enough to keep away people like Sadie, who said she wanted to come to London without George and shop in the West End. Surprise, surprise, she had no place to stay where she would be really safe and well looked after, with the bonus of a trained nurse on tap, but she changed her mind at the thought of mental patients in the next bedroom! The City of Bath suddenly offered her all she wanted."

"Bea and Dwight are here and you don't object," she said.

"They are family and you and Bea have a bond that no husband should try to sever, but Sadie, here?" He shook his head as if the idea was horrifying.

"She did say that George would not come here too?"

108

"She was quite sure that he wouldn't, if she had anything to do with it, was my impression."

"Then why would she want to visit us?"

"Elementary. She can't resist trying to find out what you have that she hasn't got."

"There was never anything between me and George," Emma said firmly.

"I loved you long before you admitted that I was there," he said. "Even when I felt that you were still in love with Guy, after his death, it made no difference. You can't dictate emotions that you would like other people to have for you. They can't help it either if they love you. George still loves you and she senses it."

"You think they should not have married?" Emma was worried and felt responsible.

"If it hadn't been Sadie, it might have been a worse match," he said. "If they have the baby, they will be like many married couples, content with that they have, able to make love and to laugh and enjoy life together, but never really feel deep down happy, as we are."

"Are you happy enough to offer me fish and chips in the cafe round the corner?" she asked.

"Don't push your luck," he said. "They may have only the famous wartime special, egg and chips."

Chapter Ten

Emma put on the plain navy blue dress that she wore when helping Paul with the patients. They'd agreed that she must be called Sister when on duty, but not wear white dresses or white coats, so that the atmosphere could be relaxed. Paul wanted his consulting rooms to be as friendly and as natural as possible, and his working clothes consisted of a rather old but clean Harris tweed jacket smelling faintly of heather, grey flannel trousers and a neat shirt and tie, giving little evidence of his good medical qualifications and status as a consultant.

Mrs Molton came early, smartly dressed and wearing a minimum of very good jewellery, well chosen and in perfect taste. She was skilfully made up as if due at a reception rather than a session with a psychiatrist, and her hat was elegant and obviously made by a fashionable and expensive milliner.

She seemed disappointed to find Emma ready in the consulting room and Paul talking on the telephone in his adjoining office. "What's keeping Dr Sykes on the phone?" she asked querulously. Mrs Molton peeped into the office and pursed her lips, then eyed Emma accusingly as if it was all her doing. Her eyes took in every detail of Emma's crisp appearance and the fact that she had a good skin, clear eyes and a very nice figure.

"He will finish soon," Emma said, and smiled. "It's good to have patients who arrive on time, and in this instance a little early, but he will be here for your appointment, at half-past two."

110

"Can't you do all that office work? He's a busy man," Mrs Molton said pettishly. "I thought that receptionists did all the dreary routine office work."

"If we had a receptionist she would do that, but as yet we haven't found the one we want," Emma said in a pleasant tone of voice. "But even if we had such a gem, there are times when a patient needs to speak to Dr Sykes personally, as you know."

Mrs Molton looked annoyed and almost threw her musquash fur jacket on to a chair. Does she really believe that she is the only patient and is special? Emma thought. Several times she had answered the phone when Mrs Molton called and had to tell her that Dr Sykes was with a patient and couldn't be disturbed. Now, it was as if she suspected Emma of having a personal vendetta against her, wanting to keep her apart from her lovely caring doctor.

"I *do* know about that and sometimes I get pushed off the phone as if I wasn't important, when you can have no idea what I want to discuss with the doctor," Mrs Molton said viciously. "You aren't a doctor so what do you know about patients? I want to see the doctor alone but you are always there spying on me, and what are you but a girl in the office?"

"Didn't I make the situation clear, Mrs Molton?" Paul appeared in the doorway and smiled. "Sister is highly qualified and trained at the Princess Beatrice Hospital, here in London. She probably knows more about certain aspects of medical procedures than many doctors do and could have taken over a big department in surgical nursing, but prefered to help me here."

Mrs Molton sniffed, but had no intention of making an apology. "I thought Sisters wore uniform, then we would all know who was who!"

"We like you to feel that you are among friends, so we have no need for hospital trappings," Paul said gently. He shot back his cuff, making it obvious that he looked at his watch. "Still five minutes early, but

111

we can begin as I have finished my phone calls," he said.

Emma laid the hat carefully on a small table and unlaced and removed Mrs Molton's shoes, then made the patient comfortable on the new green leather couch, making sure the under-blanket was smooth and the light cover was warm and tucked in to give a sense of a 'back to the womb' security. In spite of her antagonism towards the attractive young woman who patiently made sure that the pillow was perfectly aligned and that the light from the window was shielded from her eyes, Mrs Molton relaxed under the gentle hands.

Emma sat apart, out of the patient's line of vision while Paul listened, asked questions and continued after what had been three previous sessions, to encourage Mrs Molton to face the facts about her early life with domineering parents and then an equally domineering husband.

Widowed and childless, she now faced loneliness and confusion as there was nobody left to bully her and she found that when she tried to bully others in her turn, she hadn't the force and personality to do so. She was rapidly losing her few remaining friends, and was scared of being left entirely alone so early in life.

She wasn't under hypnosis but was in a dreamy state, warm and secure, with the pleasant unreproving voice so interested in her problems, causing her to recall things long forgotten or happenings that she usually preferred not to remember.

"What made you happy as a child?" he asked.

Emma's attention wavered among the memories that shed no light on the woman's present condition, as her early life had been boring and uneventful when she had taken it for granted that all children had parents who made them obey strict rules, as her parents did, and nothing really exciting had happened. She had no pets and no close friends and no brothers or sisters.

A bit like me, Emma thought, except that my parents

didn't really care what I did and I had a lot of freedom to go out with my friends, even if I hardly ever brought them home. *And,* I escaped.

School was touched on, with very few resulting clues as to her present condition of frustration and unhappiness, and her academic achievements were average rather than good, not surprising in a house where a book was hardly ever picked up and read. There was a dismal background of a colourless family existence where nothing of interest or thing of beauty was ever discussed.

Paul asked about hobbies, and she burst into tears. "I wanted to go to an art school but my father tore up all my drawings and told me I had to work in his office until some unlucky man would take me off their hands."

"And the man you married was like your father?"

"I thought at first he was kinder and would let me paint, but the war was on and he went into the Navy. My father was an important man and arranged that I must go into his office again and so avoid being sent into the Services. It was that or become pregnant, to avoid being called up, and that didn't happen," she said.

"You could have enrolled," Paul said, almost as a question.

"I tried, but he had been cunning. By that time, my father's factory was producing material for uniforms and my name was listed as in a reserved occupation, from which I had no escape."

"You lived at home?"

"By necessity only," she said bitterly. "My mother was killed in an air raid when she visited her sister in Coventry and I had to run the house as well as working, so I had no social life. I even met my husband there and married him even though I knew very little about him. I should have known better as my father approved of him, but I thought that my life would change." She sighed. "They were two of a kind."

"How long did your marriage last?"

113

"One year; six months of which he was away. I was thankful to see him go away, as he was a rough man once the honeymoon was over, and hurt me when he made love." She pushed back the light rug as if stifled. "I didn't pray for his death in the war but I wanted it," she said harshly. "I hated him and I hated my father and when my father was killed in an accident in the factory, I was glad to be free of him, but hated the thought of a long marriage to Donald. I didn't have to face that as he was killed soon after my father died."

"You had no grief for either of them?"

She gave a long shuddering sigh. "I willed them dead and so I am as guilty as I would be if I'd shot them," she said dramatically and her hands clenched into fists.

"And now?"

"Aren't you going to say I have only myself to blame for being weak, and that I had no right to want them dead?" She sounded surprised, a little shocked and almost disappointed. "You must think I am guilty and condemn me. If I confessed in church instead of to you, I would have to do penance for evil thoughts and then be given absolution. You must think me guilty and despise me."

"No."

There was silence for a full minute and she lay quite still again except for her fingers which twitched and picked at the rug. "I have no religion and therefore no church solace and you are the first person who really listened to me," she said at last. "My own doctor told me to pull myself together and take a job again."

Across the room, Emma saw Paul shake his head and knew that in his opinion, the phrase 'pull yourself together', had hurt more people than one thought possible.

"I think you've been pulling too hard," he said. "It's time to let go a little."

"You want me to be as weak as people think I am?" She sounded angry again.

114

"Your parents are dead and you have no relatives, so what happens to the factory now that uniforms are no longer wanted in vast quantities?"

"I have no worries over money, if that's what you mean."

"That's obvious by your clothes and your general good taste," Paul said. "It's not important except that it means you have freedom of choice as to what you do in the future."

"What future? Sometimes I want to die," she said.

"Put that off for a while. You are far too young and healthy," Paul said and laughed softly. "You have been forced to give everything to other people in the past, always what others demanded of you, a habit hard to break, so why not give again now, but only what you want to give?"

"You mean sell the firm and give the money to charities?" Her disbelief was comical. "I worked as hard as any for the factory and helped to make it pay well, so why should I give it all away?"

"Who said anything about selling and giving it all away?" he asked mildly. "You are still proud of what you did there even if you hate the memories of being forced into it."

"I had vision," she said fiercely. "Before we had to turn over entirely to war work, I was beginning to be an influence there. My father was ill for three months and was furious with what I had initiated, but had to admit that some of my design ideas were good; that was after we'd had several devastating rows. I lost heart when he returned to full time war work and we had to make khaki tunics by the thousand."

"So what now? I assume you employ a lot of people who must wonder what the future holds for them. Men and women with families who depend on you now." The calm voice was relentless.

"The factory is still in production," she said defensively.

"And have you worked for more orders to keep it going? It belongs to you now, doesn't it?"

"That's nothing to do with you. How dare you try to run my business for me!"

"When did you last visit the factory?"

"Weeks ago," she said impatiently. "My accountants want me to sell it all and I think they may be right."

"But you aren't convinced?"

"No." It was a sigh. "I do think of my employees but I'm so tired. A part of me wants to do something and make it a success, but I can't, alone."

"Go away now and come back next week. I shall want to know what plans you have and maybe you can tell me about some of your ideas. If you want to make fashion clothes, this is your opportunity and you have no need to do it alone. It sounds as if you have real talent and you can get plenty of expert help now that many firms are closing. Look for new faces, keen young men and women who never knew your family, and work with them, not under anyone ever again."

Emma took away the rug and helped Mrs Molton to put on her shoes, after she'd refused the offer of tea. "Two-thirty again?" Emma suggested.

"I don't know why I bother to come! All you do is upset me and make me hate myself!"

"When a limb has been hurt, it is numb and the healing process and the coming back to life is often worse that the injury," Paul said, and gently took her hand from his arm.

"A little more independent today I think, and healthily angry with you, so perhaps any fixation she had about you is cooling," Emma said when the patient had gone. She laughed. "Less likely to jump on you with loud cries of frustrated passion? Maybe next session with her, I can read a good book in the office."

"I'd like some tea and a little tender loving care," Paul said with dignity.

"It's too early," Emma said when she escaped his arms and regained her breath. "I have to ring Bea and you must alert Dwight to go straight to the hospital when he comes in to Croydon airport tomorrow after the conference is over. I think the rest has done her good. She was very bright when I rang last night and says she's met a few people from the old days and had a good natter."

"You make some tea and I'll ring the Air Base so that they can radio Dwight, then I'll get in touch with Beatties on a professional level to speak to Miller first, and they can put you through to Bea after that, if she's still available."

"You think she may be in labour?"

"Anything is possible," he said cryptically. "The twins will probably come early, however they are born." He glanced at her. "Did you know that they asked Dwight to sign a consent form before he went away?"

"For a possible Caesarian?"

"Yes. If she was ready and it was urgent while he was away, it might be difficult," Paul said. "You know the law. It's the husband who has to give his consent when a wife needs any operation on her reproductive organs."

"That's ridiculous! What if Bea wasn't married? She could sign her own consent form then. Surely if an operation was needed in an emergency to save life, the surgeon could go ahead?"

"He could," Paul said slowly. "But he would be skating on thin ice if he did anything that the husband didn't authorise, as he has the rights over his wife's reproductive organs."

"What about emergency hysterectomy? A sudden bleeding that wouldn't stop and could kill her? That comes under emergency surgery surely, just as a bleeding gastric ulcer might need immediate treatment. Anyone can sign for that permission to operate. I've seen women sign their own forms."

"In my opinion, the law is crazy, but it dates from the time when men had complete control over their wives

117

and they were considered chattels. Husbands were even allowed by law to beat them, so long as they used a stick of certain dimensions and no thicker." He grinned. "I have a stick as thick as my little finger so think yourself lucky that you weren't born a hundred years ago." He stopped smiling. "Seriously, it is a problem at times even now, as that part of the law has never been repealed. I heard of one man who was desperately anxious to have a son and when his wife was very ill with eclampsia and the obstetrician advised a termination of pregnancy, he refused to sign the consent and said that he wanted her to go full term and be delivered."

"What happened?"

"He lost his wife and the baby."

"And the law did nothing?"

Paul gave a short laugh. "He then tried to sue the hospital for incompetence but there were plenty of witnesses to his refusal to help her, and the police did give him a fairly hard time, but no real action was taken until someone alerted the Press and as he was a fairly important figure, he did suffer a bit and questions were asked in high places which helped to bring the law under review to allow women to have more control over their own bodies, but these measures take time and we are in a kind of limbo over it."

"The pig! Pregnant women have enough to put up with apart from that sort of treatment."

"Well, Beatties have a signed consent form so they can proceed with whatever is needed for Bea," Paul said. "In any case, Miller is one of the surgeons who would carry on and do whatever he thought was a life saving action and to hell with the law."

"In the war, I don't think anyone saw a consent form when the D-Day wounded and the injured from city bombings came in, half of them nearly unconscious," Emma remembered.

"That did a lot to make the old laws seem out of date and to give the medical staff more power, as they had

118

to make the decisions. I'm sure that in a case similar to Bea's, it wouldn't be enforced now, except perhaps on religious grounds," Paul said. "In ordinary cases, any relative or even a doctor called in by the surgeon can sign for consent if the patient is in no state to sign his own form, but of course minors have to have the consent of a responsible adult."

Half an hour later, Dwight's radio contact was under way from the Air Base and when Paul rang Beatties, he was told that Bea was not available for talk on the phone as Mr Miller was with her. The Wing Sister said that they were considering a Caesarian within the next four hours.

"I'll try the base again to hurry Dwight on his way," Paul said, but he tried to get through and found the line engaged time after time.

"It can't make much difference now," Emma said. "If he got the first message, he'll be here soon and go immediately to the hospital."

"If it was you, I'd want to be there," Paul said.

Emma smiled. "I'm not sure about that and Bea's not me. She knows that Dwight would hate being in a labour ward and she said she wants to concentrate on the job in hand and yell if necessary, with no person she knows anywhere near her. I think she's right. She will have to work hard at it if they are born naturally, and they don't call it labour for nothing!"

"At least give him the privilege of being outside to pace the floor in the traditional distracted way," Paul said.

Paul tried to get through to the American Air Base again and to his relief made a connection long enough to remind them that Dwight would need a fast car to meet him and convey him quickly to the Princess Beatrice Hospital as soon as he landed.

"That's all we can do," Emma said. "I'll telephone the Wing in an hour or so but they must be busy now."

Paul nodded his approval. "It does help that you know the workings of a busy department and can sympathise with Sisters who are dragged to the phone when they are in the middle of afternoon or evening treatments, and now, she will be making sure that Bea is prepared for theatre."

"You think it will have to be a Caesar?"

"Miller said that he hesitates to induce her or rupture the membranes too early. One is lying transversely and he can't turn it except as a breech presentation."

"You *have* been checking."

"I popped into see him and looked at the X-ray. I'm not a gynae man but I could see that surgery was the answer for Bea's sake as much as for the babies." He saw her anxiety. "I know you want to be there, but you can't," he said flatly. "Bea will need you afterwards when she comes back here."

Emma smiled. "There's still a lot to do if she does come here and not go to the Air Base."

"She'll be here," Paul asserted. "It would take more than the whole of the American Air Force brass hats to keep her away, if that's what she wants, and that's what she wants!"

"I must get some more distemper for the wall in that room," Emma said. "It takes days to lose the smell."

"You have at least ten days after the Caesar, as she'll stay in the Wing for that time. Remember, this will be a major operation, not a simple delivery, and she'll have to heal up inside. She'll also have to learn to cope with twins for feeding and bathing. Has she done much in the children's ward?"

"That's a thought." Emma laughed. "Bea did a stint on night duty and hated it. I haven't done a lot with kids, either, so I'd better read a few text books."

"Not too many. Common sense and a warm pair of arms and lots of love is the treatment." He kissed her. "For me too, but first I want my tea!"

Chapter Eleven

The spring evening held a deceptive peace and Emma longed to walk in the park but knew that if she left the house for an instant, she would worry about Bea. "It's all very well for you," she accused a sleepy bird, ruffling its feathers outside the window and giving half-hearted efforts at song. "Go away, and stop making a noise! Can't you see I'm waiting for the phone to ring?"

She looked up and smiled when Paul brought in the tray of coffee and toasted cheese sandwiches that he had prepared while she showered after they made love. "Talking to yourself? You need a good psychiatrist," he said.

"I'm booked with one for a few more sessions," she said. She saw that he was more relaxed now and knew that he needed her love more than she'd ever imagined possible. His expression was usually so cool and self-contained, his face smooth and his manner so full of quiet confidence, that he seemed able to absorb the tensions of other people who needed to shed their neuroses, as if he had unlimited space for their troubles and could have none of his own. But when they made love, he lost his hidden tensions and became a warm and passionate lover who needed her as much as she needed him, and often surprised her with the intensity of his feelings.

"Yummy!" she said. "They say that toasted cheese gives bad dreams but it's worth it." She poured the coffee. "I made a pie yesterday but as we shall probably be having snacks all night if we can't sleep, we can eat it later," she said.

"Aunt Emily would by now have the teapot dark brown and the whisky ready for her cup, as she does in all moments of stress but this is healthier," Paul said.

"She rang just now," Emma said. "That shows courage, as in spite of becoming familiar with the local telephone, she never likes to use it for long distance calls if she can avoid it."

"So when do we expect the twins?" Paul asked dryly. "She must have told you a simple thing like that."

"One of each and very soon," Emma said, amused but half-serious.

"She's not wrong. I was in touch with Beatties when you were in the shower and Bea is in the anaesthetic room now. Thank God they alerted Jason for the anaesthetic."

"He's the best in London," Emma said eagerly. "He gives curare like magic so that he can speak to the patient as soon as the case is over, as the patient is kept only lightly anaesthetised and has few after-effects, and yet the surgeon and patient are both relaxed during the op, with no pulsating gut getting in the way."

"You say the nicest things, my darling," laughed Paul. "Have one of my special sandwiches and shut up about pulsating guts!"

"Someone suggested a spinal anaesthetic but Bea wasn't happy about that, and I have known patients with alarming headaches after one. Besides, she didn't want to hear what was going on as she'd be embarrassed. She just wants to go to sleep and wake to hear her babies crying, missing the sights and sounds of the operating theatre."

"I cancelled a consultation for tomorrow," Paul said. "You will want to see her if possible, and that leaves me alone here. I am beginning to think that we do need a receptionist who can be in the office while I take cases."

Emma raised her eye brows. "Has someone tried to rape you, apart from Mrs Molton?" she asked and giggled.

122

Paul put on his wounded expression. "Not funny. There are a couple of people I wouldn't see alone, and one with whom I would have to have you there all the time, right by my side," he said with feeling.

"You shouldn't be so kind to them even if that is a part of their treatment."

"I'm not always soothing. As you have seen, I have to be severe at times but that seems to be a turn-on for some who have never lived without violence or humiliation in their lives. One woman was sexually abused as a child and was whipped by her father when he found out about it and who had been responsible: a trusted a close relative, I believe, and as he felt personally guilty and angry, took it out on her and told her that it was her own fault it had happened. She was devoted to her father and obeyed him in all things so long as he noticed her, so I become the father figure and she would really like me to whip her too! She doesn't want to be cured. She likes a bit of sado-masochism!"

"So you are gentle and try to make her see that violence isn't acceptable in polite society?"

"Something like that, but I had to tell her that I can do very little for her if she doesn't want to be cured. End of story for me, but not for her."

"What will happen to her?"

"I have a strong suspicion that it's happening. The last time she came here, she asked me about the VD block at Beatties as I refused to examine her physically and referred her back to her own GP. She said that she had been with several men and thought she might have gonorrhoea."

"Was she serious or just trying to shock you?"

"Serious. She was scared of being ill but said she had no intention of giving up men as it did her more good than my sessions with her!"

"Did you write to her doctor?"

"I gave her a note for the Venereal Disease Clinic, indicating that she might be a pro. They will take swabs and if she is infected, treat her with sulphonamides and paint her genitalia with gentian violet and ask her to have regular checks. As yet, penicillin is available only for the Services and severe septicaemia and some bad open surgical cases, so she'll have the longer cure. It's a miracle when penicillin is used on gonorrhoea as it clears the disease in twenty-four hours or near enough."

"If they do that, how will she work, with purple all over her?"

"I warned her what to expect and she laughed and said it would be an added attraction as the men would feel safe but stimulated into ever wilder activities!"

"You have opened another dimension in medicine to me," Emma said pensively.

"You must have met some odd people," he answered.

"Of course, but seeing people walk in here smartly dressed and looking normal, it isn't like seeing them in bed and knowing that something is physically wrong with them!"

"So do you agree? We need a third person here if only to chaperone me when women like Mrs Molton come here," he said lightly. "And to help with the paper work."

Emma nodded. In hospital it was an unwritten rule that no doctor examined a female patient without a nurse in attendance, as much for his protection against blackmailing accusations, as to be ready to hand him his stethoscope! A doctor could be far more vulnerable in his own home, away from a ward full of watchful nurses and medics.

"The agency will send a short list and I'd be grateful if you'd interview them," Paul said.

"Must it be a girl?" Her thoughts went back to the soldiers she had nursed and had found to be helpful as soon as they were convalescent. "If security is important, a man might be better, and he could act as a useful shifter of furniture when needed."

"I hadn't thought of a man," Paul said slowly. "I don't think we need a muscle-bound bouncer, but it's worth considering a man, I suppose. An ex-army clerk could do the paper work in the office, with the door slightly open, so that a patient would not feel he intruded, but would know that a third person was there." She watched his growing interest.

"Had you thought that we might have someone living in the basement flat who would keep an eye open for the house if we were away? A girl might not want that as she could be scared to be alone in a house so close to a bombed site, but a self-contained apartment with a separate entrance might be a useful attraction to encourage someone to make a job permanent, as houses are difficult to find now that so many men are returning from the Forces."

"It's worth considering," Paul said. "In fact, a married couple might do if the woman is prepared to do a little housekeeping. I have no intention of you ever working as hard as you have done in the past and there may be times when you are asked to help out at Beatties and want to do so, or want to follow a course of study that has nothing to do with nursing."

"It does depend on Bea and how long they stay in England," Emma said. "I know she'll come back here for the first few weeks, so we need help in the house; and soon."

"I'll leave the choice to you," Paul said. "You have an instinct for people and have nursed enough males to know their good and bad points."

"I'll see a few before we decide and perhaps a girl or two as well."

"Bed for you, as you will have a busy day tomorrow. I have some work to do at my desk so I'll creep to bed later or camp on the divan in the office."

"You think we may have a call from Dwight?"

"Could be, and there's no point in both of us waiting for it."

"I do love you, Doctor," she said tenderly.

125

"Remember that when you see all those paragons of masculine charm waiting to be interviewed for the job," he teased her.

She went to their bedroom and pulled the newly-hung window curtains across, partly from habit as the blackout had made a routine of darkened windows for many years, but also because she admired the heavy drapes. They were old thick velvet, patterned with soft colours and hanging from a deep bobble-edged pelmet, and must have seen many changes of fashion and people during the decades that they had hung in the manor house on the Island.

They were like the ones in Sir Arthur's bedroom when she had nursed him in that other manor house. She frowned. There had been no announcement, but his wife must be ready now for the birth of their first baby.

It was another world, she decided. She hadn't read the newspapers each day and had probably missed it, but she knew that it was a world in which she could never live happily and she was content.

Bed was warm and welcoming. She felt good after making love earlier and drifted into a deep sleep.

The door opened softly and Paul stood by the bed, unsure whether to wake her, or to leave her sleeping with a smile on her face and a sweetly curved breast pressing against the thin nightdress. The instinct that could make her fully awake and ready to face an emergency made her turn in bed and raise herself on one elbow. "Dwight rang?"

He handed her a thick dressing gown. "Emily was right," he said and his pleasure made his voice vibrant.

"One of each? And Bea? Is she all right?"

Paul sat on the side of the bed and hugged her. "Everything went well and Bea saw them before she went into a natural sleep." He laughed softly. "I wouldn't say as much for Dwight. He arrived just as they were being born and had to wait a while before they were all cleaned up and out of the theatre. Not all his top brass status could get him admitted into that holy of holies in outdoor clothes and shoes and there wasn't time to fuss over him and give him a gown and a mask and fresh theatre boots. Beatties is very fussy about infection. I think he did his share of frustrated pacing of the corridor!"

"It's good to dent his ego occasionally," Emma said, smiling. "Men are superfluous at these times," she added primly.

"He did have something to do with it!" Paul reminded her.

"Where is he now?"

"That's why I woke you. They told him that Bea would be asleep for hours and that he ought to get some rest too, before he goes in there all bright and bushy tailed tomorrow, so I insisted that he must come here at once."

Emma slipped into a sweater and skirt and warm stockings. "I'll make coffee," she said.

"What a good thing you made a chicken pie," Paul said. "The all-American favourite dish! You are getting like Aunt Emily. Why else would you bake that if there was no need for a really big pie that we could never eat up alone?"

"Do you think he'll be hungry?"

"Was there a time when he wasn't starving?"

"Pop it in the oven while I finish dressing," she said. "Cheese sandwiches seem a long way back now and I am hungry, too."

A tired but happy man arrived and rang the front door bell. He clasped Emma firmly in his arms and kissed her. "I needed that! The nurses wouldn't let me near them! I smell coffee," he said.

"Put my wife down and come in by the fire," Paul said.

"You lit the fire?" Emma asked.

"At this time of the morning, it helps keep the blood circulating and the mind bright when all the world is at a low ebb. Maybe it's long after the witching hour of midnight but it's the time when life slows down and a chill sets in."

"I kept you up," Dwight said without a shade of guilt. "Any food in this neck of the woods?"

"Coming up sir," Emma said. "How is Bea?"

"Woozy and a bit tearful," he said. "She's had quite a day."

"So have you," Paul said.

"I'm tired and starving, but I've seen the beautiful fruit of my loins," he said quietly. "I never in this world thought I'd feel as I did when I saw that pair of ugly red faces and felt the tears on Bea's cheeks."

"They take after you then," Emma said lightly, but she found difficulty in swallowing.

"Sure," he said more normally. "I can see the likeness already. Little ugly mugs," he added softly. "Give me some more pie and stop being fresh with me, Missee."

Dwight ate over half of the pie and sighed with satisfaction.

Emma scraped the dish and put the remaining crumbs on his plate. "If this had been night duty, I would have had porridge at this hour," she said almost dreamily. "We made it for the patients' breakfasts. It took a long time to cook in a huge double saucepan as the oatmeal was coarse and hard, but it was delicious and very comforting at four in the morning before we began early treatments." She saw Dwight's shocked face and laughed. "If Bea has to get up at night for the babes, she might revert to habit and you will have thick stodgy oatmeal for breakfast unless she eats it all first."

"Haven't you broken Emma of bad habits yet, Paul?" he asked.

"I'm working on it and you did have pie tonight," Paul said, wondering what was on Emma's mind, then saw her relief when he said, "You'll have to eat porridge if that's what Bea wants, Dwight. Maybe not that, but it symbolises the needs that we all have at times to revert into the safety of childhood or in this case, shared joys and troubles such as these two have had together long before we arrived to disrupt their lives."

Dwight yawned. "So when you say to me, 'porridge', I'll know I'm leaning on her, and she needs her own space, huh?"

"You are a gem," Emma said.

"Do I get to crash out some place?" he asked.

"I even put a hot bottle in the bed," Emma said.

"Never use them," he said.

"You will tonight. Sleep well and we'll wake you latish, as they won't, as Aunt Emily would say, want you at the hospital, littering up the place and getting underfoot until they are ready."

"She is like my granny," he said. "Thanks, guys. I love ya."

"Is he all right?" she asked when Dwight was in the bathroom.

Paul nodded. "Fine. This has completely restored his pride, and his ego will work overtime when he gets back among his fellow officers. Not many of them father twins, so even if they have no more children, Dwight's virility is never going to be doubted now."

"Is that so important?" she asked, but did not meet his gaze.

"To many men it is the ultimate," he said. "I can wait a while but not for too long, Emma."

She turned and held him close. "I promise that it will not be too far away, but please, not twins, if that's all right by you?"

They dozed by the dying fire and knew that real sleep was impossible. "Is six o'clock too early to ring Emily?" she asked. "I hope that Dwight got through to his family. The time zone will be OK, as it's late afternoon now over there."

"Hello," said a cautious voice as soon as the phone began to ring. "Are you there?"

"Are you there?" Emma asked, laughing, recognising the usual manner in which Emily answered the contraption she still distrusted when long distance calls came through. So early in the morning, the lines were clear and the contact was made quickly.

"I can hear you as if you are in the next room," she said in wonder.

"Bea is fine and the babies, as you said, are one of each and healthy, but I don't know how heavy they are as Dwight came away before they were weighed and bathed."

"And you have been up all night," Emily said accusingly.

"What about you?"

"That's different. I miss a night too, sometimes, and then I have a cup of tea. I was quite happy just waiting but I'm glad you rang. Besides I didn't worry about her. She's a good girl and I could see the babies clear as clear last night."

"That was the tea and whisky," Emma said with a tremor in her voice. "You will tell me when this is about to happen to us, won't you?"

"No, that's your business," Emily said. "I can't see it happening by accident to you."

"Just Bea and Sadie?"

Emily gave a short laugh. "One was carelessness and Bea was taken by surprise. By the way, George has rented a house in Bath and Sadie is looking forward to a social life there. Did you know that some Americans have taken a huge place on the hill above Bath and are making an American museum there? Sadie knows one of the ladies and hopes to spend a lot of time there."

"So she'll feel more at home?"

"Let's hope so, but if you ask me, she's a bit of a madam! George has a handful there, and he hasn't the money to serve every whim she fancies. Sadie has money of her own and thinks it grows on trees, but George wants to support his own family and will find it hard on a Naval Officer's pay when she is extravagant."

"Why doesn't he let her spend her own money on her own extravagances?"

"Men don't like to be beholden," Emily said. "And she's not like you Emma, to value quality and not waste time or money on trivial things."

"Paul and I share," Emma replied. "We find it easy."

"As I said, you are different."

"How is Aunt Janey?" Emma asked, to change the subject away from George.

"Glad to see the back of them for a while. Sadie has hinted that when the baby comes she would like to leave it with Janey for a few weeks, as she will feel so very tired and worn out and need a rest. She still thinks she is very hard done by as she didn't want a baby so soon."

"Oh! I hope she has a sudden rush of maternal feeling when the baby does arrive. Give Aunt Janey my love and I'll ring you next week unless there is something new to tell you."

"What ever happens there, George has his mother to help," Emily said.

"I know she will but she won't have to take over completely. Even if Sadie is a lazy so-and-so, she's the wrong kind to give up what is hers, although she'd like others to do any work that she wants to avoid. I've met girls like that in hospital. That's why we had a three months trial period to weed out the ones who liked the uniform and the idea of nursing glamorous men," Emma said dryly. "It worked there but this is different; George didn't take her on a three months trial and she's there for life."

Emily coughed as if she found words difficult.

"Are you all right?" Emma asked.

"Yes," she replied normally. "A bit dry so I'll have a cup of tea."

"You are worried about George and Sadie," Emma said.

"Same as I said, Janey will surely be there whatever happens."

She put down the phone and Emma stared at the silent suddenly threatening instrument. Emily had sounded vaguely Irish and a touch Isle of Wight and just as Emma knew her grandmother must have sounded, a voice from the distant past.

131

Chapter Twelve

"I feel like a Victorian model for corsets," Bea said cheerfully. She pushed back the bedclothes to show Emma the white cotton, many-tailed binder that encircled her abdomen and the dressing over the line of stitches from the Caesarian section. "I'll finally have a flat stomach once more and be able to wear real clothes again."

"There was never a moment when you looked awful, even just before you came in here, and you know it," Emma said. "But it's good to see you looking so well now." She saw the hooks on the bed end that were intended as a place for a cot to be slung. "Only room for one, so what happens? Do they take it in turns to sleep with Mummy?"

"No, Sister has all the right ideas. She likes her mothers to sleep a lot and have the babies in here only for feeding, so that we all get a bit of rest." She glanced at the bedside clock. "Almost time to see the lions fed, if that's what amuses you," she said.

"Are you going to breast-feed them?"

"At first, until my hair drops out," she replied. "Dwight is very anxious for me to do so . . . shades of covered waggons again and all the books he's reading. Sister says I'll enjoy it and that it makes the womb go back to normal quickly and will help me get back a flat tum, so what have I to lose except my sleep?"

Emma handed her a bed cape of Jap silk and fine crocheted wool that had come from Switzerland with matching pale blue silk nightdresses. A nurse pushed a trolley into the room on which were two cots and a tray of nappies, talcum powder and pots of zinc and castor oil cream, the best protection for tiny bottoms at changing times.

The chart showed that the babies had been about six and a half pounds each at birth, with the boy the first to be extracted from the womb, making him, almost by accident, the older twin. They were both obviously strong and thriving.

"There will be very little for them except for the first colostrum in there today, but when the milk does come in, you may find it better to feed both at once or you'll be tied all day, so we'll practice the method now and then you can give bottles for this feed," Bea was told.

"Stay and talk," Bea said to Emma.

The nurse eyed Emma's crisply clean cotton blouse and skirt and smiled. "You could give one bottle," she said.

"That's an honour," Bea said. "Dwight wanted to hold them when he saw them asleep in the nursery, but they were with other babies and he couldn't go in there with his germs and his old bomber jacket! But they promised that he can see them in here with me, today. I told him to wear a clean shirt!" She laughed, knowing Dwight's meticulous personal cleanliness and his care for her.

To Bea's amusement, she was supported by pillows and one baby was put on a pillow under one arm, head to her breast and the other on the other side. The nurse helped the tiny mouths to latch on to the nipples and they sucked vigorously.

"If Dwight comes here with his earthy remarks about sows with litters of piglets, I'll throw his son at him. Ouch! He has a good set of hard gums," she added.

The nurse dropped a little milk from the bottles on to her wrist to test for temperature and gave one baby to Emma to hold. "Just five minutes at this feed as they have been working hard for very little and will be tired. I'll test weigh them and adjust the feed tomorrow, according to what you have to give them, Mrs Miller."

"I hope this is catching," Bea said with a malicious smile. "Why should I suffer alone? You are my spiritual sister and may be my twin, and I want someone to talk babies with me. I shall bore everyone for months and my poor dear father will back away and send me nice gifts to make up for his lack of enthusiasm as he did when I was a child!"

"Many men make better grandfathers than they do fathers," Emma pointed out. "You need a friend who is pregnant and to whom you can give all the unwanted advice about her condition and compare sickness and later, stitches and milk yields."

"Don't laugh! That's exactly what I need."

Emma wore an innocent expression. "Shall I write to Sadie and suggest she stays with us?"

"Look what you've made me do? He's come *orf*! and I can't get him back on again."

"Time's up, anyway," the nurse said, taking the other baby away from the breast. "Bottles now and I'll collect them in fifteen minutes so that you can rest before lunch."

"Have you chosen names?" Emma was moved by the smallness and softness and the tiny guzzling mouths. Perhaps, she thought, but not yet.

"Dwight has a few family names that come out of the ark and I want Avril for the girl as she was born at the end of April, but we shall fight over it for weeks," she said happily. "I'm rather glad she wasn't born in May, which was what we expected, as I knew someone at school called May and hated her."

"What a good thing it wasn't November," Emma said. "Not Beatrice?"

"No, Dwight says that one Bea is enough in his family and I hope he mean't the name! I compromised by suggesting his mother's name which is Charlotte and we have nearly decided on Hayland for our son, a family name from way out West, and plain John for my choice. I know that Dwight will call him Johnnie as soon as the novelty of Hayland has worn off, but it will please his family. Imagine answering to that name at school!"

"I think that a lot of Americans hide their second names by using only the initial. It sounds impressive but who knows what awful ones are hidden by doing that."

"I've heard some, but they hate being teased about them, so I don't indulge in that particular hobby now," Bea said. "The more bizarre the name, the less they like it mocked, and some Yanks of Eastern European origins have no sense of humour." She patted her son on his back, making him burp in a satisfactory manner. "If they had a sense of humour, they would never saddle their offspring with terrible names," she added. "What a clever boy!" she drooled as the tiny face went red and he tried to fill his nappy.

Emma handed her charge back to the nurse. "I have to go," she said. "I have the first of the interviews lined up for this afternoon. What do I ask, Bea?"

"You ask for references and don't take excuses for not having any. If they have been honourably de-mobbed and haven't murdered their commanding officers, they will have something to show their characters and abilities."

"First impressions?"

"That's tricky. We've all been taken in by a guileless smile and a dishonest heart! Remember Morgan with the soft Welsh voice and thieving hands? He stole from the lockers of men who couldn't reach their gear for themselves, and he even took money from my desk when I was acting sister."

"Two have wives and are interested in living in the basement flat, but the other men are single."

"If you are in any doubt about references, make sure you are sitting by the phone and the telephone directory and ask for the number of the person whose reference has been lost!" Bea gave her a shrewd glance. "Never be taken in by the sob story that they have no place to live in and need the job right now. Take the one you do choose on a trial period and don't let them move in before you are certain they'll be what you want."

"We want a man who was in the Forces and can do simple booking and office work but ideally was something to do with the medics."

"Like Grade?"

"He would be fine." Emma remembered the man with two legs in plaster who had been a medical orderly and hated being idle. From a wheelchair, he had helped out when there was so much surgical nursing to be done that they couldn't cope with office routine and he knew the medical terms and what was needed to be ordered to replenish cupboards with surgical dressings and equipment.

"I wonder," Bea said, and sank back on her pillows. "I danced with his CO. Now, what was his name?"

"Go to sleep. He'll have gone back to Lincolnshire and his family's bulb farm," Emma said.

She went out into the spring sunshine and saw the rings of petals shed round the base of the ornamental cherry trees in the park, and as she looked up there were more blossoms left, pale pink and white against a blue sky. The soft green of poplars was a light hearted promise of summer against the grey walls of the old hospital and she was happy.

Even the bombed sites looked interesting, with a lot more shrubs and bird-borne weeds covering the ruins. In some streets work had begun on boarded up and useable houses to make them . . . what had a politician promised? 'Houses fit for heroes to live in.' I think I'd rather have a pre-fabricated one if I had to choose between these patched up ruins and the simple labour-saving ones, she thought. They were being erected for an eager band of applicants who had served in the Forces and so were first in line for eligibility.

But I don't have to make that choice, she thought as she drove up to the immaculate front door of her home. It would be very easy to take on an unsuitable applicant eager to live in such a attractive house in Kensington.

The first two girls who came were totally wrong for the job. One had a fear of being alone in a house and the other one whom Emma liked very much, thought they were offering a cleaning job. She had no office skills and thought she might now go back to Bristol where she had an aunt and would get a job easily, stripping tobacco leaves in the factory there.

Two men came and neither had good references but seemed to think she'd be lucky to have them work for her. One had a good story of service in Burma and talked a lot but wasn't very clean, and the other was anxious to live in at once and have a small sum in advance of his pay.

"You must have a pension?" Emma asked, as he had given her to understand just how much he'd suffered and how sorry the army was to lose him and hinted at a rank that she felt sure was far higher than he'd achieved.

He grinned. "I find the gee-gees a bit expensive," he said as if he was sure she would share his views. So he was another, 'We'll let you know,' but Emma hinted that that it wasn't likely that he would fit their requirements.

"The agency wasn't a lot of help," Emma explained when she discussed the situation later with Paul. "They seem to take anyone who appears and don't check on them as they promised."

Paul rang the agency and was firm about what he wanted and said that he would have to have better service or he'd go elsewhere for help. He said that the labour exchange could possibly be the answer, and Emma interviewed a few more candidates during the next few days.

"I'm beginning to think that a couple would be a

disaster," she said, one lunch time. "The last ones were terrible. The wife wanted at least three bedrooms so that her family could come to stay and she didn't want to do any housework other than dusting. Her husband was as bad and seemed to think we wanted a man to sit in a cubby hole in the hall and just send people up for medical appointments, like a French concierge!"

"We do need someone," Paul said. "Mrs Coster is fine for rough cleaning but this house is bigger than I expected and I seem to be inundated with new patients." He looked guilty. "You haven't seen Bea for several days as I couldn't spare you, but I asked the wing sister if you could go in tonight after we finish here."

"Bless you, I do want to see her," Emma said. "It's time you had a break too."

"I'm taking no cases for three days next week, which will give us time to sort out the paperwork and I can fit in a session at Tommie's."

"Not exactly a break, but better than nothing," she agreed. "It will give us time to prepare for Bea coming here. Dwight insisted that she stays there for another few days and really gets fit to handle the infants on her own if necessary, without being over-tired."

"Very wise. A lot of women feel inadequate after their babies are born and a lot of post-natal depression might be avoided if more people took the situation seriously."

"Emma! I thought you'd forgotten me. All fixed up with help?" Bea asked when Emma put her head round the door of her room.

"Not really. No further than I told you on the phone, and you weren't a lot of help saying that there was no rush and someone would appear when I least expect it!" Emma looked despondent. "There is a couple who might do but neither Paul nor I are keen as we feel that the husband would do nothing and expect his wife who is full of energy and I know would be reliable, to keep

138

him. Fortunately, after all our experience with soldiers, we can smell out a malingerer very quickly. Where are all those really nice boys who helped us so much and were honest and bright?"

"They exist," Bea said and smiled in an irritating way.

"It's all very well for you," Emma said hotly. "Sitting there looking like a million dollars in a peignoir that never bore anything as sordid as a utility label, and having a figure that is almost better than ever with a bit more bosom!"

"I love you too, Duckie. Dwight likes the added inches and says I am like Jean Harlow when she was at her best. He's away just now but he'll help me move in with you when the time comes. You still want me?" she asked rather anxiously.

"Of course we do," Emma said warmly.

"But you and Paul are overworked and you are worried," Bea said.

"A little," Emma admitted.

"Tomorrow you will have a visitor," Bea said. "In fact, two."

"Miranda and your father? They did say they wanted to see what we had done to the house."

"Not them tomorrow, but later when I am there. They can bring their own food!" Bea said firmly. "Rationing gets worse or so I heard from the ward cleaner who had her eyes on my biscuits!"

"We do seem to eat a lot of scrambled eggs and sausages," Emma said. "They do very good fish and chips in the cafe round the corner, but only three times a week now, otherwise it's mostly egg on chips. When do we ever get steak again?"

"Dwight knows a place," Bea said.

"He would," Emma said rudely.

"Be like that! He plans to take you both there as soon as I am out of here."

"With you too? Haven't you forgotten a couple of things like twins? Who will baby-sit?"

"Didn't I say who is coming to see you? I managed to find Grade who has been working in London for the past six months but wants to bring his wife here."

"How did you know?"

"I told you I knew his CO. Bertie keeps tabs on his men and is a really good egg, looking after their welfare. He knew where to find him and hopes I can fit him into something worthwhile. If Bertie had his way, you would take at least six of his service bods. I put him on to my father and I think he will persuade him to take on more ex-services."

"Bless you, Bea. It would be the answer to a lot of niggles and if his wife is all right we can certainly take them on. In fact, even if she's an absolute drip, I'd still want Grade and be willing to put up with her."

"Ring me tomorrow night and let me know what happens." Bea yawned. "Time for my exercises and then bed. I wake up at eleven for the night feed and sleep like a log in between. Earth mother, that's me," she said, looking as if she had stepped from a movie and had nothing more strenuous to do than sip a glass of champagne.

"If you know the man that's who we need," Paul said. "Can he add up?" Emma put an arm round his shoulders and looked down at the ledger on the desk, sensing the tiredness that Paul so seldom showed.

"As I recall, Grade is the sort who can turn his hand to anything and is always cheerful. He helped us a lot and knows about patients as he was a clerk in the Army Medical Corps. He had an encounter with a sniper, had a small flesh wound that was not serious but then fell off a high bank and broke both legs. He was so mad about it, but as usual made the best of a bad job and took to a wheelchair with great aplomb."

140

"He can manage stairs?"

"He left hospital completely mobile but had a slight limp."

"I seem to have taken on a lot of work," Paul admitted. "I want to keep up with my general medical knowledge with the sessions at the hospital but I shall have to refuse new psychiatric patients for a while, as so many are becoming long term and the diary is full."

"You shouldn't be so good," Emma said.

"A bit double-edged," Paul said wryly.

"Mrs Molton?"

"She rang twice today, unfortunately when you were out, and she has an appointment tomorrow. What time are you expecting Grade?" he asked rather apprehensively. "I need you here when she arrives dripping elegance and Chanel No 5."

"Don't tell me that she's making an impression?" Emma teased him.

"Not the kind she wants," he said.

"I thought she'd decided to hate you."

"She did but that's one stage. Now she thinks she needs me and wants my opinion, not on her mental state but about her work. What do I know about textiles and fashion? I am fast becoming a substitute for the authority she's suffered from all her life and yet in many ways she's recovering and should have no need of my services."

"Really? I thought she was after your body," Emma said heartlessly.

"That too!"

"You are scared," she said in triumph. "I never thought I'd see the day!"

"Not scared, just hungry and a bit tired," he said with a resigned smile. "Let's go round the corner and see what culinary delights await us in the restaurant. I'm far more scared of the fish cakes from the other cafe than I am of Mrs Molton. Never again!"

"When they arrived at the restaurant Emma examined

the pencilled menu and raised her eyebrows. "What's this? Spaghetti?"

The proprietor of the restaurant explained. "My son-in-law is Italian. He was interned at the beginning of the war, even though he was never a spy. It was stupid of the authorities. He's lived in England for years and worked in a cafe in Swindon. He met my daughter there and we all liked him. They wanted to be married but the war came and he was sent away. Now they are releasing some Prisoners of War and a lot of Italians have gone back to the work they did here, as England was their home for as long as they can recall. Some speak very little Italian now. My daughter still wanted to marry Luigi, so they came here."

"Where do you buy the spaghetti? I haven't tasted it, except for that soggy stuff in tins of tomato sauce, since I was in Italy with a school trip before the war," Paul said.

"Luigi makes his own and we have vegetable lasagne and Tagliatelle tonight as well as simple spaghetti with cheese," he said with pride.

"All that this needs is a good Chianti," Paul said and twirled the last of his spaghetti expertly on his fork.

"I have no drinks licence," the owner said. "If you like to bring your own beer or wine in future, that is allowed."

"I'll tell Bea about this. Dwight may know someone who knows someone with a few bottles of Italian wine," Paul said.

"Not for me," Emma said firmly when they walked back to the house. "It will be a long time before I drink Italian wine."

"Wartime prejudice? It's over now, darling."

Emma sighed. "War was so unfair. I hated the terrible things done in Germany and Japan and the results of the bombs here. We saw a lot of the results of that, but there were other things that happened that didn't make the news and were equally horrendous."

142

"Such as?"

"We had a batch of soldiers, in the ENT unit who had been given wine by Italians when we over ran an area in Italy. The locals seemed to be friendly. In fact, they assured them that they hated the *Duce* and all he had done and welcomed the British and Canadians as friends and deliverers.

"The wine was laced with strong acid and now there are a lot of men with feeding tubes in their sides into their stomachs, as they can't use their food channels. The lucky ones have to go back every month to out-patients to swallow heavy lead-filled catheters to expand the shrivelled oesophagus. They sit for half an hour with it in situ and you can imagine that it isn't comfortable, but it means they are able to eat soft food and they do improve over the months of treatment."

"So no Chianti until we have an assurance that it is acid free?"

"And lost in the past," Emma said. "If we can forget, and if we must ever let ourselves forget."

Chapter Thirteen

Emma laughed. If she hadn't recognised Grade, his de-mob suit and dull green pork pie hat would at least have labelled him ex-service, but his stocky figure and the way he held his head and the set of his stubborn jaw was the same as she remembered, when he was a patient on Bea's ward of bored military casualties awaiting the trip to the convalescent home and either a return to the Service as fit, or demobilisation and civvie street.

She watched the man and woman eye the front of the house and the man said something that made the woman smile. She remembered with pleasure, his sense of dry humour, too.

The door knocker received a very positive announcement that someone needed admittance and had none of the diffidence that had been apparent with some of the applicants for the job, overawed perhaps by the elegant green door and the bay trees, or unused to entering imposing residences. Mrs Coster, who just happened to be there scrubbing the hall floor was ready to answer the door, determined to miss nothing, wiped her hands on her apron and opened the door. "Who shall ay say?" she asked in a terrible attempt at an upper class accent, then relaxed into her usual cockney when she saw the suit. "Oh you've come abart the job," she said. "Come in and I'll tell her."

"Hello Sister. Long time no see," Grade said. "Meet the wife. This is Eileen."

"Hello," Emma said. "Let's have some tea and you can

144

tell me what you've been doing since you left the hospital in Surrey. It's all ready, as I knew you'd be punctual." She laughed and looked at Eileen. "Has he changed or does he still refuse to drink coffee even for elevenses?"

Eileen smiled and nodded and Emma felt a deep relief. She sensed that the couple felt at home without being pushy. Eileen said nothing but she listened carefully and drank her tea with obvious appreciation of the good china and the crisp biscuits.

"I met Eileen when I was in the convalescent home and she was working in the Matron's office. I helped her with the errands and the books." Grade grinned and she blushed. "We got to know each other well in the office and even if she couldn't add up, I knew I wanted to marry her, so here we are."

"How romantic," Emma said, keeping a solemn expression.

"Did you want both of us to work here or would Eileen have to get another job but live with me here?"

"That depends on what Eileen does and what she wants to do," Emma said, hoping that she would have some opinion of her own to offer.

"Fair enough. Tell Sister what you think," he suggested.

"I was an auxillary nurse until I had a badly burned hand and they gave me light office work. It's all cleared up now," she added hastily. "I can do whatever is wanted; housework, cooking, sewing, and bookwork at a pinch, but as Mick said, I'm not very good at that and I don't really like it." Reluctantly, as if the idea was repugnant, she added, "If you don't want me, I can do night duty, looking after terminally ill patients in their own homes."

"We need someone here when Dr Sykes has patients, to answer the phone and attend to the door. If I am not here and a patient needs to be examined, or even if a patient is having analysis, we need you to sit with them and just be there."

145

"Does the doctor get a lot of nymphos?" Grade asked cheerfully. "If he needs a bit more help with patients, I can sit in as I have done when I was in the Army Medical Corps. Both of us are experienced with illness and would like to keep it up," he said.

"That will be useful," Emma agreed. "Mrs Coster does the rough work but we do need a housekeeper who can cook and do the shopping and to have someone here when we go away." Emma looked at Grade. "You did some unofficial book-keeping and ordering stock, I remember. I'm afraid this job would be a bit of everything until we really know what we want."

"Got a rocket for putting my oar in with the office work, but it didn't matter. You were all snowed under with patients. It was the least I could do and I was bored stiff with reading and playing cards with the lads."

"So do you want to work for us? You know about me, and as you must have gathered, my husband is a doctor specialising in psychiatry."

Emma saw his puzzled expression, and realised that he had heard that she was engaged to Guy, way back, so long ago now in her own mind that it seemed years ago.

"I was engaged to Dr Franklin who died in Belsen of typhus," she said steadily. "I married Dr Sykes and this is our first home together." She smiled. "You are newlyweds and so are we. We want this to be a happy place."

The couple exchanged glances and looked pleased. "Think you can put up with the pair of us?" he asked. "You haven't even asked to see the house or your accommodation," Emma said cautiously.

"I'd like to look round," Eileen said shyly. "But I'd like to work here whatever it's like. Mick has told me so much about you."

"Right. A quick look at the house and then I'll leave you in your flat for a while to see what you think, and if you really want to come here, start as soon as you can."

146

Emma paused. "How do you feel about a lot of extra work if we have visitors?"

"Sounds nice," Eileen said. "From what you told us I don't think I shall be overworked."

"Do you remember Nurse Shuter?"

"Do I remember her! Smashing blonde, and very good at her work," he added hastily. "She had the men all eating out of her hand and yet had no trouble with the lads who fancied her rotten or the stroppy ones who boasted about being at Casino or said they were Desert Rats and wanted to do nothing but eat and play cards. Was it her who contacted my old CO about this job?"

"Yes. She married an American flyer and she's just had twins. Next week when she comes out of Beatties, she will come here for a while before they leave for the States."

"Twins?" Eileen laughed. "All this and heaven too! I love babies."

"She can say that and smile," Grade said, dryly. "I'll stick to the book work."

Emma left them in the basement flat. The furniture from the Island was old but well-polished and attractive and the rooms had everything necessary for comfort including good rugs. A new gas cooker, a sink with new wooden draining boards, and plenty of cupboard space, made Eileen nod with satisfaction and look round eagerly.

Emma gave them a key to the apartment and told them to bring their belongings as soon as they liked. "You will cater for yourselves and be independent here," she said. "This is your own place now, rent free for as long as you stay with us. It has its own entrance so it will be as if it is completely separate from the house, and I shall never come in here without an invitation."

"Can we start on Monday?" Mick asked. "We haven't much to bring here as all my stuff was bombed and Eileen has always had living-in work in the hospital. After that, she stayed with her aunt or lived-in again. We've stayed in bed and breakfast boarding houses when we could have time together since we got married, but it's not very good."

"So you'll enjoy a little privacy now," Emma said. "I know just how you feel."

"I'll take Dwight up on his offer of a steak," Emma said to Bea over the phone, as soon as they had gone. "We have a baby-sitter who loves babies, or so she says."

"Grade?"

"I think they are now Mick and Eileen, and we are lucky to have found them. Thank you again," Emma said. "They start on Monday and with any luck will consider themselves our old family retainers by Tuesday! I had forgotten just how much confidence that man generates and he'll be a real asset. They obviously look on the apartment as sheer luxury after the awful digs they have been in when they had time to be together, which wasn't a great deal as they worked in separate towns after the convalescent home finished with him. It must have been terrible living like that when newly married. I know the war is over, but this situation hasn't changed for hundreds of people."

"I'm glad I thought of him. He helped me out with a very nasty sailor who managed to get drunk on something foul that he brought into the ward and then tried to touch up the ward maid! Grade took one look at him and when he saw what was happening, rang for the Military Police to take him away to confined quarters. He had no authority but was so convincing that the MPs thought he must be a doctor and came running! It was just as well as the man was in for investigation of syphillis. Not nice to have him groping the hired help! I'll give Bertie a ring and tell him. He misses men like Grade but knows he wouldn't want to be on active service again, now he's been demobbed and married, but there's trouble brewing in Korea and Bertie wants to be in the thick of it if it happens and says he needs good men."

"Not more war?"

"Probably not," Bea said easily. "If they want Dwight to go through all that again, I'll shoot whoever comes for him, but I doubt if there will be any involvement there for our boys, even with firebrands like Bertie."

"My, my, she's getting to be real fierce," Emma said.

"So would you be if you had this lot to protect," Bea said. "Mother Bear, that's me."

"Well your cave is ready for your cubs and it really does look rather nice," Emma said.

"Thursday? Is that too soon?"

"Lovely. Come early to settle in and we can all eat together at lunch before Paul sees his patients in the afternoon, which reminds me that we have the dreaded Mrs Molton after lunch today so I'd better be ready."

"Find out what her factory makes, apart from uniforms, fatigues and dungarees. Pa is always looking for more outlets, and if she isn't hopelessly neurotic, she might be useful."

"I'll mention it to Paul. It's no use asking me to discuss it with her as she thinks I am part of the furniture and rather dusty at that!"

She cooked a couple of precious lamb chops and made mashed potato and cabbage chopped with a tin of tomatoes and when Mrs Molton arrived, early as usual, they were ready for her, with the inward assurance that their stomachs wouldn't rumble from lack of food in the quiet gaps of the interview. Fresh flowers made the consulting room look homely and Mrs Molton managed a smile when Emma opened the front door to her. She seemed different and much more relaxed.

Paul smiled and put down her notes and a text book, which he'd held in both hands, making it impossible to shake hands with her as he knew that once she held his hand she would cling. As usual, Emma helped the woman to take off her hat and shoes and unbuttoned her jacket before she settled herself on the couch.

"I want to talk to you," Mrs Molton said.

"That's why we are here," Paul said mildly. "Where shall we begin today? We talked about your husband the last time you were here. You haven't been here for a week or so. What happened to the last appointment? Were you ill?"

"I've had enough of that rubbish," Mrs Molton said as if her sessions with a psychiatrist were lost in the past and best forgotten. "I took your advice," she said as if she had made a momentous decision.

"Which bit of advice is that? I didn't know that I had given any. You are here to make your own decisions once you realise your own strengths. I make no specific suggestions unless I see that you are already half-way there."

"You made me think about my employees."

"That's good."

"We are switching to fashion garments that will at first have to be of a fairly basic style as we need more machines to cut delicate fabrics, but they will have to be modern enough to make women want to buy them."

Emma listened while the voice went on and on, sometimes almost incoherent with enthusiasm, and Paul smiled and contributed a few remarks of a general nature but said nothing to influence her.

When Mrs Molton paused for breath, he said, "You can't do this alone. What staff have you who will be really supportive?"

"I pensioned off two women who were only interested in making a bulk of army clothes and had no vision beyond that, and I interviewed some very lively and intelligent students who are keen to design and have a good basic knowledge of the garment-making process. Some of my old hands will service the machines and help in many ways, and what is a miracle, they all seem

150

to like the idea and are grateful to be employed! For the first time in my life, people are giving to me, instead of draining me." .

"You are still giving, but it's what you want and need to give and that's why you get back a warm feeling of achievement."

"The Government is offering help to revitalise factories if we take in a certain number of new employees from the forces, and that is easy as there are lots of jobs for both men and women, and once we get going, there will be deliveries and catalogues and all sorts." She sighed. "I get tired but it isn't the same weariness and I sleep better."

"Have you much old stock that the Forces will not need?"

"I have a big warehouse out of London that wasn't touched by bombs, and I shall keep some of the stock there as rumours are spreading of another war, in Korea. Our men may not go there, but if they do, uniforms will be needed again. I shall watch the markets too, as army surplus is selling quite well and needs no clothing coupons. We don't want to have a warehouse full of stuff that next year nobody will want, if clothes come off ration, and uniforms for other countries will be lighter than the ones we stocked for Europe."

She looked brighter and younger and animated without being manic, and she had not talked about her unhappy childhood or anything of the dark side of her life.

"Is that the time?" she said. "I have to go now. My new manager is picking me up in ten minutes and we are going out to tea to discuss supplies of rayon and possibly silk from the Far East. I need a few contacts there."

Paul laughed. "I think that you have discovered what you need to do," he said. "You need an honest entrepreneur, not a psychiatrist."

"And you just happen to know one?" Her smile was gentle and almost mocking. "Of course you do," she said.

"You are the miracle man, and I know just what you have done for me."

Paul handed her the card that Bea had given to Emma. "This man has contacts all over the world," he said. "He's a hard businessman but has a generous side and he will help without putting any pressure on you. Tell him who gave you his card and if you want to see me again at any time, we can arrange that, but now you have enough to do and will have no time to laze about on consultants' couches."

"I know the name. He was in parliament," she said. "Thank you. He will be very useful and although he has a reputation of being a devious rascal, he gets things done, and if he knows you are breathing down his neck, I shall feel safe."

Mrs Coster tapped on the door. "A gentleman for Mrs Molton," she said.

"Well, well, did you see what I saw?" Paul asked when the patient had left with a tall well-dressed man who smiled down at her as if he wanted to care for her.

"It may be more than tea and sympathy soon," Emma agreed. "Jealous? How does it feel to be brushed aside like a discarded toy?"

"I shall need a lot of comfort," he said.

"She'll still ring you for a while," Emma warned.

"Only a few times and then she will forget she ever came to seek help. That, in my opinion, makes this a successful operation."

"Like one patient who left hospital saying he had 'Good healing flesh,' as if his recovery was all due to that, when we had worked on him all one night to save his life!"

"Nobody appreciates us," Paul said. "Telephone!" he went to the office. "It's Aunt Janey, for you."

"I thought you'd like to know. Sadie has had her baby; a bit early but all is well. It's a boy," Janey said with an excited laugh. "Only six and a half pounds but the image of George. I went over yesterday and saw him."

"Sadie is well? Did she have it in hospital?" Emma asked.

"No, a private nursing home. I'll give you the address. You will write to say well done?"

"Of course. At times like this she will miss her American friends and she has no real relatives, has she?"

Janey hesitated long enough to show a little unease. "She doesn't seem to be over the moon."

"She was shocked to be pregnant so early in her marriage," Emma pointed out. "Give her time and she'll love the baby. George must be very happy now."

"Yes he is, and as far as I'm concerned, that's what is important. He does love her now, Emma, and they could be very happy together if she cheers up."

"Do you think she's got the baby blues?"

"No, not that kind of depression. She's being Sadie in a mood and she hated the birth."

"When do you see the baby again?"

"That's uncertain. I think if I'd said I'd take him away yesterday, she'd have said, 'take him for good!' I don't like it, Emma, so I'll keep away and ring each day until she gets used to him."

"Have they thought of a name?"

"That's the best part. Alex is so thrilled to have a grandson, even if George isn't his real son. He can't wait to see him. He even suggested that he be called Clive, after George's father. Alex and Clive were very close and to me they have become the same man; and Alex has been a good father to my boy. It's sad that Alex and I didn't make babies, as we wanted a large family."

"I'll write to Sadie right away," Emma promised.

"She wanted to come to me," Janey said. "Fortunately, George found a good nurse to live with them for the first six or eight weeks after she comes out of the nursing home, and I think she'll be better with a nurse at first. After that, who knows? The important thing is that she

153

is well and the baby is well and George is happy," she added as if to convince herself.

"She couldn't leave the baby with you yet if she has to feed him," Emma said.

"Bottle feeding from day one," Janey said with a disapproving sigh.

"She should see Bea with hers," Emma said and laughed. "She can feed twins and still look as if she is modelling nightdresses for Dior."

She told Janey about Grade and his wife and urged her to bring Aunt Emily for a visit if she could be weaned away from the Island for a few days. "If Bea is here it will be good and with our new helpers, nobody would be overworked."

"That makes two of us," Emma said when she went to find Paul.

He looked puzzled. "Two of what?"

"Two rejects. Your Mrs Molton no longer wants to have *you* on the couch now that she has found another man; a bit too young for her, but rather a nice-looking change from her awful husband. I don't think she's a cold person, just frustrated. She has a full lower lip and a taut mount of Venus on each hand. She's ready for a red hot affair!"

"I didn't know you felt rejected. I still want you," Paul said.

"George is really truly in love with his wife now, so that lets me out. I did have him a tiny bit on my conscience."

"It's amazing what a baby can do for a marriage," he said.

Emma avoided his steady gaze. "The baby might have the opposite affect on them. Sadie doesn't like motherhood and is very willing for others to look after the baby."

"You aren't like her. I know you need time for lots of coming to terms with your own family background but

154

you underestimate your own warmth, darling. When we have settled in here, I'd like a son or a daughter, with your greeny hazel eyes and that lovely dimple you have when you are feeling mischievous." He kissed her and misquoted . . . "'One man loves the pilgrim soul of you and all the shadows of your changing face.'"

Chapter Fourteen

"I keep wanting to call him, 'Soldier'," said Dwight as he watched Mick Grade's receding back. "It comes naturally as he is so much a serviceman."

"Not as sloppy as your boys," Bea said. "You won't catch Mick chewing gum on duty, and I doubt if he'd do that off duty, either."

"He's taken all the bags up and put my car away round the back of the yard. I didn't have to ask him, he just did it." He looked anxiously at Bea. "Can you manage the stairs, Honey?" He grinned. "Or do we ask Mick to carry you?"

"I'm fine," Bea reassured him. "I've been practising stairs instead of using the elevator at Beatties. It's a part of my exercises and it works."

"I'll carry the twins," he said. "C'mon, Nickel and Dime." He tucked one baby under each arm and almost ran up the stairs, followed more slowly by his wife.

"Do you have to call them that, even for fun?" she wailed. "It will stick, they'll be bullied at school and resent us and leave home before they are ten!"

Emma followed them, carrying a small bag and a spare low voltage lamp bulb that would ensure soft and non-intrusive light in the nursery. "When we are given permission, we hope to have a lift installed and it could be soon, as we stressed the need for its use for patients. That seems to be the magic word. We have had the phone and extensions fitted quickly, and been given extra vouchers to buy instruments and medical supplies, which can be loosely translated as hair dryers and anything else that the dealer sells, like toasters. We did need a small steriliser, a lock-up drugs cupboard, glass syringes and a few forceps for emergencies. We are now quite well-equipped."

"This is wonderful," Bea said with real pleasure. She surveyed the room, with the pretty voile curtains that were slightly yellowed with age but otherwise intact, and the heavier warm blue velvet ones to keep out the cold, any draughts and excessive light. A wooden screen covered with tooled leather made a cosy corner for the bath and changing trolley and a low Victorian nursing chair was ready for feeding time.

She smoothed the cretonne cover of the divan along the wall. Emma had placed it there so that someone could sleep in the nursery if any anxiety for the twins was bothersome, and the pine twin cot stood firmly in the middle of the carpet square. A soft American patchwork quilt that Dwight's parents had sent was turned back at the two top corners to invite the babies in to sleep.

Dwight handed the baby girl to Bea and told her to sit in the rocking chair by the fire place. He beamed at her. "That's what I wanted to see, my wife rocking our baby by the fire and looking just wunnerful!"

"Meanwhile Junior needs changing," she said dryly. "Don't forget to put plenty of zinc and castor oil on the piece of gauze before you slap it on his bum. We don't want him to have nappy rash, do we?"

"Who, *me*?"

"We share everything, Pardner," she said with a sweet smile. "This twin business is too big for the one of us."

"I think I'll make sure that Eileen has the lunch ready," Emma said hastily, and left them completely happy and wrangling over the best way to fold a terry towelling nappy.

"Settled in?" Paul called as Emma passed his office. She paused in the doorway. "Happy as sandboys," she said. "It all looks very cosy and Bea said the contrast to the American Base is incredible. We can have good hygiene without everything smelling of Lysol and looking clinical all the time. The huge armchair that I nearly left on the Island as too big, will be perfect for Bea when she feeds both the babies and needs support for both arms."

"And you are happy to have them here?"

"Too happy. I shall hate it when they go to the States."

"So enjoy them while they are here."

"Lunch in fifteen minutes and then you have a patient, I believe. A man to assess? Do you want a neurological examination tray?"

"Lay one but leave it in the clinical room. I think he's just confused and that there's nothing pathologically wrong with him but we'll see. His name is Alun Monteroy, and I'm seeing him as a favour for a friend who is worried about him, but I doubt if he needs me."

"What's his history?"

Paul frowned. "He's a medical student that a colleague asked me to see. He did well at first when everything consisted of learning and lectures about the theory of medicine, but now he is on the wards he is not settling and has fits of what can only be described as rage, which is not his usual style as he is very intelligent and has a good sense of humour. I met him once socially and liked him."

"Is he in real trouble at the hospital? A danger to patients?"

"He's good with patients, Jake said."

"Jake being your friend who sent him to you?"

"Yes, he's a registrar on Vernon's medical firm and he's worried that Monteroy might be thrown out if Vernon gets his way. They seem to be building up to a serious showdown that Jake is afraid might lead to violence if Monteroy doesn't calm down."

"A personality clash?"

"That's quite likely. I've met Vernon and he's an abrasive so-and-so. Good at diagnosis but lacks sensitivity. Personally, I'd hate to work under him." Paul glanced at the notes on the desk. "I'll hear more this afternoon. He's a bit old for starting in medical school."

"He might be ex-service. Remember? The government are giving ex-service officers the chance to take up another career when they are demobbed. I know two who said they wanted to be doctors but never had that chance as the war intervened, but could now do so with the new grant and a priority of opportunity offered to them."

"Can you spare the time to sit in with me?"

Emma looked surprised. "Of course; that's my job. The fact that Bea is here doesn't have to disrupt the whole house and practice."

"So you haven't joined the baby worshippers?"

"I'll leave that to Eileen. She's very eager to baby-sit and do anything to help. I'll tell her that Bea is coming down to lunch and maybe she would like to sit in the nursery to make sure they are not restless after the move to a strange place."

Paul watched her brisk steps as she went to the kitchen. Bea and Emma had done so much together and yet this time, Bea was doing something different and apart. He wondered wistfully if Emma would want the same experience of motherhood now that babies were in the house, and he sighed. For once he felt impatient, as if time was flying and he wanted it to give him a child now, to enjoy while they were young. Immortality was through the family and the continuation of life.

The toad-in-the-hole was almost as good as Aunt Emily's and the fresh salad was crisp and up to even Dwight's high standards. Huge strawberries, soaked in a little gin to enhance the flavour and smelling of summer, made the rather watery ice-cream acceptable as cream, and the companionable laughter added its own sweet sauce to the meal.

"This won't do," Paul said at last. "I have work to do and I'm sure you have a few babies to feed, Bea."

"I shall sit and watch and marvel," Dwight said.

"You can soak the nappies," Bea said with a charming smile.

"Learn to delegate, Honey. You'll never be a successful officer if you don't do that. I have organised Eileen, who is my best buddy from now on, and she soaks the nappies."

"They are so happy," Emma said to Paul, when Bea and Dwight had gone up to the nursery.

"And complete," Paul answered softly. "Come on, lay up that tray for examination. I may need it and he'll be here soon."

Emma put on a clean ochre blouse and a dark green cotton skirt that hugged her hips and looked smart but businesslike, and when she went to answer the doorbell, she was poised and welcoming.

"I'm Emma Sykes, Paul's wife," she said informally, as he had met Paul socially and was a member of his profession. This meant that he was not altogether a strange patient.

"Alun," he said and smiled. "Alun Monteroy. God, what a relief to see a friendly face." He looked apologetic. "I don't know why I'm here," he said.

Emma liked his smile and the firm set to his jaw. His eyes were dark blue and his thick hair dark, as if he was Celtic. Probably Welsh, she thought. Even the name Alun that she had seen on the notes, spelled in that way, was an indication of that, but his voice held no accent apart from being pleasantly cultured. Patients would love you, she thought, quite irrelevantly.

He followed her up to the consulting room. Paul greeted him with mild courtesy and asked him to settle on the couch, the atmosphere immediately professional.

Paul finds it awkward treating someone he's met, however tenuous the link, Emma decided, and sat quietly out of eye contact with the patient.

"We have met just once, Alun," Paul said. "I know nothing about you so let's start where you feel ready to to say something about your life and past."

160

"Nothing much to say about my childhood. A happy family, with ambitious parents who encouraged me but never forced me to succeed. I suppose I was bright at school both as far as sports were concerned and academically, and had no hang-ups there."

"Brothers and sisters?"

"Two brothers older than me who were good friends and good sports. We played together and shared a lot. We never really fought physically, at least not more than siblings do, and never bore grudges." He grinned. "We were never allowed that privilege. Mother insisted that we never let the sun go down on our anger, so we made up before bedtime, which was preferable to having her wrath!"

"Welsh uprisings could have done with your mother," Paul said.

"Yes." Alun laughed. "I suppose it did nip any tendency for violence in the bud."

"And was there any tendency to violence in any of you?"

Alun bit his lip. "Not really violence. We did gang up on a few boys who tried to bully our friends, but we never did them any harm. The threat was usually enough to make them cool down."

"You went into the forces?"

"The RAF."

"You chose that arm of the Services?"

"It's what I wanted to do at the time. I was a fighter pilot."

"Tell me about that."

Emma raised her eyebrows, suddenly knowing why the name was familar. She scribbled a note and handed it to Paul behind Alun's back. '*Famous Ace pilot with a lot of strikes. Wounded once and warded in Surrey but not with my department. The girls went crazy over him.*'

"I shot a lot of planes down," Alun said in a tired voice.

161

"Did it upset you?"

"No, it was exhilarating and I had a lot of kudos from that." He sighed. "We all think the good times will go on for ever, don't we?"

"When did it stop?"

"I caught a packet and was grounded while my leg healed."

"Was the wound bad?"

Alun shrugged. "Boring but not lethal."

"A famous man surrounded by pretty nurses all adoring you, can't be bad?" Paul suggested.

"It was great," Alun admitted. "I had extra special attention and it was really great until one day a new nurse arrived during a slack time and there was nobody to introduce us. To her I was just another patient with an undramatically wounded leg." He still looked as if he couldn't believe it. "She had never heard of me! I couldn't take it in at first. I started my usual spiel about being a wounded warrior needing solace and she accused me of getting fresh with her! I'd come to think it was my due to have the nurses falling over themselves for my attention and I could have had at least four of them, if I'd raised one little finger and beckoned."

"Did one girl matter?"

"No, I could play the field with no effort from me, and that one nurse certainly didn't matter, but when I looked at the other guys in the ward, I suddenly saw some men who were uncouth and coarse, but who pulled the birds easily because they too were famous . . . for killing. The best of that bunch who were my friends, were two other fighter pilots and a bomber pilot who had done a lot of missions deep into Germany. He had a wounded chest, but in addition had battle fatigue in a big way and maybe we all had it to some extent once the adrenalin stopped flowing. We all lapped up the care and flattery at that time and probably needed it."

Emma recalled the boys in bomber jackets and roll-neck

162

sweaters who were the elite of the pilots, sitting exhausted, sprawled over the leather chairs in the Wings Club when she went there with Phillip. He had spoken of them bitterly as the favoured few and envied them, but all that she had seen were tired boys who had been under pressure for too long, with a deep hurt in the backs of their eyes.

"Did that make a difference?" Paul asked.

"I got better and went back to base. I was still proud of my record and still wanted to serve my country but the glamour had gone. It was still good to be praised and greeted with acclaim and I knew I had done my duty and was proud of the fact, but I was not so blind to flatterers any more. When I managed to leave the Air Force as a wing commander with a couple of gongs, I applied to join medical school to learn to heal rather than to kill."

"Did you enjoy medicine?"

"I was fascinated and thought I'd found my niche in life."

"And now?"

"I know I can't do it, but I *don't* need a shrink to tell me. I need to change paths. I can do that alone!" he said defensively. "I know I have an obssession and am potentially violent but I can cope if I leave medicine."

"Then why are you here? Jake must have misread your situation. Do you want to leave now?" Paul's voice was conversational. "Forget the 'shrink' bit. Let's have some tea before you go."

Alun looked startled. "Is that *it*? You don't think I've lost my marbles?"

"No," said Paul.

Emma walked quietly from the room and asked Mick who was in the office for a tray of tea.

"Doing the soft approach before the interrogation?" Mick whispered with a grin. "Coming right up, Sister."

"This is not MI5," she whispered back. "We need biscuits too."

Alun sat on the edge of the couch now, as if the change

163

of position gave him freedom to talk of other things. He smiled at Emma and asked about the work at Beatties. She told him where she had worked and of her love of surgical nursing and the operating theatre.

"So why are you working here?"

"I like it and Paul and I can work together," she said. "We all have to make changes at times, some good, some bad, but I find the first few months of any change, the worst. I was in charge of my own department and thought I was Queen Bee, then left Beatties and did a little private nursing where I had to be very ready to adapt to other methods and restricted conditions, and being dogsbody at times," she added cheerfully.

"Didn't you ever want to hit the people who slighted you?"

"Not the patients," she said firmly. "I was there to help them." She giggled. "There were one or two relatives of patients who tried to put me down, and I had to bite back a few choice words, but I believe in the adage, 'Don't get mad, get even,' and it does work in surprising ways. Have some tea, and these biscuits are quite good."

"How does it work?" He stirred his tea several times and drank a little.

"First it helped me. Losing one's temper is so undignified and seldom has the right effect, although I have lost my temper sometimes and it paid off. I like to keep calm and find a weakness that can be exploited, like snobbery or a lack of humour." She smiled. "I have enough Irish in me to remember every good thing done for me, and every insult."

Alun laughed. "Awkward lot, we Celts."

Emma continued, "If I lost my temper I would know that it would mean the other person had found my Achilles heel and that would be to my disadvantage."

She saw that Paul wanted her to continue. "One woman thought I was after her son who was my patient, and she told me very bluntly to lay off as I wasn't good enough for

164

him. I said very little but then he told her that he had asked me to marry him and I had refused him. Even he couldn't quite believe it, as he had a title, land, everything. She thought that no woman in her right mind would refuse him. It was a lovely moment."

"What if I had to lose my temper or burst? If I hated a man so much that I wanted to kill him?"

"You'd need to think twice about it and walk away. No man is worth that sacrifice," Paul said. "Vanity is bad, but pride is a valuable attribute used well, and have you asked yourself why the other person is aggressive towards you? Could it be jealousy of your war record or your obvious good looks? Many things make a man goad another, to wound him and make him react in a manner that is demeaning."

"Do you know Vernon?" Alun asked bitterly.

"I've met him," Paul said. "Good at his work with arthritis and the more obscure nervous deseases but has a bit of a chip about not being accepted for the RAF."

"He tried to enlist?"

"His sight was not quite good enough."

Alun gave a low whistle. "I thought he'd chosen to keep out of it and looks down on any man who fought! He accused me of poncing about in the sky doing damn all and pulling women in my spare time while the likes of him worked their fingers to the bone patching up the ones at home, who had been bombed by people like me, as if I and not the Germans, had personally bombed Britain!"

Paul laughed. "I expect he told you that you would never make a good doctor and you'd be better off spraying crops in Australia?"

Alun looked stunned. "How did you guess?"

"This is off the record and quite unprofessional of me, but that's what he says to all the ex-pilots he meets. I rang Jake for a little background and he was afraid you'd really do something that you'd regret, like striking Vernon in front of witnesses, as he hands out his insults only when he has an audience to add salt to it."

"Why didn't Jake tell me?"

"I think he tried, but would you have listened?" Paul laughed.

"Besides, he knows I have to practice on someone and we are just setting up the clinic, so you could be a guinea pig."

"That's rubbish and you know it!" Alun glanced at Emma. "I shall pay Emma your fee. She is the one who really helped."

"You needed to stand back and see yourself objectively," Paul said. "There's nothing wrong with you, except for a bit of hurt pride and bloody-mindedness. You will change bosses soon, as they take fresh students on a firm after three months. Try for a surgical team and then you need never see Vernon except from a distance and he will have no power to hurt you."

"Don't get mad, get even," Alun said reflectively.

"That was my wife speaking, not a psychiatrist," Paul said. "I don't like the way your mind is working!"

"I do!" His smile was like Bea's when she was plotting. "Why didn't I remember what my mother did?"

"What was that?"

"My mother used to cool a situation in a peculiar way. How did I come to forget that? She didn't fight but she made the person feel embarrassed by doing something kind for them."

"With a mother like that, you don't need Paul," Emma said. "More tea?" she asked and turned away so that Paul couldn't see her laughing agreement.

"No thanks. She said that some people never forgive a good turn. Eastern countries lose face if they have to accept a favour and are duty bound to pay it back to make it even and be under no obligation."

"So what can you do?" she asked.

"He has a passion for ballet and I have tickets for the

gala at the Angel, Islington. Sadlers Wells are still there, pending the return to Covent Garden and the dancers will include Margot and Helpman and most of the greats. I was given tickets which are as gold to any real balletomane and I know he couldn't get any. I had thought to boast about going, but now, as I'd rather have opera, I can give them to him, in public, and watch the tug between wanting them and hating my guts."

"Heaven save me from more patients like you," Paul said. "I think we have sewn seeds of sedition, not healing today!"

He shook Alun's hand and regarded him soberly. "Don't give up medicine, and make sure you never forget what you have done for the country. That is still important whatever people like Vernon say."

"Can I come back?"

"No, there's no need and you have a lot of work to do if you want to be a good doctor. Make your good and bad experiences work for you and you'll be a valuable member of the profession."

Monteroy eyed Emma cheekily and she saw just how attractive he must have been to the nurses who knew his war record. He could be as attractive even if they knew nothing about him, she thought. "A pity. I like your biscuits," he said.

"I'll see you out," Emma said. At the front door they shook hands and he smiled into her eyes. She pulled away and laughed. "A word of advice. The next time you chat up a girl and really like her, say nothing about your wartime career. If she likes you and I think she might, all that can be told later. Let her judge you on what she sees, an attractive man who is studying hard to be a doctor."

"What a pity you are married," he said lightly.

"I don't think so," she said gently. "Paul and I have a good marriage. Goodbye, Alun."

Chapter Fifteen

"Are you sure?"

"Of course I'm sure, George! You are my son and Clive is my grandson. I'd love to have him here for a while." Janey sounded irritated. "You don't have to apologise, as if it will be an unwelcome imposition. I love babies and I wish I'd been able to give Alex and me what we wanted – a large family."

"I'm sorry. It's just that Sadie doesn't seem keen on motherhood, and I thought that after so many years, you might feel the same and not want squawking infants about the house. She loves the baby but not the endless chores associated with him."

"Has the nurse left?" Janey asked shrewdly.

"Yes. Sadie finds that without her she has to cut down on her visits to friends and the American Museum. She tried to take him to Milsom Street to have coffee and chocolate Mikados in the Cadena, but he yelled so much that she had to bring him home again, which spoiled her morning and made her bad tempered. I can't afford to employ a full time nurse, and I'm much too pigheaded and masculine to allow Sadie to pay for one. What happened to mothers who look after their own children? You never had a nanny for me and I can't imagine how my grandmother ever managed with her brood and the shop."

"I hope you never say that to Sadie," Janey said. "Other peoples' experiences are a red rag to a bull at these times! She has my sympathy. She's young and very pretty and has had everything done for her in the past, in a country that hasn't suffered as we did. She married a handsome Naval officer and had no idea that she would have a baby so soon. She wanted and had every right to expect a good time and a carefree and loving relationship, not interrupted by a baby crying! I hope you do your share, George," she added accusingly. "When have you taken her to a dance lately?"

"I've been very busy," he said defensively. "The days are full of boring paper work. I'm tired and not inclined for dancing at night. I just want to enjoy my home with Sadie and the baby."

"You sound very old, George," his mother said disparagingly.

"I am in line for promotion and then we'll have a Naval steward to help and we shall be able to afford a girl to help with the baby," he said.

Janey clutched the phone but spoke calmly. "Does that mean you expect to be operational again soon?"

There was silence for a long moment, then he said, "I am not cut out for desk work and they want me for a command of a new frigate based in Portsmouth."

"What does Sadie say about it?"

He laughed. "She has this cute idea that a ship in Portsmouth will stay there and hardly get its bottom wet. We'll have lots of parties on the frigate and a full social whirl ashore. She is so innocent," he said tenderly.

"You'll move again?"

"I think so, but to go back to the other matter: Sadie does need a break, or so she says, and if we leave Clive with you for a couple of weeks, we can attend a few functions that she has lined up for us in Bath. I may take a few days off and spoil her."

"You do that," Janey said warmly. "Bring the baby and stay for a weekend and then go back and enjoy yourselves. Tell Sadie I'll want a list of his feeding formulas and anything he needs in the way of teething syrups."

Janey was staring at the cot in the spare room when Alex

169

came home. "Getting broody?" he said with regret. "Too late for us now, so why don't you get rid of that? By the time we have Clive here again, that cot will be too small." He sighed. "If what I think is correct, George will be sent to Inverness or somewhere far away soon, and we shall see very little of them."

"Not Inverness, Alex. He will have a command from Portsmouth which will be better than Scotland for us all, and we are going to be entrusted with the care of our grandson for two whole weeks as soon as they can arrange it!"

He hugged her and delighted in her enraptured expression. "Promise me you won't eat him!" He looked about the room. "I'll bring in another small cupboard and we could put some of the spare rugs in here."

Janey held the cot blankets to her face. They were warm and dry and smelled of lavender and she returned them to the airing cupboard with spare sheets and a light quilt. "I'll make up the cot the day they arrive," she said.

The car horn alerted them and Alex went out to bring in the baggage and a folding baby pushchair. Janey pursed her lips but said nothing. She disliked the new baby buggies from America, with open tops and the baby facing the wind and often low down on the level of car exhausts. She left the deep baby carriage in the garden shed until Sadie had gone and concentrated on making the baby comfortable in the room upstairs.

George had told her on the phone that they would leave the baby, go back at once and not stay for a night or so.

"I have such a lot all lined up for the next week," Sadie said, her eyes sparkling and her face prettily pink and white. "There are a couple of dinners for officers and one to celebrate George's promotion, and a big reception in the Pump Rooms at the Assembly Rooms in Bath."

"Don't drink too much of the spa water," teased Alex.

"I tried it and it's awful!" Sadie said. "I hope that I don't

170

have to taste it ever again. No, this time we are having a ball with everyone dressed as Romans, as the baths are Roman, you know."

"I did know," Alex said, solemnly. "I can't imagine George in a a toga."

Sadie gave a bubbling laugh. "He'll look real cute and I have a white dress with gold bands and we shall all bathe in the King's Bath which is warm all the time from the thermal spring. It will be such fun and quite different! I shall have pictures taken of us in the pool."

Janey waved them off from the drive, with Clive snuggling against her shoulder. She asked Alex to put the baby buggy away in the cupboard under the stairs and to bring out the deep Silver Cross perambulator. It wasn't dusty but she ran a duster over the gleaming coachwork and sighed with contentment. The carriage was deep and the hood kept away draughts but allowed plenty of fresh air. Clive seemed to like it when she wrapped him warmly and pushed the pram into the garden to a sheltered spot where he could look up at the waving branches of a tree, and see the birds come to the bird table.

An almost overwhelming sensation of belonging made Janey gaze down at his smiling face. It was almost a pain. She turned back to the house, trying to tell herself that he was not hers but only on loan and would soon go back to Sadie.

"Looks just like George," Alex said. He saw his wife's trace of sadness. "Cheer up. We have him to ourselves for two weeks and when they come to live in Portsmouth, we shall be closer than we are now they live in Bath. As he grows older, he can stay with us for holidays. It's clear that Sadie will welcome that. At least she isn't the possessive mother I thought she'd be and she is very fond of us," he said, seriously. "We must be careful to keep it like that and not to make him too attached to us," he pointed out. "We are only fostering, not adopting!"

"Dear Alex. What would I do without you?" She hugged

171

him and he pushed back a tendril of her still-bright hair and kissed her. "I'll try not to want him too much," she said.

"Let's eat and then you can be the proud grandmother. I know you'll be dying to show him off in the village, and the old pram is perfect for that, even if it rains."

"Sadie said she'd ring tomorrow evening to see if Clive has settled in and to tell us about the dinner tonight," Janey said. "In many ways she's such a child and her enthusiasm is very attractive. I think that George really is in love with her now and is glad to have found her. Our first impressions weren't fair. She arrived seasick and with morning sickness too! What woman could show her best under those circumstances?"

Alex agreed with everything she said and let her talk, but knew that she was determined to find all that was good in Sadie and ignore the lack of concern that Sadie often showed for others.

"I've closed the door to Clive's little room," Janey said when he was safely tucked up in the cot. "Do you think he'd like a cat or a dog?"

Alex laughed. "He's here for two weeks! A dog is for ever plus dog hairs and mess," he said firmly. "Cats sit on babies and smother them," he said darkly, but she saw his mouth twitch.

"That's an old wives tale, and we could have a cat net on the pram," she said. "George wanted a cat, and long after he was grown up he said he'd envied the other children with pets, but it never seemed the right time to have one while his father was alive, and of course we can't have a cat: you are allergic to them."

"Not to dogs," he said. "But I think you have enough to do now without puppy training as well, and I can't help with that as I have to get back to work or the factory will grind to a halt."

Sadie rang and was bubbling over with all her news. The ball gown that a friend in America had sent, arrived in time and was a sensation, the people they met were charming and the dancing out of this world. "How is Clive?" she wanted to know. "I do miss my darling baby but I know he is in good hands. I think you are wunnerful. I'll ring again in a couple of days time. Here is George."

"Are you sure that Clive isn't too much for you, Mother?"

"Don't be absurd, dear," she replied briskly. "One small baby, who needs food and warmth and a little cuddling can't be too much for any healthy woman, even at my advanced age," she added dryly. "And don't tell me I am wunnerful," she said, laughing. "Have a good time and make sure that Sadie doesn't stay in the water too long even if it is healthy spa water and in a heated bath."

"Sadie should have married a man with pots of money, who could employ a large staff so that Sadie could do as the upper classes did before the war, have her baby brought to her, smelling sweet, for one hour at five o'clock, to make a fuss of him between social engagements, and without soiling her hands. I know she loves the baby, but she seems very happy without him," Alex said.

"She knows we look after him and so she can relax. She'll grow into it," Janey said but her tone was uneasy. "We can fill any gaps and George knows he can depend on us," she said and shivered.

"Goose walking over your grave?" Alex asked lightly. "Not catching Emily's Cassandra qualities, are you?"

She laughed and made up Clive's bottle feed and wondered why she had not heard from Emily for nearly two weeks. Janey had tried to get through twice but the phone was off the hook each time and she'd had no spare time to try again since yesterday.

"Emily?" she asked when someone finally lifted the receiver at Emily's house.

"No, this is Dr Sutton." Emily is in bed and I've insisted that she take a sleeping draught."

"Is she ill?"

"Don't be alarmed. Nothing serious, but she has had a

lot of bad nights. Even allowing for the strong tea and whisky night caps," he added benevolently. "Do you know what's worrying her?"

"I can't think of anything. Since she left work at the British Restaurant she's been fine and she loves working for you. She has no money worries and she always seems healthy, apart from a bit of arthritis."

"I know her well and I think she's on the verge of a crisis of nervous exhaustion and I can't pin down any reason for it. She has something on her mind. I noticed it when we played bridge last week and I beat her. It's become much worse now, but she isn't losing her mind, so never think that. She can still put me in my place."

"Let me know if you need help," Janey said. "I'll ring your surgery tonorrow so that Emily isn't disturbed by phone calls. I tried to get through several times but the phone was always engaged or off the hook."

"She'll sleep now and a good night's rest might sort out her nervousness. Don't worry. She's a dear friend and I shall make sure she gets well again, but I wish she'd confide in me about what's troubling her." He chuckled. "She'll hate being waited on and that might make her well again very quickly, but she'll have to put up with my housekeeper cooking for her for a while!"

"If she allows that for more than a few days then I shall be really worried," Janey said.

She went slowly into the garden where Alex was tying up and staking loose rose bushes after the rain. "Something wrong?" he asked.

"I hope not, apart from Emily being under the weather and having her pet doctor dancing attendance. He said that she has something on her mind that prevents her from sleeping and she shows signs of nervous collapse."

"That's not like Emily." He put the secateurs down and gave her his full attention. "If she's worried, it isn't about Emily Darwen!" he said firmly. "Emma isn't ill? I know we are well and Emma is the closest to Emily. Get on

174

the telephone and ask Emma if she knows anything." He smiled. "Perhaps Emma is expecting?"

"That wouldn't give Emily the wobblies."

"Mrs Barnes on the phone," Mick said and put down the groceries that had been delivered to his flat by mistake.

"Thanks Mick. They could have waited until tomorrow," Emma said. "Leave them there and I'll put them away. Go now! Eileen said that you are taking her to the pictures."

Emma rushed to the phone. "Aunt Janey? How lovely to hear from you. Are you busy baby-sitting, yet?"

"I wanted a chat about Emily," Janey said, knowing that Emma would worry if she wandered round the subject and made it seem worse than it was.

"Is she ill?"

"Not really ill but Dr Sutton says she has nervous exhaustion. He has given her a sleeping draught for tonight and insists that his housekeeper cooks for her. It's part of the shock treatment! You know that woman can't make pastry!"

"Do you think it's serious?"

"Have you noticed that as she gets older, Emily is becoming more fey? When we were children it wasn't really apparent, but it developed later, almost like old Mrs Lee the gypsy that your grandmother had in the shop and who gave her a lot of teacup readings and advice."

"You think she's had a premonition?"

"I'm relieved that you are both all right," Janey said.

"I can't think who would be in danger," Emma said slowly.

"Are you still there?"

"I was trying to recall what she said when George was about to bring Sadie to meet us all on the Island. Paul and I laughed afterwards as she said another pregnant woman would be coming to the house and of course, Sadie was in the throes of morning sickness and Emily had the sour lemons lined up ready for her in advance!"

"Was that all she said?"

Emma took a deep breath. "Aunt Emily muttered something about seeing a death, but she hoped it wouldn't happen and she was probably wrong. She refused to say more and never referred to it again so I forgot it, too."

"If George was at sea, I'd be really worried, but he is safe and we are at peace now. He promised not to go into submarines like his father did and he has been promoted to take command of a frigate. He is with Sadie in Bath, celebrating, and I have Clive for two whole weeks."

"I'm glad you rang," Emma said. "I think that her premonitions may get out of hand occasionally. Some of the things she predicts never come true."

"Not many," Janey said wryly. "Let's hope this is just a reaction to losing all of us in such a short time after we'd had such a good time together, and she's becoming fanciful, alone in that house."

"You don't believe that for one moment."

"No."

"Neither do I. I'll ring tomorrow after you get in touch with her doctor and I'll tell Paul about it. He may have a perfectly simple answer."

"People's minds are devious enough without the addition of Aunt Emily's mental crystal ball," Paul said when she recounted the phone call. "If she needs sedation, then something is worrying her in a big way. Has she many old friends who are ill and likely to die? Her generation are tough but not immortal," he said.

"There's nothing recently. It was all long ago, but after losing her mother and her fiancé, the two most important people in her life, surely nothing could affect her like this now, and she is so down to earth about birth and death as a rule," Emma observed, but she was worried.

Janey went in to see Clive at least six times during

the night, half-expecting to find him gasping for breath or worse. At dawn, Alex insisted that she stayed in bed while he mixed the early feed and brought Clive to his wife in bed.

"Just look at him," he said. "As healthy as any baby I've ever seen. Whatever Emily sees, it has nothing to do with Clive."

Each time that George or Sadie rang to check that Clive was well and that Janey wasn't exhausted by one small baby, Janey gave a sigh of relief and felt oddly deflated, as if she was worrying without cause, but she didn't manage to speak to Emily.

"I'm keeping her under sedation," Dr Sutton said. "Paul gave me a lot of good advice as I have very little knowledge of neurology and he says that she may recover fast if we give her time to block out this sense of dread."

"You don't think that she is physically ill?" asked Emma. "She could be forecasting her own illness or worse."

"That wouldn't cause these symptoms. Emily will accept death as a part of life and she is as healthy as any woman of her age I've seen. This must be personal as she wasn't as upset about any of the wartime tragedies, even the atom bomb."

Janey forced herself to wait until the phone had rung four times before she snatched up the receiver. She relaxed when she heard Sadie's excited voice. "We went to the Assembly Rooms last night and had the most fabulous time. I wore my Roman gown and George looked so *handsome* as a Roman senator with laurel leaves and all!"

"Tell me about it," Janey said. It was safer to listen and not to show her true emotions, but she was increasingly sure that Emily was thinking of George or Sadie. If it was further away, still sad, but impersonal, she would have confided in her favourite sister.

"George wouldn't go in the King's Bath as he said it smelled of minerals, but he watched us splashing about

177

in it and the water was wunnerful. I got my second taste of spa water when someone splashed me. It was no better than the first and probably a lot dirtier!" She giggled. "We had showers after the swim. They could do with a more modern shower room but I went to the ball clean and sparkling, as George said. My hair was dry as I had the darlingest rubber cap covered with pink flowers, and a new white Bukta swimming costume. Someone said I looked like a lovely waterlily! Wasn't that sweet?"

Janey listened with growing relief and spoke to George just to hear his voice.

"Hi, Mother," he said. "How is my son? Sadie was so full of herself she forgot to ask."

"She knows he's well, and she wanted to tell me about the ball. She sounded so happy just to have time with you alone, George. I think you are a lucky man. She is so in love with you."

"That's generous for a mother who dotes on her only son," he said lightly. "But thanks. We had a wonderful evening. I shall always remember Sadie floating in that pool with an absurd bunch of flowers for a cap and her slim white swim suit. Even the statues above the bath seemed impressed!"

Janey heard Sadie giggling and knew she was listening to all that her husband said, then heard her say, "I think I'll lie down, Honey. I have such a headache. It came on just now, quite suddenly."

"George?" Janey said.

"I'll ring tomorrow," he said, and the phone was silent.

Janey wiped her hand on her skirt, aware that it was damp. Everyone had headaches and Sadie was good at making sure that George paid her his full attention, so there really was nothing there to worry anyone.

Chapter Sixteen

Alex found Janey in the nursery and knew she hadn't heard the telephone. He had waited for almost ten minutes before going to her and now as he watched his wife with the baby, he was full of mixed emotions.

He waited until she had put Clive back into the cot and twitched the curtains to shield him from the slanting rays of the sun through the window and he suggested that they had some tea.

"What a good idea. I've been busy getting all his clothes clean to be ready when they collect him," Janey said. "It seems such a short time to have him here, but I suppose they want him back? He settled in so quickly," she remarked wistfully.

"I'll make the tea," he said.

"I'm not tired," Janey protested. "You haven't read the paper yet." She went to the kitchen, humming to herself, and brought in the tea tray and some cakes. She handed a cup of tea to Alex then looked at him more closely. "What's wrong?" she asked quietly.

"Sadie has been taken very ill," he said.

"How ill?" She put a hand to her stomach as if it was becoming tied into knots.

"Ill enough to make it impossible for George to take Clive home for a while."

"She'll need me to look after her," Janey said at once. She smoothed back her hair as if preparing to leave at any moment. "I can take Clive with me and care for them in their own home."

Alex shook his head. "Clive mustn't go there. They think it could be infectious, so you must stay here. In any case, she is in hospital in Bath."

"Do they know what it is? When she phoned after the Roman evening, she was so full of . . . life . . ." Her voice trailed away.

"She's on the danger list," Alex said. "They suspect a very acute form of meningitis."

"She complained of a bad headache the evening after the ball," Janey said.

"George said that she had a very stiff neck and has a high temperature and the doctors are doing a lumbar puncture today."

"It's curable now, isn't it? They have new drugs for that kind of fever?"

"I don't know. Paul could tell us a lot more. I'll ring them soon, after George has talked to them."

"Poor Paul," Janey said. "If it's as bad as it sounds, he will have to tell George the truth. That part of medicine and nursing would really finish me."

"They give good news, too," he reminded her.

She burst into tears. "I feel so mixed up Alex, and very guilty. Do you know, after the first impact of the news, I had a warm feeling and thought that we can keep Clive for a long time now."

"I felt the same," he admitted, putting a comforting arm round her. "It's not wicked. Just think that he is lucky to have loving grandparents who care enough about him to want him here, and George can feel free to be with Sadie as much as they will allow him to be. When she is over this, she can come here as well as Clive and you can have a wonderful time being rushed off your feet looking after them," he said.

"What do you mean? To be with her as much as they allow him to be. He can hold her hand and be there, can't he?"

"She is in an isolation block where everyone wears

180

protective clothing until they can say what the bug really is."

"Poor Sadie. She loves physical contact, and she loves George," Janey said. "She'll be so lonely surrounded by people she doesn't know, all wearing caps and masks and hardly speaking to her. She is still very young, Alex."

"I'll ring Dr Sutton," Alex said. "He can break the news to Emily. Perhaps this will settle her mind about whatever was making her miserable, now that this has happened. There will be one less person troubled by this if she knows the worst."

"Wait," Janey said, and Alex reached over to hold her cold hand. "Sadie is going to die," she said quietly. "That's what Emily saw; death, not illness."

"She may have been mistaken," he said weakly. "But maybe it would be wise to wait until we hear the result of the lumbar puncture in case there is more news."

Janey was weeping, tears on her cheeks and heaving long hopeless sobs, and Alex felt as helpless as he had done when her first husband, his fellow officer and closest friend, had died under the waves in a dark slug of a submarine, and knowing now that he loved her as he had done then, above all others.

While she washed the cups and saucers, insisting that she needed things to do, he quietly rang Paul and told him the news.

"Thank you," he said at last when Paul offered to get in touch with the hospital and then telephone Dr Sutton. "I am a coward. I hated the thought of telling Emily. Please let us know if the hospital says there is any chance of improvement in her condition. Janey is very depressed about it and can't stop crying."

"At least she has her hands full with the baby," Paul said. "If it's anything like it is here with the twins, there is a lot to do."

The day seemed very long and grey and Janey went about her work in a daze. Even Clive sensed the fraught

181

atmosphere and grizzled as if he had colic, but it gave Janey the excuse to hold him and pace the floor to soothe his cries until he went to sleep. She smiled wryly, wondering if she was giving comfort to the baby or he to her.

Cautiously, as if she half-wanted the number to be unobtainable, Janey rang Emily, but as before, the instrument was engaged or off the rest. "Leave it to Paul," Alex said. "Get some rest before the night feed. Clive is the important factor here, and we need to keep well to look after him, sweetheart."

By midnight the baby was fed and asleep, the house quiet and Janey was settling into a deep exhausted sleep. Alex crept down to the study and closed the door. He mixed a whisky and soda and switched on the electric fire.

At two, the telephone rang only twice before Alex had it in his hand. "Dad? Thank God you answered." George's voice was so controlled and brittle that Alex thought it might snap at any moment.

"Your mother is worn out with worry and she's asleep but I thought I'd keep a kind of vigil."

"Thanks." George gulped and then his voice was gruff. "Leave her until morning. Sadie died an hour ago. It was a virulent bug and she had no chance. At the end, she was unconscious, so she didn't suffer for very long. It was all so quick." His voice broke. "They made me stay on the other side of a glass screen. I watched her die and couldn't hold her. I don't know what to do, Dad."

"Your mother must stay with Clive but I'll come to Bath tomorrow to help with the formalities, then you must come back here to sort out your future."

"What future?"

"You have a fine career and a son." Alex sounded warm and friendly. "I have you so I know that sons are a good idea," he said. "They grow on one after a while. Get some rest and I'll be there tomorrow. I'll tell Janey in the morning and she will stay here and leave it all to me," he said firmly.

"Thanks. What would I do without you?"

"You'd manage," Alex said dryly. "But I'm glad you need me. Clive is better off away from it all just now so I'll tell Janey to stay with him and get ready for you to come here." He stopped to think for moment. "Is this the first call you made?"

"Yes."

"I'll ring Paul and Dr Sutton and act as liaison if you let me know details."

"That's a load off my mind. I don't think I could speak to Paul or Emma just now."

"Get some rest, son. I'll be with you as soon as I can tomorrow."

Alex went softly to the bedroom where Janey was gently blowing bubbles in her sleep. He slipped between the sheets and to his surprise felt relaxed. After only a few minutes, he fell asleep. He woke at seven, aware that the baby was mewing softly in the next room and Janey was still asleep. Silently, he made the feed and turned on the fire in the nursery. The shawl that Sadie's American friend had made for the baby was soft and enveloping and very comfortable as he wrapped the baby in it. Alex wondered if many people in the States would be sad at Sadie's passing and his throat tightened with grief for the girl who his family had known for such a short while and who had not really sampled life to the full, only nibbled hungrily at its edges. She hadn't had time to make friendships on this side of the Atlantic, he thought.

He fed the baby and tried to find traces of Sadie in the tiny face, but it was almost as if her dying had erased everything. A tiny George looked up at him and smiled, then burped loudly.

Janey put a cup of tea by his side. "I heard the kettle boil for the feed. You look like a contented father and son," she said.

"Almost that," he said. "Bring your tea in here and sit down."

He rubbed the small back and rocked the baby tenderly, his heart full of a mixture of deep sadness and a growing joy.

"Has it happened?" Janey asked.

"Yes, George telephoned at two. Sadie died at one," he said simply. "She was in a coma at the last, so she didn't suffer. I said I'd go there today to help George with the formalities and you must stay here with Clive," he said firmly.

Janey sat dry-eyed and stared at the baby. "We'll get a nice girl to live in," she said. "George will need time to think."

"As we did when his father died," Alex said gently. "It's as if the generations are being mixed up and we have another George to look after."

"You will be in touch with Paul and Dr Sutton?"

"Yes, I told George that I would, and Dr Sutton can tell Emily."

"I wonder how she feels today? She must be told as soon as possible. Not knowing can be worse than the real facts," Janey said. "Someone will be awake in London as Bea's babies will be fed about now." She took the baby and Alex went down to the study took a deep breath and dialled.

"I expected to hear from George and didn't want Emma to answer the phone," Paul said. "When did it happen? I knew it was inevitable. They've talked of banning bathing in the Roman bath for a long time but found no bad organisms, even though a lot of people thought that the silt at the bottom was suspect and wanted it closed. But now they will have to look into the problem again, and more closely."

"I'm doing all the communicating now, so I'll let you know what is happening," Alex said, and sensed Paul's relief.

"I'll come to the funeral and I think Dwight will come

184

with me, but the two girls are best left here with Bea's babies," Paul said.

"I agree that Emma is best out of this," Alex said. "She's too warm-hearted, and one sympathetic smile could stir up a load of trouble for George. He will be very vulnerable just now."

"I'm glad you agree. Emma has no idea what could happen if he meets her now. I like George, and if he needs us later, we are here to help in any way we can, but I think that you and Aunt Janey are better suited to cope with him and his immediate problems."

Dr Sutton was as unsurprised as Paul had been. "I'll go at once and tell Emily," he said. "But I expect she knows already! If I can persuade her to ring her sister, it will be good for her. I think she was quite fond of that poor girl and hated to think of what might happen and not be able to do anything about it. Women's instinct or something more? The older I get, the more complex the human body and mind becomes."

"Tell her to put the phone back so that Janey can be in touch," Alex said.

"I wonder if Emma could be spared for a day or so? Emily would respond to her more than to any other person and it would be the tonic she needs, just to see her. She might be able to make her eat. I'm sure that everything my housekeeper sent over was put in the pig bin. A diet of strong tea, whisky and biscuits isn't enough to keep a sparrow alive. I won't mention it to Emily until Emma is on her way, but let me know if she can come and I'll make sure someone meets her from the ferry."

Alex telephoned Emma and told her what the doctor had suggested.

"I was considering that," she admitted. "I didn't want to push in if she didn't want company, but if Dr Sutton says I should go, I can get a train tomorrow. Paul isn't too busy just now and Mick can see to the office and clients." She asked if Janey was feeling better and for

185

details about the funeral so that Paul could attend it to represent the family with Alex, and Dwight wanted to be there as a fellow American who was a family connection by marriage.

"George says that there will be no funeral here." Alex cleared his throat. "He told me that when she knew she was very ill, she made him promise that as soon as she was better, he would take her home to America. I said that it was too late now, but he said she would want to be buried in her own country. I mentioned that transport might be difficult but he insists that even if she couldn't go back alive, at least he can see that she is buried among her family and friends."

"Have you George's telephone number?" she asked.

"You aren't thinking of talking to him?" Alex sounded serious.

"No. I am not a fool, Alex. I know he is in a state now and I might make it worse, but when he's out of this awful time, he will not need me. He loved Sadie and she will always be his wife and the mother of his son. I want to tell Dwight about the funeral. He will get in touch with George to sort it out. If he can pull a few strings to arrange transport, he will, and George can go with her and settle her affairs over there."

"You were a long time talking," Janey said when Alex found her in the nursery, putting clean sheets in the cot after settling Clive in the pram under the porch.

He told her about the conversations and mentioned that Emma would be going to the Island and would get in touch as soon as she saw how Emily was progressing.

"I wish I could see her, but it will be better once I can talk on the phone. Whatever did we do before we had telephones?"

Emma packed a small case, and early the next day, Mick drove her to the station to catch a train to Portsmouth. She found a carriage that had no more than twenty cigarette ends on the floor and sat in a corner seat with the window open. It was bad enough feeling sad and wondering what she would see when she met Emily, and the dusty carriage did nothing to diminish her mood. The old velour upholstery was stained and the floor dirty and the smell was of old socks and Service uniforms and the remembered misery of war.

Dr Sutton's gardener met her, drove her from the ferry and asked where she wanted to go. "Straight to Miss Darwen," she said. "I won't bother to go to my cottage just now."

"I took some things from the doctor earlier and told her you were on yur way," the man said. "He thought you could do a bit of cooking for her."

Emma walked slowly up the driveway and saw that there was, as usual, smoke from the chimneys. She smiled. Fire was comfort for Emily and had been for her family for years. Even now that she needed no fire for cooking, as she had a modern gas stove, Emily had a fire in the sitting room.

"Anyone at home?" Emma called.

Emily Darwen came out of the sitting room, and for a long moment allowed Emma to embrace her, then pushed her away. "Nice to see you but you shouldn't have bothered," she said. "Be a good girl and put the kettle on."

She seemed unsteady and Emma saw with a pang of anxiety that she had lost weight. She made tea and Emily sat sipping it with her feet on the brass fender while Emma told her about the truth of Sadie's death.

"I saw it," Emily said. "And her no more than a child."

"Are you feeling better?" Emma ventured.

Emily turned towards her. "I knew when she died. It was like a boil bursting and the anguish of it flowing away. I hadn't eaten for days and the stuff that the old housekeeper at the doctor's made for me I put out for the birds. It was

187

kindly meant but heavy and had no flavour. I wonder he puts up with her."

"Have you eaten today?"

"I had some bread and jam. When I knew she was dead, I felt hungry and heated milk and butter and sugar and made myself some nice bread and milk like my mother used to make years ago when we were ill."

"Something smells nice," Emma said.

"He sent over some pork chops and they are in the oven with onions and apples and turnips. I fancy a bit myself now, so lay the table and we'll have some in about ten minutes when the potatoes are ready. You'll sleep here tonight?"

"Yes, it's not worth lighting fires in the cottage as I shall have to go back the day after tomorrow," Emma said.

"I ought to do some shopping," Emily said when she'd eaten her lunch and was making more tea.

"Good. If you don't need a nap, I'll see if the car starts and we can drive up to Carisbrooke and through Gunville, down Forest road and Hunney Hill to Newport for the shops, and come back home before the light goes."

Emma noticed that after good food, Emily had more colour and was brisker in her movements, and made no objections to the ride.

"I'm glad I came," Emma said. "We were worried about you, and to be honest, it's good to be away when they make arrangements for the burial. George will go with the coffin and I think Dwight will organise an American transport plane to take them to America as Sadie was an American citizen and George is a serving British Naval officer."

"I can forget it now it's happened and over," Emily said. "I'd like to buy some Westmore's buns and doughnuts if they still do them in the shop in the market square. They are the only shop-bought cakes I eat. The buns are nice when they are fresh but get stale the next day and have to be toasted.

Emma glanced at her, amused by the sudden interest in

food. "I like their lardy cakes," she said. "We can buy a mixture."

The autumn sunlight was soft and the hedges had a coating of traveller's joy on the dank leaves and leftover berries, beaded with mist. Every season here is a traveller's joy, she mused, and was glad to be at home again.

"That little nipper will take a bit of Janey's time," Emily said. "Is she up to it? Looks as if she has him for life now."

"George will pay for a girl to live in, and Janey can enjoy the baby and not have to do all the work," Emma said. She looked sideways to see what Emily's face showed. "She needs to see you and hopes you will go over there soon."

"I might, just as soon as I have my legs again," Emily said.

"I could take you to Yarmouth for the ferry and we can ask Alex to have you met at Lymington," Emma suggested.

"I could manage that. I feel stronger after that nice chop. I was silly to stop eating." She looked embarrassed. "It won't happen again."

"Promise?"

"I promise. I'll eat up my greens even when you have a baby," Emily said with a return to her old acid humour.

"You'll grow fat before then," Emma assured her with a laugh.

She left Emily by the shops in the market square and didn't lock the car in case she wanted to sit in it.

The small town was bustling and had a lot more clothes in the shops that Emma had seen for years, even if they were still utility garments with the familiar logo inside. The so-called wool in the skirts and jackets was harsh and mixed with other fibres and was what the Yorkshire mills turned out as shoddy.

Fabrics were still available only on clothing coupons

and Emma's supply of Swiss cottons and pieces of silk from parachutes was dwindling, but she needed sewing threads and hat elastic, so she went to Dabells in the High Street and lingered there, hoping to find material to match or contrast with a short length that could be made into a jacket if faced with another piece of fabric.

Emily was sitting in the car when she returned, holding court with three old friends who had been buying doughnuts and passing on family news. She looked more animated and Emma backed away for another fifteen minutes and strolled round St Thomas's Square, past the old inn on the corner and the rooms where she had learned to ballroom dance as a child. The Medina Cinema was showing 'All Quiet on the Western Front' again, and she tried not to look at the swinging cardboard cut-outs of German helmets advertising the film. Did nothing change? The war that the film portrayed was the First World War, and the previous generation had all believed it was the war to end all war.

Emily chuckled. "It was quite nice sitting here. I had a chat with a nice few people and it was like old times before I worked at the restaurant. I'll be able to have more time now to visit people and hear all the gossip."

"So what wicked things did you hear about today?" Emma asked as she started the engine.

"I must ring Janey and tell her that Miss Dyer from the chapel had a baby! Janey will remember her. I thought she was past all that but the baby came a few weeks ago and she had it adopted straight away. The doctor took it and said she'd better forget about it if she wanted it to have a good home, and that was that. Gone a day after it was born, and the doctor is the the only one who knows where, apart from the registrar of births. Miss Dyer is back at work in the saddlers and all the old biddies at the chapel are wetting themselves trying to find out who the father was."

"Aren't you curious?"

"I could make a guess. They should look no further than

190

their own choir. I don't believe in Virgin births as Miss Dyer insists it was."

"Let's get back before the mist comes down. I can make poached eggs on mashed potato for supper," Emma said. "And of course, buns and lardy cakes."

Death and birth and even a touch of humour, discussed all on one day, Emma thought as they drove back along the darkening road. Emily could cope now and was looking forward to visiting Janey.

Chapter Seventeen

Emma waved goodbye as the Yarmouth ferry left the jetty, feeling relieved that Aunt Emily had gone to see her sister with every sign of pleasure, unlike her usual attitude when faced with travelling more than five miles. She would be met from the ferry and Emma smiled when she imagined the gossip that would accompany many cups of strong tea that evening.

She turned her mind to her own affairs. I've had the easy part, she thought. I had only one stubborn aunt to sort out!

The wind had risen in the night, tearing the last of the leaves from the trees and then it had subsided as if unwilling to make the crossing to the mainland rough for Emily Darwen, but more autumn gales were imminent. The Yarmouth lifeboat had been out twice on the previous day and as always, was ready for whatever the weather flung over the sea.

The way back to the house was quiet and the roads nearly empty, a contrast to wartime when troops moved about in trucks all over the Island, to and from Albany Barracks at Parkhurst and to the ferries for Portsmouth and Lymington. The harbour at Yarmouth smelled of seaweed and fish as she remembered it. I could smell this and know where I was even if blindfolded, she thought. It had a different smell from Ryde and Sandown and even Cowes, which came closer, possibly as that too had a deep water harbour.

She checked that all the windows were closed in

Emily's house when she returned, banked up the fire with coke and ash to keep the room warm for at least another day and picked up her bag. She made sure that the house was locked and put the car into the garage which was then locked too. A note on the garage door would alert Wilf, who had a key, to make up the fire again each day to keep the house warm for Miss Darwen's return.

Emma walked along to Shide station and caught the train to Newport and on to Ryde Pier Head and the ferry to Portsmouth.

It was late afternoon when she arrived in London and wandered out of Victoria Station, hoping that a convenient bus would take her to Kensington. Paul knew that she would arrive about now, but she had little hope of being met, until she saw Mick waving his arms as if signalling in semaphore and beckoning. Thankfully, she sank into the car.

"You OK, Sister?" Mick said.

"Fine, but very glad to have been met at the station."

"Doc said you might arrive on this one and so I took a chance. Have a nice time did you? What's it like down there? I'll have to take Eileen there one day. She's always on about the seaside but I can't take more than half a day there. All that water! And I had enough sand when we were in Tripoli."

"The sea is still wet and blue, except when it rains and it turns grey and rough, but at all times the views are wonderful. Even if there is a mist, we know the views are there, and that's what matters," she said.

"Busy up at the house," he said laconically.

"Is everything all right?" she asked anxiously, and found rather guiltily that she had pushed the day to day happenings of the house in London to the back of her mind while she was on the Island.

"I guess so, but there's been a bit of what my old officer used to call 'orderly chaos' without you, and you've only been away three days. Mrs Miller is blooming and Eileen

193

is besotted with the babies, but your cousin turned up yesterday as he had to see someone in the MOD and the Admiralty about compassionate leave. He looked like death warmed up," Mick added cheerfully.

"George came to the house?"

"Mr Miller brought him as they are going to the States together, with the body."

"I see."

"You missed him by a whisker, but he didn't seem as if you'd find him good company."

"Poor George. When do they leave?"

"They've gone. They're up there somewhere now, in an American transport plane. The American arranged everything. I must say he strikes me as more efficient than I gave the Yanks credit for, but with his rank he can pull anything."

"I didn't know that Dwight would go with George," Emma said. "I feel as if I have been away for weeks!"

"Well, you are back now," Mick said as he drove in by the front portico. "I'll bring your bag and Eileen will have laid on something for the hungry traveller."

"Thanks Mick. You are a gem."

Emma found Paul with a male patient so she merely let him know she was there and went up to Bea's apartment.

"My husband has left me," Bea said dramatically.

"Not before time," Emma said.

"It's time you came back, away from that place. I can hear a hint of Emily Darwen acerbity! Dwight is flying over with George and to make it offical both of them are in uniform, doing things for the State. George being on compassionate leave, gave it an edge, or that's how they managed to wangle it."

"It seems strange to have a death with no funeral here. I've heard of people losing relatives in some way where a funeral is impossible, like a drowning or a missing person with no known grave, and they say that they can't get rid of their grief and sense of loss unless they have a service and interment to show that the person is really dead and has gone for ever."

"I had patients like that who had lost relatives in the Holocaust," Bea agreed. "They grieved because they couldn't say goodbye. I had very little to do with Sadie and I can't say I liked her, but I do feel restless as if we really can't dismiss her from our minds until she has been decently buried in a decent way."

"Let's hope that her funeral in America sets George's mind at rest."

"You almost met him," Bea said, with a shrewd sideways look.

"So Mick told me," Emma replied calmly.

"Just as well you were away. He had a hungry look about him and needed the soft bosom of sympathy."

"You exaggerate," Emma said.

"Talking of soft bosoms, mine are hard and there are two greedy mouths waiting to latch on to them. Help me as the babes are getting so heavy. I must start mixed feeding."

"They are growing so fast, Bea."

"I know. They can sit up in the pram now with pillows. I try to make them lie down and look like real babies when Dwight is here." She looked guilty. "If I'm honest, I would admit that they could have gone on the bottle and mixed feeding a month ago, but while I feed them they are still babies and much too young for our move to the States."

"I don't think you fool Dwight any more than you fool me. He will let you stay for a while but you really must get your packing organised. While Dwight is still in the Services, he can pull rank and get a plane to take whatever you need over the pond, and I have a feeling that this trip with George isn't just charity, to help a fellow officer in trouble, but a trial run for the big move."

"I know," Bea said in a small voice. "Remember the General, Dwight's godfather?"

"Is he still in Britain?"

"Off and on and he wants to visit us before we have to say goodbye to dear old England. He didn't actually say we shall fly off into the sunset, but it was all there!"

"And Dwight? He did talk of leaving the American Air Force and becoming a partner on his family ranch."

"I think he'll discuss his demob in Washington on this trip, and arrange our transport for everything we possess here. He told me that it's been suggested that he stays on the general staff at the White House for a while, be debriefed and hang up his cap. He will then put on leather chaps and I shall have to climb into my covered waggon!"

"I think all covered waggons have air-conditioning now," Emma remarked dryly. "You will be going to the country of plenty and the fleshpots, and a session in Washington with Dwight as a VIP can't be bad."

"I hate you, Dewar. I shall be as miserable as sin and I don't want jollying out of it."

"Poor Dwight and Paul, with two miseries to live with when they come home!"

"I wish you'd never seen this house. It's far too good and I can see you living here for years," Bea said unhappily. "My roots are fast becoming locked in here too. I like having Harrods close by and the park is wonderful for the babies and I shall hate going away."

"It will be a while yet," Emma said optimistically. "Enjoy what you have here. It's getting dark now and too late to take them out, but if it's fine in the morning we can walk over the park with the infants and see Peter Pan."

"Don't give me mental teddy bears, Dewar! But I agree. I want to see him and ask his advice as Aunt Emily isn't here. How is the Witch of Wight?"

"Recovered and sees nothing bad for us. She is determined that her visions of Sadie are to be the last, but how she thinks she will avoid her fey gift eludes me."

"I will take her with us," Bea asserted. "Kidnap her if necessary."

"She's *my* aunt," Emma said proudly. "She stays here

where she can enjoy her tea and whisky at night. Coffee and Bourbon wouldn't be the same."

Bea stole one of the sardine sandwiches that Eileen had prepared for Emma and brought to the nursery. "If I can't take Aunt Emily, then I shall dangle huge sums of money in front of Mick and Eileen and they'll come with us."

"Not a chance," Paul said from the doorway. "I thought I'd find you plotting here." He kissed Emma. "Good to have you back. Bea has been intolerable," he said, grinning.

"It wasn't me," she said. "There was an awful lot of movement here with Dwight packing to leave and a visitation from George."

"See what I mean? The minute you had gone, it all happened."

"Mick said that George looked, as he put it so poetically, like death warmed up."

"I gave him a sedative for the flight," Paul said. "I doubt if he realised that travelling in the same confined space with the dear departed can be a great strain, even if the coffin isn't in the same cabin!"

"When we go, Dwight can arrange to send the baggage separately and I shall take the twins in first class accommodation in a real air liner. I have terrible memories of a flight we made during the war with a lot of air crew being sent on leave, but they gave us a nice set of toilet facilities behind a curtain."

"Very down to earth," Emma agreed.

"You are admitting that you might leave England?" Paul asked, half-seriously.

"Yes." For a moment, Bea looked as if she might weep, then patted Johnnie on the back rather energetically and went behind the screen to change his nappy. "I shall take everything with me, including the four-poster bed," she said. "I wonder who could carve a coat of arms on it to really impress the natives."

"Take the bed and whatever you have in your room that

197

has become homely," Paul said. "We won't even count the silver when you've gone."

"Thanks, Paul," she said huskily. "That's you done," she told the twins. "Sleep well and please don't start teething tonight."

"No night feed?" asked Emma.

"I shall give it late and maybe have some peace in the morning if their built-in clocks don't give the game away, and tomorrow, I shall see my gynae man and ask for something to dry the milk, as it will have to be bottles from now on." She regarded her full breasts with interest. "I hope I don't go flat-chested after this. Dwight loves me as I am, even if they do feel like a pair of balloons at times."

Emma tidied the consulting room and threw out the dead flowers in the hall, leaving everything ready for the next day. Coming home was just that now, a coming home. She turned on the wireless in the kitchen while she prepared an evening meal and the soporific strains of the Palm Court Orchestra made a soft background.

The Island seemed a long way away now, although the journey from Ryde to London had taken a shorter time than it had in wartime. As I know I can go there at any time and have a cottage waiting for us, the length of time between visits isn't important, she decided. If Bea goes, will she find the gap widening too fast and forget her life here completely or will she think as I do about the Island, that she can come back at any time, and not feel cut off?

"There's a concert at the Albert Hall tomorrow," Bea said, bringing in the *Evening News*. "Dwight is a Philistine and hates classical music, but I want to wallow in Mahler, and before I go to the States I must top up my collection of records."

"I'll take both of you," Paul offered.

"I can feed the babes before we go and again late at night after the concert, and lovely Eileen will baby-sit."

Bea smiled happily. "We'll have a good evening to make up for the misery we've witnessed lately."

"Mahler's 'Song of the Earth'? You call that cheerful?" asked Paul, raising a sardonic eyebrow.

"I shall cry buckets when they sing the ending," she said. "A good cry is very satisfying if it means nothing personal."

"So tomorrow, you see about the drying up process." Emma looked at Paul. "Can you manage without me in the clinic? I'd better go with her or she'll do too much and buy up half of Bond Street."

"Even though you've only just come back, please do take the day off," he said generously. "I have only two sessions; one with a new patient and Eileen can chaperone me with her. The other is the ex-fighter pilot you met."

"The medical student with a chip on his shoulder about his sudden lack of charisma?" Emma was surprised. "I thought he'd sorted himself out. Why come here again?"

Paul shrugged. "He either wants to beat me up for giving him the wrong ideas or has a desire to talk about how well he feels now. It happens. A lot of people need to recount the good results as well as the failures." He grinned. "If he takes up my professional time for just a chat, he pays the fees!"

"Reduced for fellow medics?"

"Of course, and if he came to the hospital, it would be free."

"Give him my regards," Emma said. "We could invite him over socially one evening."

"I'll do no such thing! He took a real shine to you the last time he was here, and I can't have my patients having fixations about my wife. Eileen will sit in on the session and do nothing to stir his baser instincts."

Bea giggled. "You have to watch her, Paul. I had the bad reputation of being Beattie's prize flirt, but that calm I-am-lovely-but-you-mustn't-touch appearance, is devastating. It's still there even now she's an old married woman like me."

"Idiot!" Emma said and blushed. "You can't talk, Paul! What about Mrs Molton? She was hot on your heels and if I hadn't been there, she'd have seduced you."

"I confess! I am heartbroken and jealous in spite of her blood red finger nails." He laughed. "Would you believe it? She went off me rather quickly and now has a man much younger than her late husband, who trails after her with every evidence of lasting pleasure!"

"The new manager of her factory?"

"Yes. She tried to give me some illegal clothing coupons which I refused."

"How many?" asked Bea with an avaricious glint in her eyes.

"Lots," he said.

"Some men can be irritatingly honest!"

"I did refuse them but a special delivery came the next day. Plain brown envelope and no note, just a wad of coupons. What should I do, Sister? Take them to the Ministry, or tear them up?" he said with an air of innocence.

"Emma and I will take them shopping tomorrow," Bea said firmly. "I have known girls who sold their bodies for these! Besides," she added, "many shops are much more eager to sell clothes than to bother with coupons now, as they think rationing will be over soon."

"So you have no conscience, Bea?"

"Pa says that it's more important to revive the economy by buying things now," Bea said self-righteously. "He should know. He's had a finger in the black market for most of the war, quite anonymously of course." She held out a hand. "I'll take those off your sensitive conscience and make sure that Emma and me spend them on really, really essential clothes like black nighties."

"So long as you don't set up a stall in Oxford Street and sell them," he said dryly.

Emma answered the phone. "Long distance for you," she called to Bea.

"What it is to have priority! Hello darling," she said as soon as she heard Dwight's voice, faint and crackling over the line.

"We'll be here for a week," he said. "George has people to see regarding Sadie's estate, which seems to be considerable. At least he isn't acting like a zombie now he has practical things to sort out. Fortunately, when they got married and bought the apartment for use when they returned to the States on holiday, the lawyer persuaded them to make reciprocal wills, possibly because George was in a hazardous occupation and it was for Sadie's protection rather than his. It cuts down the bureaucracy a lot."

"Give my love to your parents. You did remember to take with you the last pictures of the babies? You must show them to your family now that you are in the States."

"I'll do that. I must fly down to my parents for a day or so. We have a lot of talking to do and I want to see the plans for our house, which is nearly finished except for the pool."

"No pool! Not with young children around. We can use your parents' pool when the babies are being looked after at our place."

"Right. My mother will really approve of that. No pool and a lethal campaign against all snakes and nasty insects," he said, laughing.

"I'll miss you but make it a good visit."

"Try to get out and have a good time," he told her.

"I shall go to all the exhibitions that bore you, and do lots of window-gazing," she promised. He groaned audibly. "We are going shopping in Liberties after I see my gynae man, and to hear Mahler tomorrow while you are at a dismal funeral," she said to tease him.

"The one that sounds like a death march? I'll stick with the funeral."

"Sometimes I wonder why I married you!"

"You know damn well! And we have twins to prove it."

"I thought it was my beautiful mind you fell for," she said. "Dwight! Not over the phone!"

He chuckled and the line went dead. She held it at arms' length. "I should think it would be cut off," she said, but her lips twitched and her eyes held remembered loving.

Emma found her rummaging in a chest of drawers. "Lost something?" she asked.

"My figure, if I can't find a bra to fit," Bea said.

"Buy some tomorrow, if you can guess what size you'll be next week. Would you like to ring Janey and tell them we heard from Dwight?"

"Sure. Get her on the line and I'll talk to her." She heard Emma call her.

"Is that one of my favourite aunts?" Bea asked. "We thought you'd like to know that they are safe on dry land in the States and George has a lot of lawyer stuff to see to before they come back, so you may or may not see them next week unless my husband runs off with a girl in a revue."

"Dwight wouldn't do that, and I hope that George doesn't try to find comfort in that way. I'm glad he's so busy. In a way I'll be a lot more calm once he is in his new command. Men can home in to work and do a lot of forgetting when they are occupied."

"Is he bringing back Sadie's personal belongings?" Bea asked her.

"He said he wouldn't. He'll ask a girl friend of hers to take her clothes to a charity and he'll put the apartment and futniture on the market through an agent, but I insisted that he brings back all the photo albums she may have had, so that Clive can grow up knowing a little more about his mother than words can tell him."

"How wise and kind," Bea said.

"It's what my mother would have done," Janey said

simply. "Emily has gone to bed early. It's wonderful to have her here and Clive smiled when he saw her, which seemed to be a big surprise to her as she says she doesn't know anything about babies. Many people find her abrasive but you can't fool a baby!"

"No bad prognostications?"

"Not a vibration! Can we now say, all's well with our world?"

"If Emily says so, I'll believe it," Bea replied fervently.

Chapter Eighteen

Bea tucked the babies into the perambulator and adjusted Avril's bonnet. "And you can keep that cap on, Johnnie," she admonished, when he dragged off his woollen cap for the third time. "It's cold out there."

"I know it's early, but a brisk walk now and fresh air for the twins will not take long. We can be in Harley Street by ten," Emma said.

"Dwight left a camera here and I shall take their pictures by the statue of Peter Pan. I want to collect everything that will remind me of England and this place in particular. He took a lot of snaps on the Island as an enthusiatic foreigner, and it nudged me into seeing things again that I take for granted." She laughed. "Little does she know, but he even managed to get a good picture of Aunt Emily when she wasn't looking. She'd kill him if she knew," she added complacently. "Dwight said she was like an African tribeswoman who believes that a camera would steal her soul if her picture was taken, but I think it's just vanity."

The gleaming coach-built pram went smoothly over the path in the park, the body slung on elegant springing as good as an aristocratic motorcar and the interior warm and covered in soft white calfskin.

"You'll take this with you?" Emma asked.

"Yes, but it really goes with uniformed nannies with awful hats and grey stockings, all *tres* snob, but that would be going too far. I think the Americans on a ranch would goggle a bit at that and the nanny would miss meeting her buddies in the local Cadenas for coffee, but I do like the

204

pram as it's safe and practical and the babies can use it for at least another nine or ten months as it's big enough for them to lie side by side for short naps."

"You'll need a nanny."

"Dwight has it organised," Bea said sadly. "Have you ever felt you were being rushed without anything being said?"

"Often, but Dwight has a rare talent for looking ahead and smoothing the way, and all you have to do is to float along and be happy. Who is she? Have you met her?"

"She's OK," Bea admitted reluctantly. "She's ex-service and has taken a course with Norland nannying, so she has the right experience with children. Dwight met her when she was working at the American Base as a nanny to one of the children there. It is unfair to think of this as an added attraction, but she lost her husband in the war and shows no sign of amorous attachments, so we might have her with us, if she enjoys America, for quite a while."

"She's British? I thought Dwight would have chosen an American."

"Bless him. He wanted me to have someone who spoke my language in more ways than speech, and who has a voice that won't influence the children to talk with a broad accent of any kind, American or English."

"So they won't live on peanut butter and jelly sandwiches?"

"Over my dead body! I shall scream if I can't have roast beef and Yorkshire pud."

"Plenty of beef in Texas."

"Plenty of everything. Plenty of too much. Lots of space and fresh air and a vast empty land. I shudder at the thought."

"You like horses," Emma ventured to remind her and Bea laughed, ruefully.

"My cunning husband has promised that he will have two Shetland ponies sent over for the twins as soon as they can sit up straight and not fall off."

205

"They wouldn't fit in here in Kensington," Emma reminded her.

"I'm being brain-washed, Dewar, but I'll have to like it. I know I couldn't live without Dwight, so where he goes, I go." She sighed. "There have been women far from home since the beginning of time, either following their men from choice or being dragged by the hair. I used to think the poem, the Solitary Reaper, was sad but improbable, but I'll know soon how she felt . . . The sad heart of Ruth, sick for home amid the alien corn . . . and I think that women are far more adaptable at pulling up stumps and starting again than men are."

The babies smiled at the ducks and the tiny London sparrows that clustered round Emma's hands as she held out pieces of stale bread for them. Bea snapped away at everything, including Peter Pan, who gazed over their heads as if they didn't exist. The twins weren't impressed by him as much as by a large dog lifting his leg against the statue.

"You will be just like your father!" Bea scolded them. "No taste for culture. Just a love of smelly animals."

"We'll leave the twins with Eileen. It's time we left for Harley Street," Emma said as they walked back to the house. "It will be easier to take taxis today, and Paul can drive us to the concert tonight unless we walk to the Albert Hall."

Bea came from the consulting room of the well-known gynaecologist with a bemused expression. "I never expected to be given a docket to obtain a special bra," she said. "He showed me one and it isn't exactly glamorous, but he said I'd need a firm support to help the milk stop, when I take these tablets. It's adaptable, so that I can haul in the slack when my bosoms shrink. I hope I don't lose them altogether," she wailed.

"You won't, but you can't feed a baby for the rest of your life, just to keep that shape," Emma said unhelpfully. "But maybe I'm wrong," she added. "One gynae man at Beatties was fond of saying that in Italy and Latin American countries, menstruation stops at marriage. As they aren't allowed any birth control there is no gap between pregnancies. The women are either pregnant or feeding babies for the rest of their fertile lives, so if you have nine children, probably nine sets of twins, you can keep that voluptuous figure."

"I hope you have triplets!" Bea said acidly.

"Aunt Emily doesn't see that," Emma said.

The babies chewed on Bikky Pegs, the hard chewing stick with coloured ribbon through the hole at the end that could be pulled out if the baby tried to swallow it whole. They were designed as a safe way of helping teeth through without becoming as messy as rusks, which soon became wet and crumbly. Avril had a shiny red cheek and Bea sighed. "She's very good but her gums are very tense and I thought I saw the tip of a tooth yesterday."

"Make a note," Emma said mischievously.

"I suppose so. What I forget to put in that Darling Baby Book, I'll make up later, but Dwight's aunt sent it and I have the task of keeping the record; but it's so *twee*."

"Lovely little cherubs on each page, all swathed in tulle and lots of rabbits and pussy cats," Emma reminded her.

"It would be more honest to show the cherubs in nappies! I think we have a slight problem in that way now. Home James!"

Baby changing and lunch over, Bea took her tablets and slept for an hour while Emma and Eileen gave bottle feeds, keeping the babies out of sight of Bea so that they couldn't smell her breast milk.

Paul finished work for the day and joined them for a light meal before the concert. The ex-pilot had been calm and grateful out of all proportion to the help that Paul and Emma had given him, recognising that he had been vain and that life could go on after the glamour of flying; and bloody-minded consultants could be treated with calm passive resistance. He also admitted that he'd

207

met a girl who showed that she liked him, before she knew of his reputation as a war hero.

"This is exciting," Bea said. "I haven't been to a proper concert for ages. It will be like old times."

The huge, rather ugly but imposing hall filled up and a frisson of expectancy swelled as the preliminary tuning up of the orchestra began.

Emma read the programme and saw what would be in the next concert: a medley of wartime music. She gulped. Were people ready for it? It was too soon to be dismissed as harmless nostalgia, made smooth by time and the softening of memories. Who could bear to hear the songs of Piaff, the Warsaw Concerto and the haunting notes of Lilli Marlene, all of which would bring a flood of memories, some good, some bad, but all disturbing?

"I wonder if they'll play Glen Miller?" Bea said. "I love the big band sound and in spite of his tragic death that no one really fathomed when he disappeared over the ocean, I can listen to that as it had no sad undertones for me, as some did," Bea said.

"You could have a good nostalgic cry and enjoy sad memories but I think that's one concert I'll leave to you and Dwight. He loves 'String of Pearls' and 'Moonlight Serenade' and 'American Patrol'. He plays them often enough," Emma said with feeling. "I don't need to hear them in a concert hall when he plays that record again and again. Isn't it strange that the ones you wish would break, never do? He even leaves the door open now since he heard that Eileen loves the sound, and the patients can hear it in the distance and they often remark on the nice background music!"

"Look on it as a valuable service that Dwight adds to my work," Paul said dryly. "I would not have thought of it, but music does seem to soothe the savage breast, or to put it more politely, calms my disturbed patients. "I think we should arrange to have muted non-vocal sounds in the office to filter through."

"Why not have a juke box and let them put in their own penny?" asked Emma, scathingly.

"No thanks! Eileen would sneak up to play 'White Cliffs of Dover' after the consultations, and that is something I couldn't bear."

The audience settled down and the enveloping waves of music filled the vast hall. Emma closed her eyes to have her own reveries but Bea watched people, to stamp the scene on her memory. The women wore a mixture of shabby-elegant and brash utility clothes, with the odd pretty silk blouse made from parachute silk; and a few pre-war fur jackets, often smelling of moth balls, added a pathetic attempt to indicate wealth and glamour.

The orchestra stage looked cold, if the pinched faces of the players were any indication, until the unheated hall was warmed up by the sheer volume of warm bodies, and the music played on, with beauty and sadness and a climax that was almost physical.

"I must buy that," Bea said. "I'll play it to the cattle and see what they have to say. Tomorrow, I must go to the National Gallery and buy prints of my favourite pictures."

"It's a good idea, but why the panic?" Paul asked when they were in the car and driving the short distance home.

"It's later than you think," Bea quoted sombrely. "I must gather what I can before we leave as I doubt if I shall find what I want over there."

"They do have culture," Paul pointed out. "In many ways the Yanks look on us now as the savages! What about Carnegie Hall and the Hollywood Bowl? Both wonderful concert arenas with orchestras like the Boston Symphony, and great musicians who escaped the European pogroms and fled West."

"Even popular music during the war came from there quite easily if anyone had a contact, as it was unobtainable anywhere here on gramophone records," Emma said. "The student who was sent a record of the original 'La Vie en

Rose' with Piaff singing, from a cousin in Boston, was much sought after for parties, and he was so *smug* about it. It was his passport to temporary popularity, as he was the only one with that record."

"I want my own British-bought selection," Bea said firmly. "Dwight's family are not very into classical music and I hope that I can find a few people who will want to listen to my records. I'll buy some good opera, too."

"Don't buy 'Porgie and Bess' over here," Emma said. "They do it better!"

"Whose side are you on?" Bea asked with simulated irritation. "Can't you see that I am enjoying thinking out things that will make me miserable and homesick?"

"You'll love it," Paul said. "Can't you imagine her, Emma? She'll swan into America and pause just long enough to plan her line of attack and then take it by storm! We've all seen her in action and motherhood has done nothing to improve her."

"Why did you marry a shrink?" Bea asked politely. "I have to take several different things over there to prove what I want them to think of me. This rather heavy culture will be fine for Sundays and Dwight's stuffed shirts of top brass and my own pleasure when I'm alone and a bit blue, but I'll take a few jazz records and some really smaltzy music that will find a lot of different friends."

"See what I mean," he said cryptically.

"Come and browse pictures with me, Emma?"

"Only if they have put away the war artists and I can have Danish pastries in Lyons Corner House," Emma said.

"I want wartime paintings," Bea said. "That's for another lot of people who have never seen war and look on it as if it might be a temporary inconvenience but not really for them." She chuckled. "Can't you imagine them, sipping cocktails and having to sit facing a wall covered with the pictures that Moore did of the figures in the undergrounds during the blitz, and the ones of wounded and burned airmen that a woman artist did at the scenes and in hospital?"

"You wouldn't!"

"I might if the need arises, and I must remember everything about it, too," she added soberly. "I can't walk away from all that and forget it happened."

"I used to wait for my boyfriends on these steps," Bea said as they climbed up to the main entrance of the National Gallery in Trafalgar Square.

"Who didn't?" asked Emma and laughed. "It's a wonder there was room for all of us. Each time I mention the National Gallery people say the same. It was a good meeting place, specially for new dates, in public in case they got fresh, and yet a place where we could talk. It was warm in the gallery, not for our benefit but for the pictures that needed to be kept away from frost! It was private in a way, as there was space and we could sit on those leather benches as if absorbed in the latest exhibition, in comfort and without being too committed to each other."

"What happened when you left the Gallery?"

"I ran for a bus," Emma said. "A quick goodbye and 'It's late; see you sometime,' brushed off the ones I didn't like."

"Me too. Taxis were a risk as they often tried to ride with me but buses were wonderful, except that I landed up in some odd places, as sometimes, I didn't read the destination on the front, in my rush to get away to just anywhere," Bea confessed.

They giggled over the fat ladies in old Masters that Bea said were painted for the benefit of old voyeurs who liked a bit of flesh. "They got away with a lot of highly immoral stuff in the name of art," she said. "The monks must have been in a constant state of arousal with some of those pictures of saints, and as for mythology, *well*! I once wondered how it would be with a wicked satyr?"

"Too hairy," Emma said. "How are you with Picasso?"

211

"Where?"

"There's an exhibition of Picasso, Paul Klee, Pissaro and Matisse," Emma read and was about to pass on, but Bea pulled at her sleeve.

"This I must see. I shall buy a print of 'Guernica' and possibly 'Peace'. I don't pretend to understand it or even like it, but I find it compelling and 'Guernica' can be my centrepiece when I invite the American isolationists to drinks."

"You've lost me," Emma said and gasped when confronted by the enormous canvasses that covered the gallery walls. They looked at the Blue Period and made comments on the 'Woman with Fish Hat' and others, but when Bea came to 'Guernica', in the original, she sat on a bench and stared at the uncompromising and harsh work about war, her face stony.

"Didn't he live in Germany or occupied France during the war?" Emma asked.

"He wasn't a collaborator," Bea said, firmly. "This is war in all its violence and grief and a lot of people were offended by it. A German officer saw it and said, as if accusing him of sedition, 'Did you paint this?' and Picasso said, 'No, YOU did.'"

"'Peace' is better," Emma said walking along the line of pictures.

"I almost understand this one."

They saw the wonderful colours of the Matisse collection and the small coloured squares on the bright pyramids of Klee.

"I'm exhausted," Emma said at last. "It's another strange world, but I'll come here again if only to see Picasso's earlier work when his females had shape and noses in the right places. Artists with skills like his can afford to take chances, I suppose. He certainly does. He is a superb draughtsman."

Bea bought a lot of prints and longed to buy an original, but knew that this was impossible. "Danish pastries, if done well are works of art in themselves," she announced. "It's our duty to sample them."

"Does this place mean anything to you?" Emma asked when they were sitting on the worn red velvet chairs in the Vienna Café part of Lyons Corner House.

"Not a lot. I came here once or twice with other nurses but most of my friends were a bit up-market for Lyons and we went to officers' clubs and hotels and some good restaurants if we wanted serious food. Places like this do have the advantage that a girl alone could feel safe from the hyenas who try to drum up acquaintances in the other places, but wherever I am, I hate eating alone."

"I came here a lot at one time, sometimes alone on days off duty when I couldn't find one of our set off at the same time and sometimes I met Phillip here." Emma laughed, "Although we were at school together, it's so long ago since I saw him that I forget him until I am reminded by Aunt Emily, who knows all things about everyone, and knows his family on the Island. She told me that he is now in business in South Africa and married into a wealthy family, so I don't have him on my conscience, but he does still ask about me in letters to his mother."

The Danish pastries were large, round and fluffy and full of sultanas. Bea ordered two and put one of them into her handbag wrapped in her handkerchief. "They don't sell them to be taken away, so this is the only way I can enjoy one at home," she said. "I love the bits of marzipan." She licked the icing from the twirls of yeasty dough.

"They are as good as ever, but some shops have stopped selling decent cakes as they say they can't get the right ingredients to keep up the standard, or like Fuller's, they sell them on three days a week instead of five, which makes for even more queues," Emma remarked. "When will rationing end?"

"I'll send you food parcels," Bea said, and Emma was reminded that Bea no longer said *if* I go to the States. She now said *when*, and it was plain that she was slowly beginning to look forward with increasing pleasure to the prospect.

"You'll be ready soon," Emma said. "When Dwight comes back he'll have it all settled."

"I know." For a moment, Bea looked bereft.

"It will be exciting," Emma told her.

"Yes."

"The twins will love the life there once they can walk."

"Yes, yes and *yes*! But I shall be so torn to bits inside, Dewar. Promise me you'll come to visit us and stay for a long long time."

Emma thought of an expression she had heard long ago. Had it been passed down from the grandmother she had never really known? She smiled. It had become an Aunt Emily saying.

"If the wind's in the right direction, we'll be there," she said.

"And if it isn't?" Bea asked, suddenly full of a kind of angry panic.

"We wait, I suppose."

"You do no such thing. You pull your finger out and make it! You put on the bloody engines and come fast . . . or you damn well swim!" Bea almost shouted, to the surprise of the couple at the next table.

"I think it's time we left," Emma said hastily, and asked for the bill.

Outside, they leaned together giggling. "Did you see that woman's face?" Bea asked.

"She'll spend the rest of the day wondering where the boat is," Emma spluttered.

"Something to tell her friends," Bea said. "Six months ago we might have been arrested as spies, suspected as having a submarine on the Serpentine or in the Regent Canal. Come on, let's take a taxi. Suddenly I feel empty," she said. "I hate these tablets. They are draining away the babies' elixir of life."

214

"You couldn't have been away for so long if they were not on the bottle," Emma reminded her.

"True." Bea waved furiously and the cab driver saw them and drove them through the London dusk that Bea would remember always as blue, under the street lights that still bore traces of the blackout paint that had dimmed the lights for so many years.

Chapter Nineteen

Emma stared at the huge station waggon in front of the entrance then hurried inside the house. The faint sound of 'Moonlight Serenade' assailed her ears and she smiled. It might be Glen Miller's signature tune but it had also become Dwight's.

"He's back," Bea called breathlessly, her happiness making her voice light and very young.

"I guessed," Emma said dryly. "Who owns that hearse outside?"

Bea came down the rest of the stairs and watched Emma take off her thick coat and gloves and smooth her hair after she'd shaken off the woollen pixie hood that gave her a gamine and rather fetching look.

"Too cold for the babes?" asked Bea.

"No fog or wind, so they could be wrapped up in the porch," Emma said. "But the estate car, or as I'm sure Dwight would call it, station waggon, why is that here? Surely Dwight didn't come in that? Wasn't he met by a chauffeur at the airfield?"

"Change of plan. I've made coffee," Bea said. "Come up and see Dwight."

Emma followed her, wondering what was on Bea's mind, and secretly dreading what she might hear.

"Emma Honey!"

Dwight hugged her and gave her a lingering kiss that made Bea mutter, "Down boy", then he went back to the twins who were wriggling on a blanket on the floor and trying to eat the wooden bricks that Dwight had brought them.

"Well?" Emma asked, looking from one face to the other. "Did you have a nice funeral, Dwight? From the size of that vehicle blocking the entrance, I wondered if you were now in the undertaking business."

"No, I'm not a mortician. The interment was not something I want to recall for too long. It was bleak and cold and there were very few people there. I'm glad I was there to be with George. I felt so sorry for that guy. He was like a zombie but as soon as he had more practical matters to sort out after we got back to the lawyer's office, he was better."

"Is he back, now?" Emma asked.

"Yes. I left him settling Sadie's affairs, and I went down to Texas to see my folks, then we met up again for the flight home and he seems OK now." He eyed Emma with speculation. "A bit raw, maybe, and you should keep your head below the parapet, I'd say for quite a while, but he's looking forward to his first command and that will sort out his future."

"Did he talk about Emma?" Bea wanted to know.

"Not a lot," Dwight said laconically. "But when a guy has your picture in his billfold, and talks about the Island and the time you met him there . . . all mixed in with what his mother said and what Emily said, he's covering himself with mental cobwebs that need brushing away. If he's to meet another woman to love, you'd best make for the hills as soon as you see his dust cloud, ma'am," he added.

"Don't be silly. He's in mourning," Emma said and hoped it was true.

"He said goodbye to Sadie and he was fairly shattered, but he has said goodbye, it's final and that's over for him now."

"He has a son," Emma said.

"That will help, but sons need mothers, don't they Hon?" he said with a fond glance at his wife.

"Mothers don't need sons who sick up their rusks!" Bea said, wiping one small red face. "Oh, clever boy, it wasn't

217

rusk it was a piece of paper from the box that came with the bricks!"

"Well I thought he'd like to help unwrap his present," Dwight said defensively.

"And you'd trust foxes in a chicken coop? *your* son is a baby delinquent! Pour some coffee for Emma," Bea ordered.

Dwight beamed. "That's my girl! I thought I'd missed something when I was with my nice polite family."

"How are things in Texas? "Emma asked, relieved to change the subject from George and his hang-ups.

"Great! I showed them the pictures and they can't wait to welcome Bea and the twins." He looked more serious. "First I have a stint at the White House and they have arranged an apartment for us close by."

Emma saw Bea's face lose its glow as she asked steadily, "When do we leave?"

"You have another three weeks here, Honey. What do you want to do?"

"I'd better see Pa and Miranda," Bea said in a flat voice.

"That's one day! And the rest of the time?" he asked gently.

"I'll pack, I suppose, and just be here, where I want to be."

"No visits to friends?"

"There are a few I'd like to see again from Beatties," she said slowly. "And if it wasn't for the twins I'd love to say goodbye to Aunt Emily."

"Why do you think I bought that old station waggon?" Dwight said. "We can pack them in with their diapers and cots and bottles and stay in Emma's cottage if she'll spare it." He looked apologetic. "If you are tied up here, Emma, I promise that Bea won't burn down the house."

"Isn't she invited?" Bea asked.

"No," he said firmly. "George is going there to take a present from America to his dear aunt, and to be close to

218

Portsmouth for a few days before he takes over the ship. He said that the ferry would be convenient for him as he may have to make several visits."

"It is just as convenient to drive to Portsmouth from Aunt Janey's house in Hampshire, and he'd see more of baby Clive," Emma said.

Dwight shrugged. "My fault I guess. When we were coming back, we discussed our future plans and I told him I hoped to take Bea down to see Aunt Emily to say goodbye. I think he took it for granted that you would be there."

"Oh dear!" Emma said.

"Do you mind not coming with us?" Bea asked.

"I can't spare the time," Emma said hastily. "Paul and I thought we'd go there in the New Year."

"We can show the twins all the places I love," Bea said. "I shall convince them later that they remember it all!"

"I rang Aunt Emily from the airfield," Dwight said calmly. "She expects us tomorrow for four days, and Wilf will see that the house is warm."

"You devil! I am utterly speechless," Bea said, halfway to tears.

"That's a change," he said and dodged a damp bib. "We have a meal with her the first night."

"Will George be there?"

"Yes. I think that Aunt Emily was pleased to know we would be there at the same time. He went home to see his baby and his mother but arrives almost as soon as we do and we can help out with him, as she didn't fancy having him there alone. What can you say to a man who has just been to his wife's funeral and is a wee bit morose and depressed?"

"You are forgetting a couple of unimportant items," Bea said caustically. "If we eat with them, what about the twins who should be fast asleep in bed by then?"

"Wilf's wife was the oldest of seven children and she

knows all about babies. She will baby sit any time we want her," Dwight said.

"You can go mad and dance to Ted Westmore's band," Emma said.

"Only if he plays Gershwin and my favourite big band tunes," Dwight said.

"He's quite good," Emma conceded.

"I shall collect some glass lighthouses filled with coloured sands from Alum Bay," Bea said and laughed. "Some local pottery and a bit of lace, if Emily can spare some she made, would be nice and I'll buy some views painted by local artists, like the ones they have in the railway carriages."

"But they are ghastly!"

"I know that Emma, but when I get to Texas I shall solemnly say they are our local native art form and very sought after. They'll lap it up."

"Some are a bit primitive," Emma agreed.

"We'll come back and pack and take the waggon with us, loaded with stuff and drive it on to the transport." Dwight consulted a note book. "We travel on a separate plane with a lot more comfort and it flies from Brise Norton at twenty hundred hours, three weeks today."

"A night flight? We can sleep across the Atlantic?" Bea said. "I hope the twins co-operate."

"Janet Bruce will be at the airport ready to share the load and take the babies whenever you are tired of them," he assured her. "Throw a few things into a bag for yourself Honey, just enough for the Island and we'll start early tomorrow." He yawned and drained his coffee cup. "I'll nap for an hour and help load the waggon later with the baby things."

"Are you sure you can't come with us?" Bea asked.

"Paul would let me go but I doubt if I want to meet George, and if you are there together, you can show off and make Dwight believe that you own the whole of the Isle of Wight!"

"If there's a sale, we might see what treasures we can buy and take them with us to Texas."

"Emma? You're wanted," Dwight called, and Bea turned to the babies who were trying to crawl off the rug.

"Who wants me?' Emma asked on the empty stairs.

"Here!" Dwight said in a conspiratorial whisper. "If I order food and wine, can you get a party together for sometime during our last week? Remember the parties we had with my godfather in Epsom? He'd like to see us before we leave, and you rate high with him, so he can come and also organise the smoked salmon!"

"What a marvellous idea! I have a few addresses of old nursing friends who trained with us and Paul can ask as many extra men as we need."

"You aren't setting up a marriage bureau!" he laughed. "I might have known. You and Bea have so much in common."

"Can't have wallflowers, can we?" Emma replied. "Of course, some of our set are married and I've lost touch with some others, but we can certainly make a pleasant party if I ring around. You'll ask people from your Base?"

"Sure. All the ones with acne and those who don't lust after my wife, if there are any!"

"Have that nap you planned and I'll make a list tomorrow after you and Bea have left, or she'll find out about it."

She walked slowly along to the consulting room where Paul was saying goodbye to his last patient of the day. "Hello," she said when they were alone.

"What's up?"

"Just a fit of the blues. Bea and Dwight are leaving very soon and tomorrow they are going to the Island for four days."

"You want to go with them?"

"No, Bea needs this time with Dwight in places she loves, and besides, George will be there, a bit miserable and up the creek without a paddle."

221

"Good. We can go to a hospital dinner, to which we have been invited but we can't take guests."

"Is this a sudden decision to make me feel good and take my mind off Bea?"

"Partly," he confessed. "But I don't want us to lose touch with our old stamping grounds and our old friends who will be here long after Bea has left us."

"That's sensible, but it doesn't help now. I shall miss her so much."

"We could go over there next year," he suggested. "There's no need to think you'll never see her again." He took her in his arms. "Keep that thought in your mind," he said. "If you know you can go to see her when you need to, then it will feel possible . . . and it is. Travel is easier now and nothing like it was a few generations ago when a lot of people emigrated to the States and the Antipodes and knew they'd never come back again. They were cut off from their families for ever, but we are fortunate enough to have the means to travel if we want that."

Emma fingered the marcasite and gold pendant on the slender chain round her neck, that she wore often, and treasured as it had been a gift from Aunt Emily's brother Sidney. She had met him briefly in America just before he died of tuberculosis, and she knew that the one dark patch in Emily's heart was the fact that once her favourite brother had left England to become an actor in America, she had never seen him again.

"Do you think it's possible next year?" she said with considerable doubt.

"If you can stand a partly working holiday. I've been invited to lecture and we could combine the two."

She sighed and kissed him. "You are wonderful," she said.

"I do my best," he replied modestly, but with such a wide grin that she knew he was very pleased with himself.

Emma told him about the party and they made a list of possible guests, but hid it when Bea came down to find them and said that the babies were asleep. "Come and help me pack for the Island," she begged. "You know you do it better than I can, as I forget necessary things that I take for granted, such as knickers and toothpaste."

"I've asked Eileen to make sure that all the nappies are aired and ready and you can go down to the chemist now for some more talc and zinc and castor oil cream."

"I can get that when I am down there."

"Not if it's early closing day. When you arrive you may find not a single shop open."

"Right. I'll buy my sweet ration for Emily and use some points on the ration cards for some cans of meat in case we are stuck in with the babies. I can't expect Emily to feed us all the time. Even green vegetables aren't easy in winter, apart from sprouts which Dwight can't stand, but Avril has taken to sieved parsnips and potatoes and spinach with gravy, very well, and my little horror Johnnie, eats anything so long as he thinks it's forbidden, but likes rusks with a little jam on them with his milk."

"They have such different personalities already," Emma said.

"I never thought I'd love them so much," Bea admitted.

"Does that mean you want more?"

"Later," Bea said and laughed. "Surprised? Personally, I am *very* surprised, but we'll have to wait a while as we have such a lot to do and I want to feel settled down before I make another nest."

"They say that when a mother is feeding a baby, she has no need of birth control. Paul says it has some truth but it's really an old wives' tale and risky to believe implicitly."

"So you want to make sure I have a nice new diaphragm to shield me from my fertile husband?" Bea laughed. "Would you believe that Dwight thought of that first and made me get fitted before we made love after the six weeks post-natal period! He thinks he might sire quins next time and is scared!"

"Take this to Aunt Emily from me," Paul said later, handing a bottle of whisky to Dwight. "Grateful patients bring strange offerings and hate being refused, so I have whisky which I never drink. Emily can have it in her tea and be relaxed when she is alone with George."

"Maybe he'll go away if he sees that Emma isn't with us," Bea said. "I suppose you have a more sophisticated clientele in a city, who have good black market whisky to spare: not like Dr Sutton who finds dead rabbits on his door step."

"I'd swop," Paul said. "If he has some to spare when you come back, please bring them. I don't mind skinning them and we could do with a change in our meat diet."

"Mention it to Wilf," Emma said. "He has a shotgun and if you pay for the ammunition, he'll be delighted to have the excuse to go shooting. What could be fresher?"

The twins were remarkably good when they were strapped into cots in the back seat of the estate car and were hemmed in safely by piles of blankets and towelling nappies, muslin squares and lots of clean clothes.

"Aunt Emily said she'd borrow a pram and has put buckets and Dettol in the kitchen and Milton for sterilising the bottles."

"She said it's no bother to her as she wanted to have everything ready for when Janey brings Clive to stay," Paul said when Bea began to protest that she could take all that was necessary.

"It will seem odd to have babies in that house," Emma said.

"Perhaps she has an eye on the future, as usual," Bea suggested and Emma felt her own heart beat faster, but whether with panic or anticipation, she couldn't tell. She tried to appear enigmatic when Bea eyed her with raised eyebrows and a quirky smile.

"You'll need a bottle of boiled water and one of orange juice in case they are thirsty on the journey," Emma said. "Have you packed the fresh batch of concentrated orange from the baby clinic?"

"Yes, and I bought cod liver oil drops from the chemist. The official stuff is too smelly and they gag on it. When it's spilled on bibs and clothes it's very difficult to remove the smell and the stains, so if you know of someone who is addicted to cod liver oil, there are four unopened bottles in the nursery cupboard."

"At least the Government supplies really good care for infants and nursing mothers," Paul said and grinned. "Psychologically, rationing is a good thing and these supplies for babies are too, as nobody likes to take less than their due if it's free and so the babies have cod liver oil and orange juice that the mothers might never buy if it was left to their own choice."

"I'll give the cod liver oil to the grocer," Emma said. "He has a new puppy and will use it for him. It's amazing how many pups owe their strong bones and teeth to the handouts for babies. That stuff is revolting, but like food rations, nobody refuses her quota."

"What do I say to George?" Bea asked.

"Give him our regards and say that if he has to come to the Admiralty, we shall be pleased to see him," Paul said before Emma could reply.

"Paul! You can't be serious." Emma looked scared. "I can't have him here if he tries to disrupt our lives."

"You have to meet him again Emma, and we are secure enough to be generous. He's all mixed up now, being torn between his son and his loss and the new exciting career ahead of him. He can only enjoy that when he can lose his feeling of guilt about shunting his responsibilities on to his parents. He needs friends and family Emma." Paul regarded her solemnly. "If you keep him away now, he'll build up a mental picture of you that isn't healthy. He'll keep you in his mind as his lost love, and feel permanently distanced and frustrated."

"You are one hell of a shrink," Dwight said with a vehemence borne of his own experience when Paul had convinced him that he personally had not dropped the bomb on Hiroshima. "I think he's right, Emma. Go along with what he says."

"We needn't tell him he's invited to stay, just to pop in if he happens to be in the district," Bea said with a sweet smile. "I'll make it causal as if it doesn't matter to you if he comes here or not. You are just taking it for granted that all he wants is friendship." She laughed. "You can't have him here mooning over you for a few days. He might get ideas and embarrass you."

"Hey, I'm the psychiatrist around here," Paul said. "She's right," he told Emma. "And you may find that he values our friendship now as we know his background. With us he has no need to put on a brave face about his loss as he might with strangers. Let's face it, darling, he needs family now, and I like him."

"Spoken by a man who beats his wife and knows she will never dare to leave him," Dwight said with a grin. "Just like me," he said and side-stepped Bea's pinch.

Emma waved as the station waggon started up and slowly left the front entrance. She had a lump in her throat. "It's a rehearsal for them leaving for good," she said and Paul hugged her close.

"Not for good," he said reassuringly. "And not yet. We have work to do," he added bracingly. "With them out of the way, we can start arranging the party. Dwight alerted his godfather who seems to think it's *his* party now." He shrugged. "I'm not fussy. Suits me if he brings all the food!"

"I'll ask Eileen to unpack that tea chest of china that we brought from the Island. It was a job lot, contents bought unseen and I haven't seen what's in there yet. If it's useful we'll need it when we have a crowd here.

I doubt if there is anything that's worth much as we had it so cheaply."

Paul watched her back view as she hurried to the basement where the chest was stored, bracing herself to tackle the work ahead with her usual confidence, and he smiled, knowing that a challenge for Emma was the best medicine.

Chapter Twenty

Paul's appointment diary was full over the next few days as he wanted to be free just before Bea and Dwight left for America.

"We'll have to tell Bea about the party," Emma said firmly. "They'll be back this afternoon and if she sees the tables set up in the drawing room, she'll want to know why. I think she'll enjoy the planning, more than she would the surprise, if she knows nothing about it until the day."

"At least we know who might be coming," Paul said.

"A few gaps that are sad, with girls who have moved away, married or left nursing and doctors who have left Beatties and have no contacts there."

"It does show that we must keep in touch with our old colleagues, or we could be isolated here in private practice."

"When I rang one Admin Sister at Beatties, a Sister who stayed on and is now a fixture there, I was offered a part-time job even before I invited her to the party!"

"Do you want to take it?"

Emma frowned. "It's good to know they still value me but I'll have to think about it. Let's leave it until the day of the party and see how many of them I could bear to work with," she suggested.

"Would it be surgical?"

"Not exactly. I would be relief Casualty Sister, for three mornings a week in Cas and for a couple of surgical out-patient sessions."

Paul laughed. "They certainly know what to offer you, as you thrive on drama and gore and my clinic lacks a lot of that."

"When Bea goes . . ." she began and bit her lip.

"Exactly," he said quietly. "Consider it carefully and take the job if it helps the transition. If you don't have full control of the department and all the responsibility that comes from running the whole thing, it will mean that you can give notice and leave when you've had enough, but running individual clinics means that you do have control of the sessions in which you work. That should satisfy even your organising zeal!"

"What about your clinic?"

"You would be here for afternoon sessions if I needed a trained nurse here for neurological investigations and for some mornings. I can arrange that schedule to fit with you. When I am doing routine analysis, Eileen is very good now. She sits and doesn't fidget and looks calm and helpful. She makes a good chaperone when Miss Backer has an appointment, and Mick helps with the disturbed males. Miss Backer is my worst case at present and has a firm belief that she is being followed and needs a body guard; me preferably! I am trying to persuade her to go into hospital as a voluntary patient for treatment."

"So you don't need me for many sessions?"

"I need you for a lot of professional expertise, but far more important, are things like love and friendship and I need you as my beloved wife."

Emma buried her face in his shoulder. Such love was almost daunting. She could hardly look at his face as she knew that soon she must make up her mind about having a family of her own, even though Paul had no wish to press the situation.

"Work!" he said.

"Eileen has bought some powder that she swears makes good meringues. It can't have any egg whites in it and I

229

doubt if it will be edible but she wants to try it, so don't ring for her for a while as she's busy down there now in her own flat, messing about with what looks like plaster of Paris!"

"The General insists on bringing cold meats and smoked salmon and some of that famous angel cake and devil's cake that the Yanks seem to like. I hope you make a sponge cake with jam in the middle. I can't eat a puffed up synthetic bath sponge!"

"Mick is arranging for beer and cider and Dwight has enough music to suit everyone," Emma said. It was all coming together and she felt excited at the prospect of meeting old friends again.

Lunch was late; just home-made vegetable soup and soda bread with cheese, and when Emma heard the sound of a car horn, she glanced at the clock, amazed that Bea and Dwight were home so soon.

She dried her wet hands and left the rest of the china that she had been washing. The tea chest from the manor house on the Island had given up treasures. There was an almost complete tea service of blue and white Willow Pattern china, several large serving dishes and a three-tiered cake stand of impressive proportions on which Eileen hoped to display her meringues and small cakes.

Paul had looked puzzled when he found a large cup with a ledge along one side that looked as if it would strain fluid into the cup but Mick told him that his grandfather had had a cup like it and it was a moustache cup for the use of men with verdant growths of hair on their upper lips. Inside at the bottom there was a picture of a very well-moustached man in the uniform of the Boer War with the name Earl Haigh under it.

Paul laughed when Emma washed it. "That's one cup we can spare. I have no intention of growing a huge moustache."

"I shall send it to America," Emma said but put it aside when she heard Bea's voice and went to greet them.

"Go to Auntie Emma. I must have a pee," Bea said and thrust Avril into her arms. "Who'd have smelly twins?" she said and kissed Emma's cheek.

"Smelly but nice," Emma said and Avril gave her a smacking kiss. "Mick is making tea and I'll change the babies while you tidy up," she said, and Dwight followed her to the nursery with Johnnie.

"How's Emily?" Emma asked.

"A bit skinny but fine. George stayed for one night, saw that you were not with us and went back to his parents and Clive."

"How is he?"

"OK," Dwight said firmly. "I think he suddenly realised that he had lots to do before he takes his command, and he did miss his son."

"What did Bea say to him?"

Dwight dropped a soiled nappy in the bin and wiped one small bottom with cotton wool. "You guessed she'd say something?" Emma nodded and nuzzled the soft hair of the now fragrant child in her arms. "I really didn't hear and I haven't asked," Dwight said seriously. "But he seemed a bit subdued after Bea made him walk with her up to the house to fetch something she said she'd left there with Aunt Emily on the last visit."

"Thank you, Dwight," she said.

"Has my godfather been in touch?"

Emma laughed. "He sent a staff car from Berkley Square with enough cans of food to feed an army and a heap of rather nice paper table napkins and large covers for the tables. The perishable food will be here on the morning of the party and he will arrive early to be with us for tea as he says he wants to catch up on all our news and see your next generation," Emma said.

"He's a great guy," Dwight said and grinned.

"We'll have to tell Bea about the party," Emma said. "If it was me, I'd feel left out if I was kept guessing until the actual day. Half the fun is the planning, and

Bea is good at it." She saw his expression. "You told her!"

"Mea Culpa! She got all misty about her old friends and I had to tell her. She was cross because I hadn't said anything but she was thrilled to know we are having a party."

"I have a souvenir for the man in the picture of your family that you gave us; the man with the handle bar moustache."

"What the heck? You never met Jud, even if he did join your air force at the beginning of the war and got led astray by the other bomber pilots and grew that terrible fungus."

Emma put the babies down to sleep and said that Eileen would feed them at their usual time. "Come with me," she said, and he followed her to the kitchen where Bea was pouring tea and helping herself to biscuits.

"One moustache cup," Emma announced and handed it to Dwight.

"You didn't tell me!" Bea said in mock horror. "You aren't growing a moustache when you join the White House?"

"It's wunnerful! Jud will go mad. Who's the picture?"

"A terrible General who sent a lot of boys to die in awful conditions in Africa and later in World War One," Bea said. "You needn't tell him that. Just say he was a famous soldier."

"A bit off-putting to finish your tea and find him staring up at you," Paul said.

"That was the idea," Emma explained. "Emily told me all about the emotional blackmail that went on, with posters accusing men of not serving their country and not being ready to protect their wives and families if they remained civilians."

"Was there a draft?" Dwight asked.

"Later, there was conscription," Emma agreed. "But at the beginning there was a surge of national emotion and

232

pressure on civilians to join up and take the Queen's Shilling. Aunt Emily blamed men like Haigh because her own father went to war and left her mother with a large family and a shop for two years while he was in South Africa." She laughed. "From what she said, I believe he wanted to go and was persuaded to enlist, not so much through ardent patriotism, but under the influence of strong ale and the urge to be a non-commissioned officer with the Royal Horse Artillery once more, as he had been before he married. She said he was a fine horseman and he was offered his old rank if he volunteered."

"Are you sure that Emily can spare this? It's a memory of those wars," Dwight said.

"She has forgotten most of it, and the tragedy of losing the one man she ever loved has dimmed over the years; that is until she sits with Janey over their awful tea and whisky and they reminisce."

"Besides, Emily has no moustache," Bea said firmly. She chuckled. "Texas will be shocked and puzzled when I give them my gifts." She proceeded to show them the souvenirs she had brought with her from the Isle of Wight, including a few saucy postcards and some very amateur paintings. The glass lighthouses and model ships filled with the layers of coloured sands from Alum Bay would be something unique, Bea was convinced, and she ignored her husband's remarks about the wonders of the rocks in the Grand Canyon.

"I keep telling her they will not understand the warped British humour in those cards," Dwight said plaintively. "They'll just see fat broads with huge butts and tits and read what's on the cards but not see the inuendoes."

"You understand them. I saw you roaring with laughter by the shop that had them on a stand."

"I'm almost a Brit now and I've been brain-washed," was his excuse.

"Did Aunt Emily give you any lace?" Emma asked.

"Nothing like that wonderful quilt edging that you have

233

and that I would love to steal but know I can't," Bea said. "She did give me some tray cloths and four linen towels with deep crochet ends that will look elegant in guest rooms, and I shall treasure them as they are beautiful and she made them."

Emma glanced at the clock. "Look in at the babies," she told Bea. "I'll start cooking the meal. Eileen will have fed the twins but wants to get away."

"What's her hurry?"

"Don't you remember? Two nights a week are sacred. No Dwight, she isn't religious although it is a kind of religion. She is obsessed by the cinema and joins the queues in rain or shine and comes back with stars in her eyes as do thirty million other people. We seem never to have enough of it, and I confess it is nice to go to a film occasionally."

"What's on tonight?" Bea asked when she went up to the nursery and found Eileen washing baby bottles. "Leave that," Bea said. "I'll sterilise them and clear up here after you've gone.

"It's Bing Crosby, Bob Hope and Dorothy Lamour in *On The Road To Morocco.*" Eileen sighed. "I've seen all of their films twice over. Bing Crosby's voice sends little thrills all up and down my spine," she confessed. "It must be wonderful to work as they do in such lovely places, with all that sunshine and sand and blue sea."

Bea closed her mouth, then agreed weakly that it must be fun. It wouldn't be fair to disillusion her and tell Eileen that she had been to a studio where the wind came to tease the heroine's hair from a wind machine and the sand was heaped on the studio floor with a bright synthetic sun shining over a painted backdrop of the ocean, or library pictures of seascapes were added to lend authenticity, and all done in Hollywood studios.

"I went last Thursday when they changed the programme, as they do in that cinema in the middle of the week, and the second film was all about New York gangsters . . . You will be careful, Mrs Miller? There is a lot of violence over there, with people getting shot. You aren't going to Chicago, are you? That's where most of the gangsters are and there's violence in the streets there every day . . ."

"Eileen lives in cloud cuckoo land," Bea said when she came down to supper. "Anyone would think she'd never been in a war and had her family bombed out. She seems to look on that as normal violence if there is such a thing, and an act of God, but she is frightened of burglars or when she reads in the papers of attacks in public parks."

"A little escapism isn't a bad thing," Paul said. "At least she keeps her dreams away from her life here and does a good job, and she feels safe here."

"Mick seems contented enough," Dwight said. "Perhaps she closes her eyes and thinks of Anton Walbrook or that guy with Greer Garson who had all the women in the cinema weeping when he lost his memory, and that film with the guy who was blind, was a real tear jerker."

"I wept too," Bea said defensively. "Ronald Coleman's voice is really beautiful . . . and so English," she said mockingly. "Do they show our films in Texas?"

"They show anything," Dwight said dismissively. "You'll have the theatre in Washington and some fine concerts if that's what you want."

"I'll want the cinema too," Bea said. "And popular music and music hall."

"They call it burlesque over there, and it isn't quite the same," Paul said, teasing her. "No cockney songs like 'My Old Dutch' and 'Any Old Iron'. Nothing with double meanings and a broad wink, and no blue sketches. Do they have statuesque nudes as they do at the Windmill, Dwight?"

"We have wholesome revues by Busby Berkley amd girls who dance in wunnerful costumes. Our musicals are the best in the world."

"We have them too," Bea retorted. "What about the

Tiller Girls with the longest legs ever and the Bluebell Girls?"

"You have Phyllis Dixy, specially for our boys," Dwight said. "Very basic and cheap, but we have Fred Astaire and Ginger Rogers."

"Fred is British," Bea said triumphantly. "But I like a lot of things on both sides of the pond. I agree with Noel Coward that cheap music is very potent and it stays with me longer than more worthy songs do," Bea said. "Just as well as I have to listen to Glen Miller and Hutch all the time."

Dwight whirled her round the kitchen. "Don't tell me you don't melt a little when I play 'Deep Purple'?"

"Eileen drinks it in," Bea said.

"So do you, you little snob! Stop pretending."

"Come on Bea, I want you to look at the party room and tell me if you think we have enough tables for the food. Stop wrangling, you two!" Emma ordered jokingly.

"Emma, I think you come from a long line of puritans," Dwight said. "You never fight for fun."

"How right you are," she said calmly. "I've seen too much of real rows."

That evening, the telephone rang again and again, first with news of friends that Emma had been unable to contact and who might be able to come if they could find somewhere to sleep on the night of the party, and then the General took up the air-time, planning what he looked on as a major military operation.

"What we need, General, are billets," Bea said crisply and grinned at Dwight. "Beds for eight unless they sleep here on the floor. All our accommodation is tagged for the first ones who contacted us."

"Leave that to me. I can take at least twelve," he said with relish. "How big is your yard? And access?"

"Big and wide at the back," Bea said.

"Well, give me priority with parking," he drawled. "I'll

have my ADC drive a trailer over and you can use that. We don't seem to be using so many for on-the-spot accommodation in camp just now and some will go to Europe soon. You'll find them comfortable. American senior ranks don't like discomfort even on army manoeuvres when they are only observing."

"Ask for the moon and he'll say it's a doddle," Bea said as she put the phone down.

"He retires soon so he can stick his neck out and bypass the rules," Dwight said. "You may find you are using a trailer that saw action in the desert with Monty or in Italy at Cassino," he said, impressively.

"Or in Hyde Park by the anti-aircraft balloons," Bea said. "Twelve? Do we segregate the sexes?"

"Be nice! Give them a break," Dwight said with a grin. "Who cares? They can blame Uncle Sam for anything that happens."

"You hypocrite!" Bea said. "You don't let a man look at me for five minutes, leave alone touch! And before Emma was married, you watched her escorts like a hawk!"

"That's different," Dwight replied with a maddeningly superior smile. "I pull rank all the time. Head of the herd, that's me."

"Well keep it to one, in your harem," Bea said. "Remember, the female of the species is deadlier than the male, so don't go out collecting more little fawns."

He shuddered. "I wouldn't dare."

"Have you started packing?" Emma asked. "There isn't a lot of free time after you've been to St James's for a whole day with your father and Miranda, and then we have the party. I don't want you to go, but you'll hate it if you have to leave in a rush and have a few loose ends left."

"I know." Bea looked tearful for a moment, then braced herself. "Putting it off doesn't make it easier and I'm better if I'm busy," she agreed. "What else was in that tea chest?"

"Treasures galore. Some large jugs that will be useful for lemonade and cider, some small cups and saucers that don't match but would make a good coffee set as they are the same size and individually pretty, and a lot of table linen that someone used for packing the china."

"Any spares?" Bea asked wistfully. "I'd like something from that place. I shall pretend it's from our old family home and show it to everyone when they see our four poster bed. The Yanks are suckers for history and are much more snobbish than we are in spite of our class distinctions." She moved restlessly. "It's true Emma, I need something to hold on to from here. I have no real family roots except for Pa, and he isn't what I call close."

"He's never denied you anything and he is fond of you, Bea."

"I know. I've had so much and yet so little. Even our houses or apartments have never been home. They were just places where we made a smart house and lived there until the next one. I want my children to have things that they'll remember from infancy, like the rocking horse we had made at the Base and the things that Aunt Emily and Janey gave me that are homely and good . . . comfortable things," she added with a droop of her shoulders. "I am used to moving about so that's no problem but I must put down roots somewhere now, and I also want to remember all that we've done in the past few years together."

"That's a lot," Emma said shakily. "I don't think I'm ready to recall a lot of it."

"It's there and when you come to visit us we'll sit with our feet on the brass fender as Emily does, and drink strong tea with whisky and talk about the past."

"You peeped," Emma said, convulsed with laughter.

"What *is* she talking about?" asked Bea.

"Look in there."

Emma opened a cupboard and dragged out some roughly tied up parcels. "For me?" Bea said suspiciously. "You shouldn't have bothered."

"Yes, for you from the manor. I hid it but thought you might like it even if you find it awkward to fit into your new home."

Bea tore off the wrappings and stared at a complete set of hearth tools complete with a wide brass curb with fretted sides for the front of a fireplace, and a hanging rack of brushes, pokers and shovels all gleaming from long polishing.

Dwight and Paul found them sitting on the floor, laughing hysterically, with tears running down their faces.

"It will be perfect," Bea said. "We must have a fireplace made to fit it!"

"Sure," Dwight said indulgently. "We'll turn on the fans high enough to make you cold and then light the fire."

Chapter Twenty-One

Two laconic GIs trailed a cable into the basement to fix it to a power plug and tested the lights in the trailer. Eileen watched fascinated then ran into the house to tell Mick about it. "There's even a fridge and a lavatory in there and the bunks look really comfortable."

Mick broke a meringue in half and tasted it. "Not bad, considering," he said.

"Considering what?"

"The fact that it's not your usual ones. It's crisp and sweet and tastes of vanilla, and if it's filled with that creamy stuff that came with the rest of the American food, I suppose some won't know the difference," he said doubtfully, then grinned.

"Don't say there's a war on! I think the peace is worse. I've dug up a patch out the back for some vegetables. 'Dig for Victory', they said and now we have to dig if we want onions and parsnips. Onions are like gold all over London," he added. "Even Covent Garden only had pickling onions and none of the big fat ones like my father grew."

"Before the war we had men from Brittany, selling onions off bicycles," Eileen said. "I wonder when they'll be back, if there are any left now. My father called them Johnny Onions and always gave them a pint of ale if we bought from them. Long strings of nice mild ones they were, with firm flesh and they made wonderful thick cream of onion soup when we had colds. My mother swore they did us good."

"Your dad spoke their lingo?" Mick asked with a new respect for Eileen's family background.

She laughed. "No more than 'How much?' and 'Do you want a drink?' which is fairly easy to say, mostly with hand signals. They showed us snaps of their families and I wonder what happened to them when the Germans invaded France?"

"Probably went to forced labour or worse," Mick said, then changed the subject when he saw his wife's expression. "What's that?" he asked.

"Give it stir, there's a love. It's tinned salmon with home-made salad cream and a drop of lemon essence to put in the sandwiches. The Yanks brought a load of salad which looks nice and will be lovely and crisp with the savouries and cold meats and make up for the lack of potatoes."

"Do they need you upstairs?"

"I'll take up the meringues and cakes and see if they want help with the twins. I'm going to miss those little darlings," she said wistfully. "This house won't be the same without babies."

"Pity we don't seem to have any," Mick said.

"I didn't mind, with the twins being here," Eileen said.

"Well you never know. Maybe they'll oblige soon." Mick looked upwards and grinned. "In their way, they are as devoted to each other as the twins' parents are. Not as showy but it's all there."

Eileen changed the babies while Bea set out the china and glasses, and Emma held back and allowed Bea to organise everything. It's really her party, she thought. It means a lot to her.

The General arrived, made a fuss of Bea and Emma and tried to dandle the twins on his knees without much success as they were now at the stage when they wriggled and tried to pull his hair.

"I don't know if I rescued the General or my offspring," Bea said when she asked Eileen to take them to the nursery. "Coffee will revive him," she decided and the atmosphere was more peaceful until the General, in his bluff and tactless way waited until Paul was out of the room and then asked Emma all about Guy and his death.

"That's a closed book, General," Dwight said when he overheard the questions. "Paul is a very lucky man and they are really happy." He gave him the benefit of his special boyish smile. "A fact of war that had no right to deprive Emma of happiness," he said. "Agreed?" he continued with an edge to his voice and Emma glanced at him gratefully.

"Sure . . . Sure," the other man said, suddenly embarrassed. "I can't keep my big mouth shut!"

"Thanks Dwight," Emma whispered when she followed him into the kitchen for more coffee.

"He attacks everything as if he's still driving a tank," Dwight said and grinned. "I recall the first time you were at one of his parties and he hinted that all British girls were on the make with American servicemen. He never learns, but he's really fond of you and Bea, so be nice to him."

Emma changed into a slim-fitting dress of pale green with a deep plum-coloured belt and small velvet collar. The marcasite pendant she wore caught the colour of the collar and she felt as if it was a talisman.

Bea wore a light-textured two-piece suit that brought out the blonde sheen of her hair hanging over the coffee-coloured jacket and both women had precious high heeled shoes and nylon stockings that did marvellous things for their legs. One by one the guests arrived, then a party from Beatties who had shared a car and could get back to the nurses' home that night.

Squeals of laughter came from the trailer where doctors and nurses who had left their training schools and were now scattered out of London, re-disovered each other, talked of old times and and took pleasure in the emergency arrangements for their sleep that night.

Paul's crowd from St Thomas's made new friends and

as Bea said, exchanged all the signs of mutual attraction! "The noise reminds me of the dances we had in Surrey when we took over that old mental hospital and had nothing to do while we waited for the balloon to go up and bring the wounded from D-Day when the invasion of Europe started," one Sister said.

"All we need is that terrible record of 'An Apple For The Teacher', the only quickstep we had until someone added to our record collection. Anyone with a decent record was welcome, however spotty he was," Bea recalled.

"That I could bear," Emma said. "Its only snag was that it jogged us up and down and if a partner was in rough khaki uniform, and he was taller than me, it was like having sandpaper rubbed briskly over my face."

"These OK?" Dwight asked. "I went through them with Bea and vetted a few that might bring tears to your eyes," he said kindly. "Can't do with weepy women tonight."

"No, this is a happy time," Emma said and her eyes sparkled.

"Made up your mind about going back to Beatties?" Paul asked later.

"It could be fun," Emma admitted. "It's flattering how much they seem to want me."

"We all do that," Paul said. "You underestimate yourself, even now when I thought I'd built up your ego." He was only half teasing.

"Who was on the phone?" she asked. "A bit late for patients or their doctors to ring."

He looked over her head at the crowd of people talking and laughing and eating the food from the very good buffet and he wondered if she was ready for what he had to say.

"It was George. He will be in London tomorrow seeing someone at the Admiralty, and he wants to see us." Emma tensed and he put an arm round her shoulders. "I asked him to lunch," he said. "It may be an effort but it will do you good as well as him."

"It's a good idea. I'd rather see him when we have

a house full with Dwight and Bea and the twins. They know him, which helps. That will make it easier and the longer I put off seeing him the worse it will become, but I can't think why it should bother me as there was nothing between us and he did love Sadie," she said pensively. "I do feel very sorry for him, but he will have a very good career and Aunt Janey says that the baby is fine and very lovable so he was no worries about Clive, with her to look after him."

Paul laughed. "At least there will be plenty to eat. The General was far too lavish with the food and we shall have leftovers to eat for days after this party."

"I haven't opened the cans of food as there was enough fresh meat and that cold roast turkey, so we have a good store cupboard full as well," Emma said. "I'm not offering to send any back!"

Eileen and Mick ate with them and helped clear the dishes with Mrs Coster washing up. She had eagerly volunteered to help as she wanted to see who was there, what they were wearing, and added darkly to her husband, "What they got up to." She viewed the sleeping arrangements in the trailer with the deep suspicion and rigid moral values of the average honest East-Ender.

Bea flitted from one group to the next avidly listening to news and giving her own stories, and a few of her closest old friends were taken to peep at the twins who were fast asleep and so for once, quiet and still.

Midnight came and went and gradually the party lost its pace and many guests went home. The rest took the hint to leave when Paul put on the record of 'Who's Taking You Home Tonight?', the traditional wartime last dance tune that Bea and Emma recalled from the huge dance halls opened for the Services in Covent Garden and The Astoria in London.

One of the guests drove Mrs Coster home, laden with brown paper bags full of food from the party and eager to tell her husband that one of the doctors brought her home, right to her door as if she was Royalty! Eileen put away the leftover food in the refrigerator and the cool larder, before going back to her own quarters and Bea sank exhausted on to the big settee in the drawing room while Emma made up the bottles for the twins and gave them to Dwight.

"Come on Honey, get your ass off that seat or you'll go to sleep. Let's feed the twins and get our heads down. I'm bushed."

"You have to be full of warm hospitality again tomorrow," Paul said.

Bea groaned. "Not another party?"

"Just George coming to lunch," Emma explained.

"We'll be there," Dwight said firmly. "I'd like to see him again before we go."

"Now I know how Aunt Emily felt at the British Restaurant," Bea grumbled when the party from the trailer and the spare rooms came into the kitchen hungry for breakfast early the next day, saying they had to get away to go on duty or to meet other commitments. "Talk about feeding the five thousand!"

It gave Emma little time to think about George and she realised that after they'd cleared away and laid up for lunch, she had barely time to change into something that didn't smell of burned toast and was clear of spilled coffee.

Mick brought George up to the kitchen where Bea was drinking tea and complaining that she had gone off her dear friends, who left such a muddle, ate everything in sight and went off with bright smiles, leaving the breakfast washing-up to others.

"I left my car by the curb as your back area was full of a huge trailer," George said.

"The Americans have just arrived to shift it," Mick said. "If you let me have your keys, I'll park your car inside as soon as they have gone," Mick offered.

"That's good of you," George said.

"Do you want to have the twins down here?" Mick asked Bea. "Eileen is quite happy up there if you want to leave them until after lunch."

"Thank you Mick. They are getting a bit of a handful so it would be nice to have lunch in peace."

Dwight and Emma came into the kitchen together, and Dwight went forward to shake George by the hand. Emma smiled, raised a hand in salute and said, "Hello George, it's good to see you," then stood by Bea, making a closer meeting impossible as Dwight was in the way of George touching her. Dear man, she thought. Dwight was so unexpectedly sensitive at times. So, no embrace between old friends and certainly no kiss of greeting. She breathed a sigh of relief.

"What did they leave in the way of drinks?" she asked.

Paul ticked off on his fingers, "Bourbon, Bourbon and Bourbon, a little gin but no tonics left. However, we can make a good gin and lime juice, or a gin and orange if you don't mind synthetic juice; there's a lot of sweet sherry and some Fino and a bottle of Campari which everyone looked at and said, 'That's nice,' but didn't drink it."

The slight tension broke with George saying that Campari and gin might just pass for a gin and It and they mixed it in a jug and added lemon juice to take away the sweetness.

Emma went over and sat across the opposite side of the deal kitchen table, facing George. She felt his eyes almost boring into her and she smiled. "How is the baby?" she asked and knew that Paul approved of her question as it was to do with the future. She had no intention of touching on his tragedy unless he wanted to talk about Sadie and her death.

His face lightened. "He's a fine little chap," he said. "My mother says he'll grow tall."

"How can she know?" demanded Bea.

"She said that if a baby has big knee joints he will be

246

tall, as he'll need the strength in his legs to bear the extra height and weight."

"I'll never call Johnnie knobbly knees again," Bea promised. "By the size of his knees he'll be eight feet tall!"

"Old wives' tales," Emma said.

Bea smiled, with a sly wink at Emma. "What do you know about it Dewar? You haven't even one baby, George has a son and I have twins! After lunch, I'll take you to see Johnnie's knees and you can tell me what you really think," Bea said.

Dwight asked pertinent questions about the frigate that George was to command and by the time they sat in the now tidy drawing room for coffee after lunch, the conversation was easy and Emma found that she had no difficulty in arguing happily with George about the merits of uniform or mufti off duty.

"We were never allowed to go out in uniform because of the risk of cross infection on the wards," she said. "The only exception was on Alexandra Rose flag days but we had to change all our uniform and send it to the laundry on our return. I must confess it was fun but we were a bit vulnerable as some men wanted to chat us up and make dates."

"I can imagine," George said.

"You are lucky. You can swan about looking glamorous on duty and off." Emma glanced at the gold rings on his sleeve. "Do you ever get overcharged in shops?" she asked. "They must think you are very rich."

"During the war it was often better to wear uniform as some people believed we were civilians shirking the call up if we went out in mufti," he said. "Now it's different and we can relax. Already the armed forces are a bit *de trop*. Kipling had it right with his poems about the change in attitude of the public when danger has passed . . . I forget how it goes, but it's something like . . . 'in peace it's Tommy this and Tommy that and Tommy go away, but it's thin red line of heroes when the band begins to play . . .'"

"But all the nice girls love a sailor, in peace and war," Bea suggested.

He shot a meaningful glance at Emma. "Not all of them," but she saw that there was humour in his eyes and she knew that he wasn't upset.

He looked at the clock on the window ledge. "I have an appointment in an hour," he said.

"Come and see Johnnie's knees, "Bea said and led the way to the nursery, hurrying ahead to warn Eileen that they had visitors.

Emma felt George's hand on her arm as they climbed the stairs. "It's wonderful to see you, Emma," he said quietly. "So much has happened since I went to America and I've gained and lost a lot in a very short time."

She looked up at him, her face aglow with affection and compassion and he bent and kissed her gently on the lips.

"I'll love you for ever," he said. "But you have nothing embarrassing to fear from me. I want your friendship now, and hope you and Paul will never deprive me of that when I come back on leave. Today has been a light in the darkness. I can think straight again and I know that you have done well to marry Paul."

"We're here," Bea called from the nursery door. She held one twin on each arm and beamed with pride. "Bet yours isn't as nice as mine," she boasted.

George took Johnnie from her and solemnly examined his knees.

"Clive is younger but he'll grow just as big . . . and as dribbly," he added, wiping away the moisture from his sleeve. He handed the baby to Emma. "My Lords of the Admiralty will take away my command if I arrive with baby spit on my uniform!"

"Come again soon," Emma said at the front door.

"May I?" George asked, looking at Paul.

"Of course. You and Emma are cousins and have a

special family bond," Paul said. "We'll see you on the island and maybe you can bring Aunt Janey and Clive with you to see us here."

"Thank you, Paul." George hugged Emma and kissed her cheek, then smiled with a cheeky lift of one eyebrow. "Love you till hell freezes," he said and was gone.

"I think the heat's out of that situation," Dwight said as he and Bea appeared as if by magic from where they'd been listening to the goodbyes. "I want a decent cup of coffee, then a walk in the park with the perambulator. What a good word that is . . . perambulator. You needn't come with us, if you are busy, Bea. I nearly picked up a very pretty doll in the park the last time I went out as she wanted to gaze in at the twins."

"Wait for me! I want to say goodbye to Peter Pan."

"I knew she'd been meeting someone," Dwight said. "If he's smaller than me, I'll take a swing at him."

"They'll never change, thank God," Emma said to Paul when they'd gone out.

"Happy about George?" asked Paul.

"Very pleased. He has calmed down a lot and knows that he can have a good future. In time he may meet someone to take the place of his love for his new ship and be a wife and a good mother for Clive. Someone to make a home for them."

"He has Aunt Janey to look after Clive."

Paul kissed her and said, "Come to bed. Bea will stay out for a while and we have no patients or visitors."

"Love in the afternoon?" Emma smiled. "Take the phone off the hook."

She slipped between the chilly sheets and shivered. "Cold?" Paul asked, enveloping her in warm embracing arms.

"No," she said in a low voice. "Just a little scared."

He gazed at her in the dim light of the curtained room. "Why?"

"When I was with Aunt Emily, I hugged her and was

shocked to feel that she was all bones and seemed frail
She's better now and all that tannin in her tea will preserve
her for years, but George has to depend on his mother to
bring up Clive and I had a sudden terrible thought that
both the sisters can't live for ever, and you and me have
no future generation."

"So?" She could feel his tension.

"As from now, we make love to have a baby," she
said. "No more doubts, Darling. We need a family of
our own."